# THE HEMATOPHAGES

## STEPHEN KOZENIEWSKI

# SINISTER GRIN PRESS

# MMXVII

# AUSTIN, TEXAS

Sinister Grin Press

Austin, TX

www.sinistergrinpr

April 2017

"The Hematophages" © 2017 Stephen Kozeniewski

Cover Art by Matt Davis

Book Design by Travis Tarpley

ISBN: 978-1-944044-55-8

# ACKNOWLEDGEMENTS

As always, my thanks go out to Matt Worthington, Travis Tarpley, and everyone at Sinister Grin Press for taking a gamble on me. Special thanks to Carol Tietsworth for her edits. And, as always, thanks to Brian Keene and Dave Thomas for opening up this opportunity for me.

Thank you K.P. Ambroziak, Trista Borgwardt, and Nia Wright for graciously allowing me to use your names in vain.

Thanks to Mary Fan, Elizabeth Corrigan, Meghan Shena Hyden, and Stevie Kopas for being there for me to bounce ideas off and just generally to listen to me.

To Kenny Hughes, Aaron Brooks, Ron Davis, Alicia Stamps, and all my fans: thanks. You make it all worth it.

This novel is dedicated to Brian Keene, who's never given me bad advice.

# ONE

"What is your greatest weakness as a researcher?"

It's a stupid question. One that's been asked at job interviews since time immemorial. Briefly, the image of a protosapient Neanderthal in a pantsuit made from leopard-hide leaps to mind, asking an applicant what her greatest weakness as a mammoth hunter is.

I take a deep breath. The air is oxygen-rich. Richer than we keep it on Yloft. That's good. That's to my advantage. My pupils are dilated; my senses sharp. I'm tempted to tap the button on my armband, which will deliver a nice cocktail of adrenaline and chemicals directly into my bloodstream, but some employers don't take too kindly to cranking, at least, not during interviews, and the tapping motion is pretty obvious. It goes off every hour while I'm wearing it anyway, so my desire to crank manually is just a nervous habit.

I refocus on the question. That creaky old horseshit question, old as the hills.

The purpose of this question is to turn it around and reveal a secret strength.

"Truth be told, I've found that there are times when I become too obsessive about my work. Burning the midnight oil. Sometimes when I get too wrapped up in a research project I can end up neglecting my personal relationships, leisure time, and, yes, even hygiene. I don't smell too bad right now, do I?"

Everyone chuckles. Work humor. The joke wouldn't even elicit a smile with real human beings. At the office, it brings the house down. Something inoffensive enough to laugh at. A mild panacea for your daily drudgery.

The next woman on the panel clears a rather unpleasant clog of mucus from her throat to refocus our attention. I realize I've forgotten every single one of their names. I think this one is the Equal Opportunity Representative. I'm originally from the Horizant Belt. I'm not sure if that makes me an under-represented population on the *Borgwardt* or not. I can't tell from the way the EO rep is looking at me, either.

"Tell me, Dr. Ambroziak, as a counterpoint, what is your greatest strength?"

I'm not a doctor. I should probably correct her. But I don't. Is this part of the test? Should I correct her? Are they probing for assertiveness?

No, by the five sets of dull glassy eyes staring back at me I can tell they're not pulling any flashy *corporation nouveau* tricks out of their collective sleeve on me. They (or just the EO rep) had probably just misread my résumé.

The purpose of this question is to show restraint, that you're a humble team player, not a braggart.

"My greatest strength?" I repeat, trailing off as though I've never given the matter a second's thought.

I re-cross my legs so that they are reversed. The panel is staring at me, sympathizing. If I make them wait much longer I'll seem like a dummy, but I need to make them wait just long enough to feel like I'm really digging deep. I exhale painfully.

"Well, if I had to pick *something* I suppose my greatest strength is that I'm wise enough to know my own limitations. I know when to ask for help, whether from my supervisor or my peers. I'm not the sort of person who's going to get in over her head and then keep pretending like I can swim my way out of it. Of course, you all know the story about the mice and the bucket."

The panelists exchange glances with each other.

"The mice and the... bucket?" the EO rep asks tentatively.

"You've not heard? I thought everyone knew that old chestnut." I look from face to face. All blank. "Well, you see, one day two mice fell into a bucket of milk. The first one couldn't scrabble up over the side, so she gave up and drowned. But the second one kept paddling and paddling and eventually she churned the milk into butter and then just stepped out. The point is: never give up and never quit trying."

The low murmur that follows is like a symphony of mild acclaim. So far I've been asked four questions, and so far, I've knocked all four out of the park. There are five panelists and if I knew anything about interviews that means one final question is coming.

"Are you ready for the final question?"

I nod.

"What is the meaning of life?"

I'm not taken aback. Thank goodness, they haven't strayed from the script in the slightest. This is just Corporate Interviewing 101. Not a single one of them has given their questions any consideration, and every single one has an objectively "correct" answer. I'd be surprised if they hadn't come from a pre-made list.

This is the "spoiler" question. The purpose of the spoiler is to judge whether I'm easily confused or thrown off my game. The answer doesn't matter. Just answer confidently, as though they had asked you about your education or qualifications.

Without missing a beat, I say, "The meaning of life is to persist."

The hatch behind me opens with a hydraulic hiss. That definitely throws me off. I hadn't thought much about being seated with my back to the entrance, but I also hadn't expected to be interrupted. Out of the corner of my eye I spot a woman easily twice my age, limping with some difficulty on a pair of crutches. Her hair is iron gray, every strand so uniform it seems like she was born with it that way. The director.

I try not to trip over my own tongue. This is the spoiler question after all. Perhaps the interviewing acumen of the employees of the *RV Borgwardt* is a bit higher than I gave them credit for.

But it's too late. The director has already noted my stumble.

"Please go on, Paige," she says, settling with a sigh into the corner.

I clear my throat and take a sip from the alloy cup set before me. Recycled water, not imported like Yloft's. Almost pure $H_2O$. Of course, it had once been sweat and piss and shipboard vapor, but if you ever think too hard about anything you could find reason to be disgusted.

I try to pretend as though the imaginary lump in my throat is the reason for my pause, and not the director's interruption. I doubt they're buying it, though. Hopefully I haven't shown myself to be easily shaken.

"Of course, Diane," I say with a smile. You can bet I remembered the director's name, unlike these other mendicants. "As I was saying, the purpose of life is to persist. The desire for self-preservation is pre-eminent and supersedes only the desire to procreate – that is, the desire for one's bloodline to persist."

"So, we exist to exist. It's a tautology. A terrible answer."

Suddenly I think the director isn't playing an interview game. Certainly, all of the panelists have stopped taking notes on their jotters and are riveted on the conversation. Are we having a real academic discourse? If she wants to throw down, I'll throw down.

I raise my finger.

"Only if you're thinking in terms of the individual."

"What other terms should I be thinking in?"

"The biome. Look, the individual organism's existence is essentially meaningless. You or I could die today or tomorrow and life would persist. The point is that life itself persists. We originated as a bacterium in a puddle, but a bacterium can't persist in a puddle. It must spread to other puddles or there is the threat that a simple lightning strike or rockfall would destroy all life. And so, we spread to all the puddles. And then the question became what of the fate of Earth?"

"What of it?"

I lean back in my chair and press my fingertips together.

"Our ancestors knew only one thing with certitude: life on Earth would end. At some point the sun would explode, but the possibility of catastrophe before that was approaching a hundred percent. And if Earth was destroyed, whether by the hands of humankind or nature, life would cease to be. All life on Earth, therefore, was in the pursuit of a single purpose: to colonize new worlds with new biomes. To persist, as I said initially."

The director sighs heavily.

"So, interstellar travel is life's greatest pursuit?"

I shrug.

"You could say that."

The director snorts.

"I hardly think a cetacean would give a damn about interstellar travel."

"Save the whales, you mean? As I said, the individual – even the individual species – is meaningless in the greater scheme of things. Whales exist to provide an atmosphere for humanity to create interstellar travel. All life from the beginning of time has striven to create a species capable of thought, capable of technology, that would eventually travel to the stars and bring other species with it. To ensure that life itself persists."

The director doesn't blink, doesn't pause. She just speaks.

"I want to offer you a job."

I nod.

"I'll certainly consider it. Send me the particulars and..."

"I want to offer you a job right now. You just have to answer me one question: can you do it?"

I look at the faces of the five panelists. They've all turned silent, realizing that they are a kangaroo court, a rubber stamp that need not be employed on this particular document. It may as well just be me and the director alone in the room.

"I suppose that depends on what it actually is."

"If I tell you and you don't take the job it could be considered corporate espionage. On your part."

Espionage. Hestle Corporation is notoriously strict about enforcing mandatory capital punishment for spies, with torture and dismemberment at the discretion of the disciplinary committee.

I uncross my legs and rise, making a show of shaking the hands of each of the women on the panel as I go. They each in turn pretend to smile back at me. The director lets me get all the way to the open hatch before calling me back.

"Wait."

I turn. Her face is puckered up as though she's just suckled a particularly bitter lemon.

"Would you agree to thirty-six hours of house arrest and having your assets frozen for the same period?"

"In exchange for *hearing* your offer?"

The director nods. I can't deny it. I'm intrigued. Why pretend I'm not? I suppose I can suffer the indignity of a day and a half of detention if I have to turn her down. I get the impression it's not an offer I'm going to be turning down anyway. I re-take my seat.

"Ladies," the director says, "is there any reason Ms. Ambroziak is disqualified from employment at Hestle?"

I notice she, at least, knows I'm not a doctor. The hiring committee members scowl, but none pipe up. They obviously don't like being treated this way, having their absolute uselessness pointed out to them. But there's nothing they can do.

"Good. Thank you. And Connie, will you see to setting up that lien and freeze? Thanks."

The hiring committee shuffles out, faces long, puffy, and distended. The director doesn't even wait until the hatch has slammed shut.

"I need someone who knows her way around a seed ship. Someone who can tell us what's left, what's right, what's up, what's down. Someone who won't get lost."

I'm taken aback.

"I'm not... I don't. I can't. I can't do that."

The director scowls. She limps over and struggles into the seat across from me.

"I know that. There's no one living who does. The question is: can you get smart on it? And more importantly: can you get smart on it without anyone in the Yloft library noticing?"

"Maybe?"

The director turns sideways and lifts her (presumably) bad leg up to let it rest on an abandoned chair.

"And most importantly: can you get smart on it in twelve hours?"

I shake my head.

"No. Absolutely not."

"I'll assume you're a smart kid and you've made all the correct logical leaps."

I have. An old derelict seed ship's been discovered somewhere. Word isn't out yet, but it sort of is. The megacorps are scrambling to see who can get a ship there the fastest. The seed ships came from a time before any standing salvage agreements were signed. That means the race doesn't go to the fastest. No one can just show up and claim first salvage rights. Whoever can get there first only wins if they can actually salvage the ship first.

"I can do what you ask if you give me...twenty-four hours."

"That's including transit time?"

I mull it over. What's really baffling about this is the question of why they don't just tow the seed ship to a friendly chop shop. Sure, you'd need protection, but a tugboat and a couple of fighters should be able to make it there in record time. Why even set foot on the ship?

"Three hours in the Yloft stacks and fifteen hours with the data, yeah."

"And six hours for...?"

"Well, you don't expect me to lead an expedition into a crashed derelict seed ship without my beauty rest, do you?"

The director almost smiles. So, all of my surmises are right. The seed ship didn't die in space. It reached its destination and came down hard. Or maybe went off course and landed in the wrong spot.

"Your friend Peavey said she'd need thirty-six hours to do it. With no sleep."

"Peavey's a lazy shit. And she thinks she doesn't need sleep which just means she sleeps more than she means to. You've noticed the..."

I gesture at my eyes, indicating Peavey's signature purple bags. The director really does smile this time.

"All right. I'm going with you. That's 35,000 chits. *Per anni solaris.*"

"I was promised fifty."

She nods.

"For a Ph.D. You're a grad student."

"If you're really into splitting hairs, just go with Peavey. I'm sure she'll take the lower rate. And you'll be trying to fight off AginCorp and the skin-wrappers and everybody and their grandmothers while trying to somehow simultaneously run a salvage operation. Because you trusted Peavey. And lost twelve hours doing it."

Squeak. Squeak. Squeak.

She's unscrewing her leg from her hip. She twirls it a few more times, like taking the cap off a plastic bottle of liquor, then sets it in front of her like a meal.

"I'll give you your fifty. And if the mission is successful I'll give you a bonus thousand. Gross."

I purse my lips.

"If it's not?"

"If it's not you're going to be answering questions to committees for the rest of your life. The whole thing's on you, Paige. The whole thing. You're young and full of piss and vinegar. You want to prove yourself, get your honorary doctorate, a big fat fast-tracking job, and, oh yeah, a little spotlight in the history books, this is your chance. Fuck it up and..."

She shrugs. Just a tiny, dainty little movement.

"You know, most people when they tell you this is a once-in-a-lifetime opportunity, it turns out they're just trying to sell you used tyres."

"I'd venture to say 99.9% of people," the director says coolly, "But look in my eyes and tell me if I'm one of them."

I look into her watery grey eyes. Sure, there's the cynicism. The "I've dealt with a million little whippersnappers like you." But there's something else, too. Sincerity. And... excitement. She at least believes her own hype.

I nod.

*Alea iacta est.*

# TWO

I detest standing in the prophylactic airlock after leaving a ship. There's nothing particularly bad about it — it just consists of standing around waiting, not even in line, but I despise it nonetheless. It's like giving blood or getting a needle. No matter how much my mind advises me that there's nothing to worry about it, it's still squishily unpleasant in some deep, reptilian part of my mind.

It's probably because of the story. Everybody knows the story. And everybody hears it at a time when they're an impressionable child, so it settles in and burrows down into some deep, dark recess of your brain. But I don't want to think about that right now.

The *RV Borgwardt* is behind me. Ahead of me lies Yloft, the place I've lived my entire life (less a few unremembered years of my early childhood) and know like the back of my hand. To the left and the right are hatches into open space. I can tell because of the tiny portholes in each.

It hasn't been longer than usual to get clearance back into the station, but I'm still tapping my toes. I know everyone on Yloft and everyone on Yloft knows me. I haven't even flashed my transit chip yet. Why would they even ask? But still, I know there are procedures, and if I expect someone to actually just let me on the bustling way-station without sweeping for germs and checking credentials, I'd have to grease palms. Not that it never happens. Just what would I be paying for? Quick access? I'm not smuggling anything.

Sighing, I walk to the right facing airlock and press my nose against the porthole, my breath fogging the lower half of the transparent plasteel. I haven't actually gotten a good look at my future home yet.

The *Borgwardt* is just like every other Hestle vehicle: huge, blocky, and utterly unbeholden to aerodynamics or aesthetics. It's made of retrofitted material cheap enough to be unbearably ugly, but not so cheap as to fall apart under pressure. It's functional. An office building with a motor.

Made for deep space salvage and "rescue" (a joke if I've ever heard one), the *Borgwardt* and all the ships like it in Hestle's fleet spend ninety-nine-point-nine percent of their time in the ink. During the brief periods when it makes planetfall, powerful repulsors on its nominal underside make it defy gravity. I think of old fairy tales of magical castles flying above the clouds and wonder if they were inspired by something like the *Borgwardt* once.

As I pull my face away from the airlock it's too late. It's already happened. The story's come back to my mind.

A lone survivor.

She made it through some arcane war or crash or perhaps was marooned for a dozen solar cycles on a dead ship before finally being found. Sometimes she was cryogenically frozen for an improbably long period of time. Sometimes not. The story has many iterations but the important point is always that she's defied all luck to make it back to Yloft or someplace like it.

Her ship is dragged back by a salvager or a mercy mission. There's the interrogation, by a security goon in her signature glasses. Only goons and Gore-Fa gangsters wear spectacles these days. No one wears them for corrective reasons, and the Gore-Fas only wear them for fashion. You can always tell security by their impression glasses, telling them your heartbeat, whether you're lying, and a hundred other improbable things that they probably don't actually do, but goons love letting ordinary people like us believe they can.

The interrogation goes painlessly, because, of course, the lone survivor isn't lying. She really did make it through that war/collision/space lizard gullet. So, they let her out into the prophylactic airlock.

Her ship, the one she was marooned on for however long, is behind her, just as the *Borgwardt* is behind me. To the left is the interrogation room, where she just left the bespectacled goon behind. Ahead is the way-station, possibly Yloft. Actually, always Yloft in the tales we told as kids, though someone's cousin's best friend had always heard another dry dock or possibly a carrier vessel.

Then, the fourth airlock, the one facing nothing, slides open. After all of her trials and travails, usually much amped up by the storyteller, and often featuring aliens and skin-wrappers and unlikely cosmic events not so rarely involving quasars, wormholes, and interstellar organisms, she's spaced.

Maybe she knew something she didn't. Maybe it was just a mistake on the part of the Yloft systems controller. That part, the moral of the story, is as murky as the origin of the disaster, and usually depends on whether the storyspinner is trying to make it sound like a wicked joke or a cautionary tale or something else entirely.

I gasp at the telltale sound of airlock hydraulics hissing and opening. For a split second, I'm certain it's the hatch into space, as I'm certain every time I'm standing on a prophy. You know. Just for a split second. I blow out all my breath so that my head doesn't explode upon exposure. But then, instead of chill and evacuating air, my ears pop and the prophylaxis's pressure has equalized with Yloft's.

"Welcome back, Paige," Veronica, one of countless station bunny controllers says over the intercom.

"Thanks, Ronnie," I reply, waving hastily in no particular direction and scurrying onboard.

Maybe it's sad, maybe it's pathetic, but it takes me more than fifteen minutes to pack up the accumulated belongings of an entire lifetime. I look at my toothbrush, in particular, so old that not a single bristle is vertical anymore, like a haircut parted straight down the middle. It might be the nicest thing I own.

Scratch that. The dark gray pinstriped suit I'm wearing is the nicest thing I own. Like most station bunnies I mostly wear an array of speedsuits, jumpsuits, and coveralls, our fashion sense shown off by their bright colors and arrays of usually meaningless patches. I slip into a bright turquoise pair that fits like a glove, marked only with a large hippocamp patch on my back – the symbol of my alma mater. I think of these as my "school clothes" – always safe for going on campus, and not bearing any aggressively provocative designs that the professors might find objectionable.

I stuff the suit I just slipped off into a duffel with all the rest. I don't know what fashion's like on the *Borgwardt*. Every deep ink vessel has its own sense of shipboard haute couteur, and like to laugh at all the others, not to mention station bunnies or fresh virgins brought on board with no sense of whether fedoras or fake eyelashes are the thing to wear. Fine, they'll laugh at me until I can get the feel of the place and finally do some shopping. I'm not going to guess about it now, and I haven't got enough spare chits to try.

I drag two duffels and my steamer trunk outside my quarters. These, and a whole lot of underutilized education represent my entire life to date. With a deep sigh, I press a button I've never used before. It's a little yellow square with a person wearing a hat next to an arrow pointing at what could be a ship.

"What the hell, Peggy? You hit the button by accident?"

I jump, startled, and clutch my heart for extra effect. The Yloft Stevedores Union is known for being slower than flash-frozen molasses, yet here, in her little toy soldier uniform and shako, is one of my old gambling buddies from middle school, Sally. I would've known it was her, anyway. She's the only one who ever calls me "Peggy" aside from my grandmother back in Horizant.

"Sally Ann Collins," I state through gritted teeth, "Have you ever known me to strike a button or lever that I did not intend to?"

The next act in our little Kabuki show is Sally acting as though I've killed her dog, complete with quivering lower lip, and featuring every bit of the spectacle save maudlin violin music.

"Say it ain't so, Peggy!"

"It is. It is so. I never intended to stay a station bunny all my life. I'm off to surf the ink, find my fortune, maybe even my place in history."

Sally snorts and rolls her eyes. She rubs some kind of imaginary gunk from her hand off on her uniform in the customary gesture before sticking it out at me. I rub the non-gunk off my own hand before taking hers.

"Well, kid, can't say we've kept up all these years, but I'll miss you nonetheless."

I'm a little touched. More than I expected to be. Am I really leaving Yloft? I know everyone here, down to their middle fucking names. What the fuck am I thinking?

"Thanks, Sal, I... that really means something."

"Yeah, sure it does," she says, miraculously stuffing a duffel under each armpit and somehow still hefting the foot locker by both handles.

Stevedores. They are a breed apart.

I think I've never even noticed my old friend's muscles. She could probably knock out a full-grown bull.

"Where you starting your illustrious career? The good ship *Cynthia Ryder*? *Mistress of the Stars*?"

"The RV *Borgwardt*, if you please, wharfie," I say, tipping an imaginary cap.

Sally wrinkles her nose.

"Hassle Corp?"

I frown.

"What's wrong with working for Hestle? Good pay. Good upward mobility."

Sally just shakes her head as if she knows something I don't.

"Better you than me, I guess."

Whatever. I don't say it, of course, but I wouldn't be content as a longshorewoman. Sally's settled into a rut on Yloft and I refuse to. Where moments before I had been questioning my decision to leave, panicking and rethinking everything, now I'm re-energized. I pull out my wallet wand

and press it to her badge, ready to transfer a nice, fat tip. Partly it's because she's an old friend and partly it's because I can't believe she's carrying all my stuff at once, but mostly, if I'm being honest with myself, it's because I know I'm better than her and I want to rub it in.

"Hey, forget it," she says, pulling her badge away just as I'm about to make the transfer, "This one's on me. You better come back though, because this is the only time."

"Yeah," I say, "Yeah. Hell yeah. I'll be back all the time. Not like I'm dead."

She trundles off down the corridor, stomping left and right like a piston-driven machine. I feel a little ashamed of myself. But as I'm standing there, reddening, I hear her shout back at me.

"Hey!"

"Yeah?"

"Why don't you stop by the Mercado tonight? We'll play a quick round of bones. For old time's sake."

I scratch the back of my head. It actually sounds good. But, oh shit.

"I have to onboard in three hours."

As much as she can with no hands, Sally makes an "eh, what are you going to do?" gesture. Then she eyes me up and down real quick.

"You said the *Borgwardt*, right?"

"Yeah."

"You got hair bows?"

I run my hands though my hair. I always keep a ponytail.

"No."

She snorts.

"You should probably stop by the Mercado anyway. Bon voyage, Peggy."

"Thanks."

●●●

Shit. Why did I let Sally guilt me into this? I swore I wasn't going to worry about shipboard fashions, and here I am in the Mercado, buying bows instead of downloading my last bits of research from the library.

"Ah, hell," I say, tossing a bunch of bows up in the air, "I can't fucking decide."

The merchant looks me up and down. Her name is Opal. I've always felt like she had the look of someone desperately clinging to too little remaining youth, but her fashion sense has never failed me before.

"Let me guess: *Borgwardt.*"

"Yeah," I admit.

"First time in the ink?"

"How many times you been in the ink?"

She doesn't smile, but there's a twinkle in her eye.

"Never. No desire. But, here, take the green ones."

I grunt a thank you and run my wand across her register, already blinking with my charge. The Mercado is its usual mess of hawkers, gawkers, tourists, ink surfers, and station bunnies. A disproportionate section of the marketplace is devoted to foods, both exotic and down home cooking. Ink surfers fresh off a long jaunt are an easy mark for a bowl full of some steaming, spicy or bland stew. And the Mercado is deliberately centrally located so that everyone boarding or deboarding a ship must pass through it and consider delighting in its wares.

I pass by a group of bewildered tourists, all with maps of the station pulled up on their jotters, looking around like they've never been on Yloft before. Maybe they haven't. Maybe they've never been off-planet before and Yloft is their first taste of the greater galaxy. If so, it's a shitty one. I can tell by their clothes they probably belong to the luxury liner *Mistress of the Stars*, which they're doubtless trying to get back to. It would only take me a minute (a second, really) to help them, but if I stopped to help every bewildered tourist on Yloft I'd never have time for anything else.

Like the station bunny I am, I have no trouble navigating the Mercado, even with the dozen or so "under construction" roadblocks in place. The roadblocks are mostly deliberate fakes, an agreement between the construction workers and the merchants' council to keep commerce congested in the Mercado. I don't dare duck under or over any of them – why ruin the illusion and piss off the construction union and the chamber of commerce at the same time?

"Ambroziak!"

I'm at the corridor leading to the archives. And who should be there to block my way but my erstwhile peer Peavey?

I spit her own name back at her with a semi-cordial nod. She's got that skeletal, scarecrow-thin look to her that some ships encourage but I've always found a bit grotesque. Her look is the result of eschewing food and relying on stims and tranqs to get her through school. I'm hardly a straight arrow – nobody at our alma mater is – but Peavey takes it to an extreme. Her veins must be full of nothing but chemicals.

Her arms are folded over her breasts. She wears her speedsuits tight, but just baggy enough that she seems to have an ordinary supermodel's figure rather than her own gaunt, cracked-out one.

"I heard you got my job on the *Borgwardt*."

"You applied for that one, too? I had no idea. Wouldn't have snatched it from under your nose if I had."

Her lips seem to disappear, her mouth becoming a narrow slit.

"Anyway, good to see you," I say. "Got to stop by the stacks one last time. Say goodbye to Professor Pendleton for me. I'd do it myself, but, you know, fuck her."

I press the two middle joints of my first two fingers to my temple in a mock salute and attempt to skirt past Peavey. It's not hard – she's not exactly a soccer goalie, and her stick-thin figure doesn't really block the entire hallway.

"Ambroziak."

Sighing, I turn around. I don't even pretend to hide the aggravation in my voice.

"What?"

Not only has Peavey's lower lip reappeared, it seems to be trembling. It's always hot and cold with her. She's always halfway around the astral plane or laser-focused on some book. I've never seen her show genuine emotion before.

"I just wanted to say... I mean... we've known each other all our lives."

"Oh."

Crap, I'm an ass. First Sally Collins and now this. Her arms aren't folded anymore, and I can see she's trembling, her entire wireframe body all aquiver.

"Listen…" I try to dredge up her given name out of my memory banks, "Yadira, it's not that big a deal. I mean, I envy you. You get to finish up. If this doesn't pan out for me, I'm fucked. You walk away with your doctorate either way."

She runs her hand across her nose.

"Yeah, I guess you're right."

Tentatively I open my arms. Peavey and I have never hugged. I don't think we've ever shared anything more intimate than an eyeroll behind each other's back. But she seems to need it right now.

Slowly she steps into my guard. I have no idea how long this thing is supposed to last, and I seem to be the only one doing any embracing. I'm just about ready to start patting her lower back to indicate that we're all finished up here when I feel her hands rubbing up and down my back. Okay, I guess she didn't just need this, she *really* needed this.

I nestle the side of my head against hers, but roll my eyes as I do so. The fact that she's suddenly broken down and proven she's got a real heart pumping real blood in that beanpole body of hers doesn't change the fact that this is still fucking Peavey.

Suddenly she's brushing away my ponytail and wrapping her hand around the back of my neck. Has all of Peavey's nastiness all these years really been because of sublimated desire?

"Peavey…" I start to say, not sure how to let her down easy.

But no. Of course not. How could I have allowed myself to think the best of someone? Suddenly Peavey isn't just stroking my back, she's clasping my waist and her bony fingers are securely gripping my neck. I try to jerk out of her suddenly rigid grasp, but I feel lightheaded. Cigarette burns fill my whole field of vision and I can feel something icy cold seeping into my bloodstream.

I attempt to wrench myself out of her grasp, but only succeed in jerking once before I realize she's holding me like a ragdoll. There's a burning sensation, circular, on the back of my neck. The hug had been an excuse to sneak in for the chance to clasp the patch secreted in her palm to my naked skin.

My arms are dead weights. I try to bat at her, but they're asleep as though I've been laying on them all night. She smiles at me. It's not even cruel. It's like she's genuinely sympathizing with me, as though sitting by my side in the infirmary room at the end.

"Shh, shh," she whispers, running her hand through my hair, "Your whole body's just going to sleep. I coded this one especially for you. It's like anti-Ambroziak. There won't be a trace of it. Everyone's going to think you weren't able to handle the pressure of going off- station and your heart just gave out. Too bad. So sad. Bet you wish you'd paid more attention in pharmacology."

"Over a job?" I want to shout at her, but my lips won't move.

Her eyes dart around but no one is paying attention to the two lovers in the alcove by the entrance to the archives. She hustles my body over behind a cutlery dealer's canvas tent. She slowly lowers me to the ground.

"No one's going to find you here. Not for a while."

She pats me on the cheeks, again, the actions of a faux lover. Maybe she really did want me and could only consummate the mad, twisted relationship in her mind with a murder.

Well, shit. I guess this is it. I'm reduced to the point where only my eyeballs can move.

Pseudocoma. Locked-in syndrome.

In a few moments my lungs will stop moving. It's kind of peaceful, really, in a bizarre way. Especially considering Peavey could have given me something really nasty, made me choke on my own vomit (which would've just been embarrassing) or target my pain center until my heart just couldn't take it anymore (which would've been unusually cruel).

No, she was content to just let me fade away. It's surreal now. I can't even feel anything, like I'm floating on clouds. It's sort of like I'm tumbling, but not in the heart-thumping, skydiving kind of way, just as though I were tumbling away into space.

They say your life flashes before your eyes in your final moments. I never really knew what that meant. Like a slideshow? Or just the happy parts? That you just get to reminiscing? Or is it really supposed to be your whole life, relived in that tiny moment, through the magic of time dilation? Well, I'm even less clear now because it isn't happening to me. I just feel myself drifting away, like floating on a current without even a tube or a canoe.

My eyelids start to flutter and I just let the end settle in. Then I feel a prick in my arm and a cold, familiar dose of crank bleeds into my veins. My heart starts racing and I sit up like a shot. My hands are quivering as I roll up my sleeve. My armband has a clock on it, and the hour's just passed. Peavey's mistake had been in trying to kill me quietly and discreetly. If she had just out-and-out poisoned me a dose of adrenaline, stims, and vitamins would have done nothing. Instead, my body is now a mess of conflicting impulses.

My left arm is numb and refusing to move but I manage to drag myself up and stumble back into the Mercado. Australia is supposedly a dealer in clean crank and other personalized synthomeds. Every station bunny or ink surfer who frequents Yloft, though, knows to meet her around back when you needed something illicit.

"Holy shit," the narco dealer says as she presses her palm to my forehead old-school style, "You look like shit, Paige."

"Thanks," I mutter through my quavering lips, "You look gorgeous yourself."

"What happened?"

"Bad dose," I lie.

She fixes me with a look like she believes that about as much as she believes in the Giant Space Baby. She pricks my finger with a mousetrap needle I'm guessing wasn't particularly well-sterilized and then sucks the end of my finger with her mouth. Australia was born a super taster – a genetic abnormality to begin with – but a few genetic grafts and even good old fashioned subdermal chips had turned her tongue into a potent diagnostic tool. And that tool's determination is...

"You're a mess."

I can tell. I shiver even as the sweat pours down my forehead and into my eyes. She looks at me.

"This is going to cost you."

"It's all right. I've got a job."

Australia gives a short, abbreviated, delighted grunt.

"Do you now? I suppose you'll want my standard Unincorporated Data Company horseshit line on your invoice?"

"If you don't mind."

Australia runs my wand for me. I don't mind. It's not so much that I trust her as that I just want to lay down and die, and the worry of her cheating me is the least of my problems right now.

●●●

I grab Peavey's head by the ear and slam it onto the desk. Her mouth works like a fish's as she tries to get a grasp on the situation, then extricate herself from it, but I hold her fast. I lean down and whisper in her ear.

"Nice try, asshole."

"Ambroziak!" she mumbles through half-depressed lips.

"Yeah, it's me. You're only about a quarter as clever as you think you are. I guess that's why I'm still alive."

Panicked, her eyes begin to circle around her limited point of view.

"You called the goons on me?"

I shake my head and then, realizing she can't see the gesture, release hers and sit down opposite her, straddling a chair.

"No. Security's not coming for you. That's pedestrian. I don't do pedestrian."

Slowly, her left hand shaking so badly she has to slap at her armband for a shot of calming crank, she raises her head to look at me. Bearing the look of a cornered ruminant she reaches up and gently rubs her crushed-in jaw.

"What... what are you going to do?"

"Right now? I'm going to finish up a couple of hours of research, then report to the *Borgwardt.* You remember, that job I stole out from under you?"

I stand up and fling the chair along the tile so that it slams into her knees. Not a hard knock, I know, but a cathartic one.

"Wait!"

All eyes in the archives are suddenly focused on us. I raise an eyebrow and plant my hands on my hips, waiting. She glances around, embarrassed at her outburst, though she seems to already know she's in deep shit. We have grown up together, but I've always been better connected than Peavey. I have friends. People like me. They just tolerate her.

She approaches me. The interested eyes, seeing that we're colluding out of earshot, flicker away.

"What... I mean... what are you going to do to me?"

"Do to you? Why would I do anything to you?"

She stares at me.

"You're not going to get me back?"

"Academia's a minefield, Peavey. A viper's nest. They told us that the first day. I can't go flying off the handle every time I get bitten, can I?"

She almost seems to relax.

"Does that mean we can let bygones be..."

I jam a finger into her sternum.

"That being said, don't you forget this is a minefield, either. Keep both eyes over your shoulders, girl, because you'll never know when the explosion's going to take you out."

I make a low rumbling sound from the back of my throat like a bomb going off and pantomime it in the air. Peavey turns a shade of white normally reserved for porcelain latrine stalls.

I strut smartly away, smiling to myself. I don't really have any plan for her. A few ideas have crossed my mind, but none that I can put in motion before I leave the station. Peavey will keep. Or maybe she'll run. But either way she's going to be looking over her shoulder for a long, long time. And that's ample payback for now.

# THREE

The hatch opens. I don't look up.

"Howdy, there, stranger!"

A roommate. Maybe I should have specified no roommate in the employment contract. I didn't, though. I grunt and roll over in my bunk, turning my back to her.

"My name's Zanib. What's yours? Hello? You ain't deaf, are you?"

A country girl. Probably a cornhusker from Tafra-Nell or somewhere. Great. I roll back to face her.

"Listen. Zanib, is it?"

She smiles and her head bobs like a bird's. She's a pretty girl. Dark skin. Brown eyes. Hair in two identical pigtails. Maybe I shouldn't be so harsh. But, no, this is me we're talking about.

"Can we just skip the part where you try to be overwhelmingly chipper, and I try to communicate through body language that I don't want to be bothered, and then you pretend like you don't notice or maybe you do notice but you believe in the overwhelming power of kindness, and next thing you know I'm sort of taken by your effervescent charm and start to come out of my shell and just skip right to the part of the movie where we get in a fight and I regret hurting your feelings and not talking to you anymore?"

The country girl lets out a single, halfway forced, "Ha!" It's not a laugh. She drops her bags in the corner and scrambles up the ladder before flopping in the top bunk.

"I should've known you'd never been in the ink before."

I scowl. She's baiting me, but it's not enough to peek my head out from my bunk. No, I'm lying, it is enough.

"I've been in the ink before."

She shakes her head.

"Nope. If I had to guess, I'd say you've never been off Yloft."

I roll my eyes.

"I'm from Horizant."

Zanib shakes her head.

"Your mum's from Horizant. You moved here when you were, what, twelve?"

"Eight."

"I can tell from the accent."

"Still, that was a long trip."

"Taking a trip once when you were a kid is not the same as being an ink surfer. Don't worry, virgin, I'll be gentle."

I cluck my tongue and glance down at my jotter. I only have eighteen or so hours before I have to make good on all of my lofty promises. And yet, the sewage and plumbing systems of ancient seed ships has never seemed so boring.

"I told you, I'm not a virgin," I say, fighting the urge to power down my jotter.

"Mm hmm," she grunts, "I guess that's why you're messing with your roommate. The first rule of the ink is don't mess with your roommate. Especially when she knows things you don't. But don't worry, virgin, I'll teach you."

I snort.

"What are you going to do? Beat me up? Steal my shoes?"

"Nope."

She has me curious now. She's a complete shit-eater, sitting up there, bouncing her bent leg across her knee like that.

"What?"

I look up at her. She's thumbing through something on her jotter. Ignoring me.

"Oh. The freezeout."

She smiles and finally looks down at me.

"Don't worry, virgin. I know how important it is to keep your roommate happy. It's the code of the ink. I would never freeze you out. Mmm... speaking of which, you hungry?"

My stomach doesn't quite growl in betrayal, but as with any time I've ever been focused on my work for hours at a time, I haven't even been thinking about my gastric functions for so long that they seem to hit me all at once like a brick. One time, in the archives of Yloft, just out of my undergrad, I was transfixed watching holovids of Shoggoth-Yug disease blister popping that I didn't realize I had to pee until I had almost pissed my pants. I didn't, but I made it no farther than the corner of the periodicals section. I blamed it on a derelict, which I felt bad about, because really I don't mind if derelicts sleep in the archives and they were banned after that.

But I digress. I am hungry. Damn hungry.

"What do you have in mind?"

●●●

Zanib flops down into the seat next to me instead of across from me. She's one of those. I stare at her, psionically urging her to sit down in the proper spot, across from me, but she doesn't budge.

Her tray is littered with calories. She empties a tiny paper ramekin of butter on top of a fat ribeye. Fried eggs confuse me as to the matter of what meal, precisely, she believes she is eating. A bowl of heavy whipped cream and strawberries only makes the matter more Heisenbergy.

Before tucking in, she glances at my own tray, clucks her tongue, and shakes her head.

"Poor virgin. I told you to eat the fresh stuff now. You'll have plenty of that freeze-dried crap when it's the only thing left on board."

I shrug, and stir my noodles around. Ramen is what I'm used to and Ramen is what I'm eating.

"I haven't got..." I grab her receipt and turn it towards me. "Holy shit!"

She snatches the receipt away from me.

"I don't spend my chits on much. I like to eat."

Her body doesn't disagree. She's got an athlete's build. I fantasize about fucking her. I wonder briefly if she'd be into a scragged-out academic like me. Maybe, if the trip is long enough. Which reminds me.

"Well, anyway, I don't have twenty-five chits to spend on galley food, and besides I have it on good authority this mission's only going to be about twenty-four hours travel time. Two days, out and back. 'Snot so bad."

Zanib snorts. She glances around the galley. Even though it's empty, she makes a big show of putting her head on a swivel for two full rotations.

"It's not the travel time you need to be worried about, virgin. I have that on better than good authority."

I shovel a chunk of something green that might once have been a vegetable into my mouth.

"Well, don't leave me in the dark, roomie. What's going to keep us on mission for so long that we're going to run out of steak and cream?"

Zanib pushes her half-finished (!) tray to the side and leans in conspiratorially.

"I guess it doesn't matter. We're all going to be briefed soon anyway. You know what my expertise is?"

"Biology?"

She's mentioned it once or twice already in our brief acquaintanceship.

"Theoretical xenobiology," she clarifies, emphasizing each syllable as though it were more important than the last. "That means predicting the nature of alien life."

"In other words, horseshit science."

Zanib's eyes narrow.

"It's real science."

"What kind of alien life are we going to come across, then?"

She shrugs and leans back in her chair, folding her arms.

"How would I know? I'm a horseshit artist."

I cock my head. Accompanied with the "Oh, really?" look it's more than enough. The cornhusker is just as eager to spill her secrets as I am to hear them.

"All right," she says, "Are you familiar with the Gaia hypothesis?"

I quirk my mouth to the right. It rings a bell.

"Something about... Earth being a person or something?"

Zanib shrugs but also wears an expression suggesting I'm not far off.

"Yeah, pretty much. If your body's made up of cells that make up tissues that make up organs that make up...you...what's to stop us from thinking that an entire planet isn't essentially a single organism made up of plants and animals that form ecosystems and ecosystems that form a biome and so on."

"All right."

"So Meyerhofer took Gaia one step further and suggested that what climatologists considered a metaphor or a useful way of understanding the world, xenoclimatologists might consider a literal possibility."

"A planet-spanning organism?"

Zanib's eyes light up.

"A blood star. A fleshworld."

So, that's what she's getting at. I wave the silly notion off with an abrupt gesture.

"That's an old canard. We're not living in the Information Age any more. Nearly twelve per cent of the galaxy had been charted, and nothing even close to a fleshworld has been..."

Then it strikes me like a meteoroid. My spoon clatters into my bowl and pirouettes out, splattering me with juicy Ramen broth from chin to crotch on its way to the deck. Zanib snatches my spoon off the deck when I make no move to retrieve it. She eyes me warily.

"What's wrong with you?"

I look her in the eyes, as though seeing her for the first time. I think she must see the excitement in my own, because her expression changes.

"*The Manifest Destiny*," I whisper.

"Not possible," she whispers back.

"You're a fleshworld expert?"

"Well... if there is such a thing."

"They hired me as a seed ship expert."

Her lips quiver.

"I didn't know there were experts on technology that outdated."

I shrug.

"I'll be as much of one as there is in a few hours."

She looks around the room, though it remains aggressively empty. She leans in conspiratorially towards me.

"You know the old anecdote about the three blind women? And one thinks she's found a snake and one thinks she's found a tree and..."

"And it's really an elephant?"

"Do you think that's what we're dealing with here?"

"If you're saying no individual one of us was supposed to piece together what we were doing until we were on board... and what it really is, is salvaging *The Manifest Destiny*... hell, yeah I do."

●●●

I snort awake when my chin strikes my chest. I fell asleep with my finger on the scrollbar so I have already scrolled to the end of the document I had been reading. The jotter is repeatedly advising me that I have reached the end of the document, and it sounds as vexed as an inanimate object is capable of sounding.

I look around the room. The lights are out, but something flickers up on Zanib's bunk. I force myself out and stretch widely. Zanib is surrounded by a halo of holograms, stretching out in a circle around her. I wave until I finally catch her attention. She pats her bunk, so I shrug. What the hell?

I climb up and she moves closer to the bulkhead so I can lay down next to her. Her jotter projects the movie all around us, swirling left and right or up and down along with the camera pans. The point was you never had to move your head to watch the action in front of you, but if you ever felt like it, you could look left or right and still feel like it was happening all around you. She depressed the button so the audio would stop projecting directly into her brainpan.

"We can still make it back if we turn around now!"

"We were never meant to make it back!"

The special effects are hokey and the acting is over-the-top, but there's a reason why everyone still watches the classic version of *The Manifest Destiny*.

"What's got you watching this?"

"Shh. This is the best part."

The semi-legendary seed ship, shaped like a mushroom with a fat circular cap, is already caught in the atmosphere of the fleshworld. The captain fires all rockets in a last-ditch attempt to break free of the planet. Soon the fuel will run out and they will crash, and then comes the big promise scene and the fade-to-black, hinting at the bleak fate the crew actually suffered. We're practically at the end.

We watch as the filmographer wildly cuts back and forth between the exterior of the ship with boosters on full blast, the sweat-dripping face of the captain as she watches the fuel gauge, and the fuel gauge itself as it slowly, painfully degrades. I'm instantly captivated again. No matter how many times I watch it, no matter how certain the outcome, it's impossible for anyone to rip their eyes away from the screen.

The image pauses.

Unless you're Zanib, I guess.

"Do you really know all about this stuff?"

I shrug, remember how bunched up my muscles are, and the shrug evolves into a stretch.

"I guess. That's what they pay me for, anyway."

"So, this company, this United Stakes of America…"

"Country."

"What?"

"Nothing, it doesn't matter."

"Okay. So, what do they hope to get out of sending the seed ship to Vilameen? I mean, sure, they didn't know it was a fleshworld, but they did know it was barren, right? What was the profit?"

I nod. I guess I do have to explain the whole "country" thing after all.

"Well, they weren't really worried about profit. This was back before…I mean, they really didn't understand the importance of profits. It was old-fashioned. They were worried about things like honor and pride and, I dunno. Old-timey stuff."

Zanib nods.

"What was the goal, then?"

"Well, just to establish a self-sustaining colony."

"I don't get it."

A smile flutters across my face. I've been in academia so long I've almost forgotten how to explain complex, antiquated concepts to laywomen.

"Well, back then people weren't thinking in terms of benefiting their companies."

"They weren't?"

"Well, some were, of course. But there were also these nation/state things that were concerned with stuff like mass warfare and cultural hegemony. America wanted to expand its reach to other worlds partially for the prestige and partially just so there would be more people loyal to their flag."

"That flag?" she asks, pointing at the banner in the background behind the captain's head.

"That's the one."

"What about the livestock? I mean, didn't they know it was a waste of space and..."

"Zanib."

"Yeah, virgin?"

"I have to talk about all this stuff at the meeting tomorrow. You're going to be there, right?"

"Yeah."

"Then ask me questions then. Right now, I want to find out if they break orbit or not."

I lean my head on her shoulder and she starts the movie again.

# FOUR

"Anything to add, Zanib?"

I thrust my elbow with such shock and verve into the soft spot under Zanib's ribcage that I'm surprised she doesn't shout. Luckily her eyelids snap open before every head in the room turns to her and she manages not to jump at my elbowing.

Without missing a beat, she says, "I think the xenoclimatologists have covered it. We really worked quite closely on this presentation. But if there are any specific questions...?"

Elegantly played. There's some light murmuring.

"If there is alien life on the blood star, what can we expect?" a watery voice lips.

This is Helena, our security chief. Like all goons, she wears glasses, supposedly rattling off vital stats about the people and environment around her. She's a light-skinned mountain of a woman, and she once suffered some kind of terrible, smashing injury to the right side of her face. Her right nostril and the right side of her mouth are asymmetric, and several of her teeth are made of metal alloy. Such long-term disfigurements are so rare with today's plastic and dental expertise that my only guess is that she was patched up in the field by a less-than-expert hand, and no amount of reconstructive surgery could fix the lasting damage. I doubt she minds. It makes her look intimidating.

Zanib nods.

"Thanks for the question, Helena."

Groaning, Zanib hoists herself out of her seat and steps to the front of the conference table. I don't know why she's so tired. I'm the one who's been up researching feverishly for the last day. But while crank, coffee, and the sheer excitement of the mission keep me teetering on the edge of crazy, Zanib is succumbing to the usual soporifics of interstellar travel.

"Right, so, if we think of the fleshworld as basically a giant, um, blood blister, there is a, uh, sort of a something you might consider skin but that's kind of a misnomer because it's really just the pressure of the atmosphere causing coagulation at a very surface level. Basically it's just something a bit thicker than blood, through and through. Porridge. Am I, ah, misrepresenting the case at all?"

She glances at the xenoclimatologists, who had zoned out as soon as their briefing had been completed. The scientists largely wear lab coats, if for no other reason than to identify themselves as such. Some of the accountants and other white collar types wear skirts, pumps, dresses, and the like. I'm not entirely out of place in a jumpsuit, as security and some of the more hands-on laborers favor utilitarian wear. The only universal is the green bows in everyone's hair. In that respect, at least, Opal didn't lead me astray.

"Oh, yes," one of the xenoclimatologists agrees, nodding her head urgently, "Very good comparison. Sludge, or, yeah, oatmeal."

"Right. So, the center would be unlivable. Maybe it's easier to think of it like a cherry with the pit still in. The actual blood part is the top layer. I apologize, everyone, if I'm mixing too many metaphors. You know, theoretical xenobiology is more art than science."

That causes a titter of laughter. For the first time, I realize that Zanib may not even have caught the initial question. She's just vamping for time, going over the same ground the xenoclimatologists covered.

"So, if there is life..." I say, more a statement to be finished that a question.

Zanib nods. I hope no one else can read the gratitude on her face.

"Right, if there is life..." She seems to notice the slideshow for the first time. "Have we got my slide uh... G... uh... are these my slides?"

"Here's G-7," the slide controller says, bringing up a crosscut of a fleshworld, not unlike the pitted cherry Zanib just described.

"No, it's uh... like two or three more."

The slides move forward at a deliberate clip.

"There! Stop there."

The slide that comes up is a series of anatomical drawings of the mouths of animals, eight or ten, lined up in discrete ranks, each one more disgusting than the last.

"While we have no way of knowing with certainty anything about the creatures we might encounter on a fleshworld, we do know that they essentially live in blood. Or, at any rate, a solution so similar to what we could consider blood as to make no difference. They don't just occupy it, they live off of it, they thrive on it. They must move through it and survive on it. So, what we can extrapolate about the creatures we encounter on any given fleshworld is that they will likely resemble, in at least some respects, terrestrial hematophages."

Silence drops over the room like a funeral shroud.

"Hemato..." Helena starts sharply.

"Hematophages," Diane states, as though it were the commonest word in the lexicon. "Blood drinkers."

"Yes, very much so, Madam Director," Zanib agrees. "Forgive me if I slip into Latin. It's an old habit of, ah, all theoretical xenobiologists, and as we all know, *mores mori difficile*."

"The term's Greek, actually," the director states flatly, "but please continue. This is not my briefing, after all. Although I was hoping to benefit from it."

Zanib sobers up quickly. The laughter which had abetted her half-assery has dried up.

"My apologies, ladies. As I stated, any creatures we encounter will be hematophages, meaning blood-drinkers, and therefore we must surmise that their behavior and appearance will mimic one of the common blood-drinking apparati of terrestrial fauna. I've brought a small menagerie of these creatures on board for observation."

"Why?" I can't stop myself from asking, surprised that no one else has the same question on the tips of their tongues.

"Ha! Good question, Paige. It's common practice for theoretical xenobiologists to keep sample species on hand so we can examine their behavior. If the behavior of the xeno species perplexes us, we can observe the behavior of the analogous sample species in the same environment, and try to glean clues from that. *Macht Sinn*?"

I nod.

"Don't worry, I've cleared all of the analogue species with health and safety. Let's take a look at a few. Starting from the top, the mosquito, you're all, no doubt, unfortunately familiar with, has a proboscis, or elongated nose for sucking out blood. Here you'll see the silhouette of a vampire bat, although I suspect it's rather fanciful to expect a flying, bloodsucking mammal..."

"Perhaps you could stop wasting all of our time, then."

Like a chill wind on a hot summer night, a change comes over the room. It's as though everyone who's either been playing along or hadn't noticed Zanib flying by the seat of her pants has suddenly wised up. And Zanib herself feels the change and her demeanor sharpens. All it takes is ten words from the director to do all that.

"Yes, of course. Most likely any creatures we encounter will be designed by evolution to churn through the swamplike conditions of a fleshworld's surface. The closest terrestrial analog would be any of the thirty-eight species of petromyzontiformes known as stone-lickers or lampreys. Next slide, please."

I nearly retch when the slide changes, but a huge part of me is transfixed, fascinated. Admittedly, it's been a long time since I've studied terrestrial zoology (only the most useful and therefore dull stock ever makes it into the ink) but I don't recall ever seeing anything like this. The grotesque creature displayed from several angles resembles an eel, or an especially tubular fish. I have no special love of eels, but this one is particularly repulsive, being jawless. Its mouth resembles a great circular pit of teeth.

"How large will they grow?" someone whose name escapes me asks.

Zanib nods, as if she had been anticipating the question.

"Well, there are no limitations. In an ocean of essentially blood, a hematophage could grow to be the size of a terrestrial shark or even a whale."

Helena snorts and rolls her eyes.

"So, giant leech-monsters the size of busses. That's what we have contend with?"

"Potentially," Zanib agrees. "Of course, the big ones aren't the problem. We have biomonitors that can detect them and a simple electric shock should be more than enough to ward them off. The real concern would be smaller hematophages, tiny ones that could get into our systems."

"And how would we defend ourselves against that?"

"Not enter the ocean."

"How glib," the director says.

"N... no, I'm serious..." Zanib stammers.

"I know you are. But we've all already jumped to the next move of the checkers match. There's nothing much to be done about native microfauna in any case, and in a slapdash expedition like ours it's just one of the risks. Now, Paige, I believe you're next."

I nod, straighten my skirt, and rise, words on my lips, when the hatch opens and the directorate secretary, Myrna, comes strutting in as fast as the three-meter aluminum ramrod crammed up her ass allows. She clutches in her hand a piece of actual stationery – expensive beyond all reason in our current paperless environment.

"Inappropriate, Myrna," the director says through clenched teeth, until she spots the sheet in the agitated secretary's hands. "What's that?"

"It's a memorandum, ma'am."

"I can see that."

Diane snatches the sheet of paper out of Myrna's hand. Her face barely changes as she reads it top to bottom, eyes moving left to right like sensor bot heads. Just the tensing of her jaws is enough to make me retake my seat like a deflated balloon. I look at Zanib questioningly, but she just shrugs.

After taking a few seconds to mull over the document, the director clears her throat.

"Right, well, we'll take it from here. Thank you, Myrna."

The protocol officer rises tentatively from her seat at the foot of the conference table.

"Shall I reschedule the meeting, Diane?"

The director shakes her head, sharply, only once.

"No, no need to dismiss the cats and then herd them all back in. Although, ladies, if any of you have a reasonable accommodation for nausea on file, please wait outside."

I look at Zanib again, my eyes wide.

What the hell?

"Skin-wrappers!" she mouths.

I sit stock-still, as though petrified by Medusa's glare. A few of the attendees rise and leave the room in an orderly fashion, as though this were all very by-the-numbers. I don't have a reasonable accommodation, but I start to rise, tentative, wiggling my butt in the air in indecision. Zanib grabs a trash basket and shoves it into my lap, forcing me down. I wrap my arms around the basket as though it were a woobie. I'm really not sure what to expect, but clearly Zanib doesn't want me to miss the experience.

The director fusses in her chair, trying to strike a dominating pose by leaning forward on the conference table and balling her hands. It's the closest I've ever seen her to out-of-sorts. If the stories about the skin-wrappers are true, I'm in for quite a show.

The main vidscreen turns on. The woman next to me immediately turns and pukes her guts up into the garbage basket between my legs. I hand it to her.

"Thanks," she whispers, wiping her mouth.

# FIVE

The skin-wrappers are not sitting around a conference table like us. In fact, unless I miss my guess, skin-wrappers would never sit.

They occupy what appeared to be a large, open plasteel dome, free (or as free as possible) of gravity. I can't shake the feeling that as they stare at us through the vidscreen, they are also periodically glancing through the transparent plates of their command center to look at the *Borgwardt* directly. Each of the skin-wrappers I can see beyond the looming face of their (I presume) leader, are in various stages of total cutaneous debridement.

The leader herself halfway resembles a mummy of ancient Earth. Every centimeter of her flesh has been flayed down to the meat, but she's wrapped most of her body loosely in gauze, possibly for our benefit. The way the bandages float in the zero-G still leaves great swathes of her glistening red flesh exposed, and her face in particular has the look of a ghoul.

The others behind her have not taken such pains to set us at ease, and are everything from barely wrapped for medical purposes to completely exposed in all their glistening, sickening glory.

"Good morning, madam director," the leader of the skin-wrappers hisses through her exposed teeth in a dry, rotting voice.

I watch Diane for some sign that she's shaken up, or at least off her game, but there's none. She doesn't even check her watch.

"Good morning. And what am I to call you?"

"You can call me Nia," the skin-wrapper responds so snappily as to be almost peevish, "and shall I call you Diane?"

I feel a shiver run down my spine. They know our complement. This is no chance encounter.

"Yes, that would be fine," the director responds acidly.

Nia pushes off lightly from her bulkhead, tumbling through zero G with a precision and ease that could only be gained from years of practice. She comes to a rest maybe a meter further back from the camera, and for the first time her floating, intravenous robot comes into view. She reaches out and fondles the thick, plastic tube connecting her to the whirring device which even now is delivering a steady stream of nutriments and medicines directly into her bloodstream. It's a device not unlike my own armband, writ large.

Likely she has terminal cancer. The skin-wrapper subculture evolved from the victims of various burns and diseases which were better treated in zero G. The corporations, ever seeking cost-cutting measures, gradually withdrew funding and staff from their own hospital ships. The skin-wrappers gradually became healers and patients both, tending to their own and welcoming only their own. An entirely spaceborne people, their limbs grew long and their muscles weak, used to no gravity. Nia herself is particularly gaunt-looking.

"It doesn't surprise you that I know who you are?"

"Hardly. There are plenty of spies on Yloft for anyone willing to pay."

"I prefer to think we don't have spies so much as friends. Friends who wish us well."

"Friends who... slipped you our manifest?"

Nia turns back and a wave of gauze flutters away from her face, exposing cheekless jaws and naked nostrils. She doesn't bother to replace the wrapping.

"You make it sound so tawdry. We merely patrol these shipping lanes, collecting tolls. Your corporation is reasonable. Surely they don't object to paying what they owe?"

Diane purses her lips. We all wait expectantly. It's an extortion job, plain and simple. While some corporations charge docking and orbital fees at planets and way-stations they own outright, being in the ink is supposed to be, for all intents and purposes, free. Claiming a tax on a shipping lane is a not-so-subtle bandit's tactic.

And this is the dark side of the skin-wrappers. No matter how tragic their origin, they've become a plague. Over time, they took to piracy, reaving for supplies from the corporations that had abandoned them to their fates. They don't have children, their ranks gradually replenished by volunteers who judge a few years of swashbuckling better than dying in a planetbound hospital.

"They'd be happy to. Please issue them an invoice."

Evidently Diane has decided being extorted is better than being boarded. She reached for the kill button.

"Actually," Nia replies, "we're low on supplies and would rather accept barter."

A smile curls across the director's lips.

"Barter implies an equitable trade."

"Free passage will be yours. Dump half your fresh fruits and vegetables. A quarter of your meat and dairy. We're not savages, after all."

The director holds out her hand without a word. As though psychically bidden, a woman in chef's whites slinks up and presses a jotter containing what I presume to be the galley manifest into the director's hands. She scans it as though running through routine paperwork, even taking the time to scroll down and adjust her glasses once or twice. Finally, she slaps the jotter down on the table and looks up.

"I'll give you thirty liters of milk and two crates of eggs."

Milk and eggs. Both perishable. We can spare it and it may go bad anyway. I've never dealt with pirates before, except the sort who have abandoned the life to take up jobs as objects of curiosity in the Mercado, and I always assumed those were more bark than bite. I'm not sure whether Diane is making a reasonable offer, insulting the skin-wrappers, or attempting to haggle.

"What am I supposed to do with that?"

"It's a good faith offer. As a show of good faith, you should take it."

I can almost picture Nia's missing lips curling in displeasure. Her two naked rows of teeth part from each other, strands of dry, mucusy saliva connecting the mandible to the maxilla like rubber bands in a retainer.

"We need something green."

The director doesn't have to double-check the manifest.

"I'll give you a dozen heads of cabbage. And a liter of strawberries. The alternative, of course, is to board us."

I find myself transfixed by Nia's eyes. They sit caged in pockets of meat, lidless, browless, staring, but no less expressive for being so. I wonder how the skin-wrappers sleep at night, with their eyes open to the world like that.

"Blow it out your airlock and be on your way. We'll recover the goods from space."

"Have a pleasant morning," Diane responds, a blade of a sentence that could have sliced through the bulkhead.

She punches the kill switch and the grotesque visages of the skin-wrappers disappear from the vidscreen. She jerks a thumb over her shoulder.

"Go."

The chef nods and sprints for the hatch. The protocol officer rises and clears her throat ostentatiously.

"Shall we adjourn for..."

Diane cuts her off sharply.

"We haven't the time to adjourn and we've already wasted more time dealing with those pirates than we should have. I want to find out what our golden child has to say. After all, this expedition is depending on you in so many ways, Paige."

I rise and smile.

"That's kind of you to say, Diane."

# SIX

Wait patiently for the absent parties to shuffle back in, heads hung just a little low in shame. A reasonable accommodation isn't supposed to be shaming, but for some people there's just no getting over it. Smile at each of them as they go by. Welcome them with mindless pleasantries. Okay, that's sorted.

Introduce yourself.

"Hi, everybody, I'm Paige Ambroziak, although you probably know me better as the golden child."

Chuckles. Good. The director is unamused. Fuck her. She doesn't care what I have to say. This little gladiation match is for the mob, anyway.

Prove you're worth a damn.

"I am a Ph.D. student from Yloft. I wish I could tell you I'm a doctor, but you're not paying for degrees, you're paying for results. Slide H-1, please."

Take control. Make them eat out of the palm of your hand.

"Actually, could I have the remote? It'll be easier that way. Thank you. Ladies, what you are looking at is a seed ship, circa, oh, let's say, one hundred and fifty, two hundred standards ago."

"Could we be more specific, Paige?"

She's trying to throw you off. No worries. Don't miss a beat. Don't hesitate. Make some shit up.

"A hundred and eighty-five, to be more specific, madam director. Of course, this particular model spans the time frame I just laid out, but we're looking at *The Manifest Destiny*, so why futz around about it?"

They're fussing. They're buzzing. They know the movie. Of course they do. Who doesn't? I've got their interest. That's not the same as them being interested in me. That's only reflected glory, like the moon and the sun. But they're listening.

"Yes, this is *The Manifest Destiny*. Some of you may remember the movie. Fewer of you, I'll wager, remember the book."

More chuckles. Good. Easy crowd. Work jokes work on them.

"*The Manifest Destiny* was named after a 19th century nationalist philosophy, blah blah blah, this is all flavor text. You can read it on your own time."

Click through the slides. Imply that you've got more information than they could ever need. Make them hang on your every word. The words you vocalize are the important ones then, yeah? The slides can completely contradict what you're saying, but say it confidently and they'll believe you and not their own eyes.

"Here's where it gets interesting. Everybody's favorite topical: technical specifications."

Mock groans. Good, they're playing along. Better than sleeping.

"Now, now, ladies, it's not so bad. I'm supposed to be briefing you on seed ships in general, but I've chosen to use *The Manifest Destiny* as an example in most of these slides for two reasons: firstly, because it's a nice, middle-of-the-road example of the thinking of the engineers of that era. Secondly, well, I'll let you guess about secondly."

A light titter. After the presentations by Zanib and the xenoclimatologists there's scarcely any doubt left. I glance at the director. She remains unmoved, made of stone. Fair enough. We're all playing along at this point. We all know damn well it's *The Manifest Destiny* actual we're all going to salvage, but the first person to say it loses the game. Childish. But when aren't office politics childish?

Fall on your face. Make yourself seem human. They're wanting to dislike you, but they can't dislike you if you're just like them. Or you make them feel better about themselves.

"Next slide, please. Oh, I forgot, I have the remote."

I shake my head like I'm a ditz. Click the button. There it is. *The Manifest Destiny*. A reversed mushroom in shape, the "cap" consists of a bundle of cylindrical tubes, like cylinders. The "stem" is crap, just a huge reservoir of fuel and water. I say as much.

"If they had to jettison the central portion, it wouldn't really have affected any shipboard processes. In fact, that's not just true of the central portion. What we call a single seed ship is really dozens of interlocking, self-sustaining miniature pods. If one malfunctions, it can be sealed off and jettisoned from the main mass instantaneously. In practice, they likely would've taken the few minutes required to drain the fuel and water from the malfunctioning pod and possibly save the crew members before jettisoning it."

The director leans back in her chair and folds her arms. Is this... could it be? Is this my moment?

"That seems supremely wasteful."

It is! It's my moment. It was bound to happen. Do it. Leap on her. Eviscerate her. But do it in a deeply respectful manner.

"Actually, it's the entire purpose of the ship. The point is the built-in redundancy. Each individual pod could, in desperate circumstances, serve as a seed for a stable community. Let's take a closer look."

Next slide. One of the cylinders, sliced in half and looked at sideways.

"Here's the engine. Not much room for fuel, hence the central carrier. But in a pinch, one of the pods can act as an individual craft. Throughout you see the sewage systems and the hydroponics systems, intermeshed, in fact, with filtration systems throughout. While in the ink water is far too precious to waste and even human waste can be broken down into its component vitamins and fed to the plants. Precious little waste has to actually be discharged into space. To put it simply: they literally shit where they ate."

A few chuckles. Good enough.

"Despite extensive scouting, the colonists of a seed ship would not have expected even theoretically habitable planets to have alien life capable or even worthy of domestication. It's the age-old problem we still face: what good is discovering aliens with a silicon- or sulfur-based biochemistry when we can't eat them? Maybe you could find beasts of burden. Maybe you just find nuisance animals. In any case, their solution was terrestrial chickens."

Next slide. A silly comic featuring a chicken in an office setting. The sort of thing you'd pin to your jotter wallpaper if you're over fifty. A pun about eggs. Not very funny, but still good enough for a laugh. Just the fact I've included it is good enough for a laugh.

"Chickens bear meat. And eggs. They don't eat much and perhaps most importantly they provide for an important diversity of diet. If we go even further back than the seed ship era, there were interstellar flights attempting to base successful colonization on hydroponic agriculture alone. Radishes and onions and beans are fine, but ultimately for healthy, expansive colonization, livestock had to be reintroduced on some level.

"And on *The Manifest Destiny*, that level was poultry. About a hundred females with a far greater diversity in frozen seed material. As long as you keep an eye on it, track genetic markers for a generation or two, and mandate diverse breeding and multiple births that's right around the bare minimum to establish a stable gene pool."

The next slide is a chart, not a lot different from a family tree, outlining how two individuals, even with the introduction of outside seed material, failed to generate a stable gene pool. The next slide is more crowded, with ten individuals also reaching a terminus. The third is even more crowded, but shows how a hundred individuals generate a self-sustaining population.

"And not coincidentally the crew of each pod was about the same size. One hundred females, young, of childbearing age, with nurseries and room to expand the population even in mid-flight. The only difference of course, is that all that stuff I just said about chickens with mandated breeding and a mandated number of children starts to sound an awful lot like eugenics when you apply it to people."

"Presumably these pioneers volunteered for the task."

I hadn't thought Helena had been paying attention.

"Exactly so. Just coming from a time when our species was all but earthbound, simply a chance to see the ink was enough to inspire people to give up their life, their family, even control over their own bodies.

"Now, as I was saying, one pod could theoretically function as a base for a colony. It would be cramped and terrible, but it would suffice. Twelve allows for all the vagaries of space travel and still the certainty of a basis for an extremely strong colony.

"A seed ship, as you can probably guess, is an extremely expensive venture, one that our modern corporations would find fiscally unsound. Only in the time of jingoist nation-states would such a venture have been undertaken. Even bearing that in mind, the loss of a single seed ship would be a catastrophe. In addition to the human and physical cost, the loss of prestige worldwide and to be frank the lack of will to start again – the shaken nerves, if you will – make *The Manifest Destiny* itself such an extraordinary case. How did the USA so poorly mis-scout Vilameen as a colony?"

The director clears her throat.

"All fascinating background, Paige, but no need to focus so exclusively on a single case study. Maybe you could cover a little more general ground."

I'm supposed to be unflappable, but this has me seriously... flapped. Why would they have us learning about fleshworlds and seed ships if we weren't dealing with the most famous seed ship disaster in history? Is it possible we're not actually going after *The Manifest Destiny*? Is there a smaller incident I missed in my zeal and certainty? Have I really wasted all my time putting in the research on it?

I can't tell from Diane's countenance. I want to harden my heart and my grimace, but I can't. She's actually gotten under my skin.

"Yes... well."

I flip through the next few slides, covering some rather in-depth background on *The Manifest Destiny* itself.

"Ah..."

I can't even talk anymore. I'm toast.

"The, ah, each... pod is functional. As a shelter. If need be. Goal being of course to... break down the pod eventually and use it as raw supplies for building a town. Hopefully you land somewhere with lumber, but if not, there's the pod. Hopefully you land somewhere with a breathable atmosphere, but if not, you can stay in the pod. It's not ideal, but, um..."

I trail off. My mind is a literal blank. I discharge a long breath of air from between my two front teeth. I've lost them. It's not so much that I've lost them. In fact, it's quite the opposite. They're all focused on me like lasers, like scavengers sensing a weak meal about to become carrion. One mocking comment is all it'll take now and I'll be a laughingstock for the rest of the voyage, if not my career. And I can see one forming on Diane's lips.

Only Zanib seems to be worried for me, seems to be encouraging me, is mouthing something but I'll be damned if I can tell what. Maybe it's something specific. Maybe it's nothing more than "keep going." Or maybe it's "sit down." If I sit down now do I lose or win?

I can hear the director filling her lungs in preparation for the withering remark that will cut me down and cost me not just my pride but my bonus. But instead of words the air is suddenly filled with a buzzing alert over the intercom.

# SEVEN

Helena is on her feet instantly. She snatches a telecommunication device off the bulkhead – an analog throwback only included in these offices to make the security personnel feel better – and begins shouting.

"What the hell is going on up there?"

Our ears are flattened against the sides of our heads, desperately listening, as though the room is silent, even though the monotone drone of the emergency alert is deafening.

Helena hangs up the phone. Her eyes are locked on some far distant object she can't see through ten rows of bulkheads. She presses a few buttons on the phone and the alarms cut out. She kneels down next to the director and the two exchange a feverish whispered dialogue that none of the rest of us can overhear, strain though we might.

Helena nods, rises, and points to two of her officers who rise and follow her out of the room. Like groundhogs our heads all snap towards the hatch in unison as we hear Helena and her goons seal it behind us.

"My apologies, ladies, but the security director has advised me that we'll be safest in here at present, at least for the duration of the emergency. I'm afraid I need to negotiate with the interlopers. Those of you who wish to leave but are unable to due to the emergency situation... please feel free to file a complaint with Equal Opportunity or the union after the emergency has concluded."

She does not need to add the obvious caveat "or shut the fuck up." As she depresses the button for a third time that day, even the women who had left the room earlier due to their reasonable accommodations are transfixed. Nia seems to have been waiting for us to re-establish contact. Her naked teeth are bared in what the musculature of her face suggests is a ghoulish grin, but otherwise is impossible to identify without the normal hints of the skin.

Nia holds a potato peeler, sharpened to monofilaments, across our chef's neck. The chef is quivering in her whites, a wet patch over her crotch and tears blobbing away from her eyes and floating off in the zero-G hinting at the true level of her panic. Still, she doesn't move in the skin-wrapper's grip.

"Delilah," the director says deliberately, "are you all right?"

"I wouldn't say I'm all right, madam director," the chef fairly shrieks.

"I don't want you to worry. I want you to relax. You're going to be..."

Whatever Diane was about to promise the chef she was going to be didn't really matter, because Nia had decided she was going to be a peeled carrot. With a single, more than deliberate gesture, she flays Delilah's neck, once from lower left to upper right and then again from lower right to upper left, forming a grotesque red "X" across her neck. Blood begins to spray from the nicked jugular, forming into irregular blobs in the zero G like a child playing with cleaning solution bubbles. Nia shoves the chef's neck directly into the camera, turning our view into a literal rose-colored world.

Nia waits for the gore and bloody chunks to drift away from the camera feed before letting go of the chef's lifeless, exsanguinated corpse. Delilah drifts off thoughtlessly into the background, while globules of her blood continue to pirouette around one another.

"You were saying, madam director?"

The skin-wrappers behind her toot up in a horrible chorus of gallows laughter. They sound just like the ghouls they look like as they chortle over our chef's terrible fate.

Diane raises her hands up, palms toward the ceiling, in a show not of supplication, but of frustration.

"You executed the hostage. What do you think you'll get from me now? You've got no leverage."

Nia takes the time to painstakingly remove all of her bandages. Her appearance is even more grotesque than I had imagined. Whatever ailment she suffered from in life – I remembered thinking it was cancer – it must have been sheer agony for her to prefer being flayed and floating, never to be able to rest comfortably on a bed or even a chair, zero G being the only buffer between her and endless agony.

Only her eyes betray something like humanity.

"This isn't a negotiation. It never was. That was your first mistake."

Nia points a remote control at the screen. I expect her to cut the feed, but instead it is replaced by a recording. I check the chronometer on my jotter. Judging by the time scrolling by on the screen this was just a few minutes ago.

This is the outside of the *Borgwardt*. As the camera turns left and right, I see skin-wrappers, stripped down to less than their skivvies and floating in space sheathed in just thin layers of plastic, inflated to just a few centimeters off the skin. They remind me of packaged meat at the grocer's.

Then I see an arm gesturing. I realize the camera is being directed by one of the pirates. She gestures for her two comrades to lie flat against the *Borgwardt*. With a grace and expertise that can only be gained from a lifetime in zero G, they barely even use their propulsors and move, one to either side of the airlock hatch.

The airlock hatches open with a whoosh and the tiny spritz of lost oxygen. As though being fired from a shotgun, crates of milk and eggs shoot out into the ink. The camera turns left and right, reminding us that this is shot from someone's point of view. Then the camerawoman deftly dodges a pint of strawberries that seems aimed at her. When she refocuses on the open airlock, the skin-wrappers who had been hiding on either side of the hatch are gone, already inside and standing on either side of the inner hatch. Through the porthole on the inner hatch stands Delilah, the chef, staring anxiously.

The camerawoman raises her grotesque, skinless arm and signals a thumbs-up. From Delilah's perspective, the signal was to her, but, of course, it's really to the infiltrators. Delilah nods, barely containing her shuddering, and turns away from the porthole. The outer airlock hatches seal shut and the infiltrators are on board. Several of the women in the room with me gasp in horror. Even I can't help glancing back at the bulkhead hatch sealing us in. How secure is it, really? How secure will it be when the skin-wrappers take over the command center, or the core? Our lives are only a button press away from the skinless pirates.

The pre-recording disappears and Nia's odious face replaces the image on the screen.

A thump sounds on the outside of the bulkhead. We all jump. It could have been anything, really, some unimportant piston somewhere popping or the ship settling, but it's incredibly timed. There's no shaking the fear that it's a skin-wrapper, just outside the hatch, and not only that, that they're hungry to eat our flesh like the inhuman monsters they resemble.

"Now do you have an inkling, madam director, of what's really going on? Oh, or did you know and were just hoping no one else would figure it out? Not wanting to cause a panic, are we? Don't worry, girls. I'm sure your security personnel are perfectly safe, and are taking care of the problem as we speak."

From above the camera's view, Delilah's pale, rigid corpse suddenly appears. The crown of her head bumps into the camera and, except for Diane, everyone in the room gasps seemingly as one. If one of Nia's disciples didn't push the body at the camera to get that exact effect, then it was a fortuitous coincidence for her. We are well and truly shitting our pants. All eyes, rather than looking at our captor, are locked on our director, our rock.

A thump sounds at the hatch again. Like prairie dogs we turned to look at it in unison. A second knock was no accident. Only Diane is still staring forward when we look back. Zanib is pale and visibly shaken.

"Suppose I take it as a given that you've infiltrated my ship. Suppose I take it as a further given that, granted sufficient time, you'll be able to gain access to this meeting room. Aside from terrorizing my employees, I have to assume there's some purpose to this communication."

Nia nods and wags a finger at the camera.

"You're right there, madam director. There's always an easy way and a hard way to get through any situation. Even a situation as in the bag as this one. You can still be an irritant to me."

"How can I avoid being an irritant? And what does it grant me to do so?"

Nia locks eyes on Diane.

"We can dig you out, like digging a tick out of skin. But this meeting room of yours also functions as a sort of a panic room, doesn't it? That's where you'd send your people to keep them safe. But it's going to take us time, lots of precious time and effort that I'd rather not expend to get at you. And you can make it even easier on us by telling your security personnel to stand down, and then giving us all your codes."

"And if I do this, what are you going to do for me?"

"We're taking your supplies. We're taking your fuel. But we can leave you oxygen and send a beacon to your corporation to retrieve you. That's the best you can hope for."

Another thump at the hatch shatters the last of my frayed nerves. I look into Zanib's eyes. I'm no doctor – medical or otherwise – but I can tell she's going into shock. Her pupils are hugely dilated and she looks like all she wants to do is bolt like a hare. I feel a gnawing at the pit of my stomach as I realize that if my experienced ink surfer roommate is this scared, we are in true danger.

"You'd rip us apart just for the spite of letting us die in space?"

Nia turns back to one of her floating protégés.

"Tell Hannah to turn on the can opener."

A tendril of blondish-brown hair drifts into Nia's earhole, tickling her just enough to be annoying. She slaps Delilah's floating body away.

"And someone get this thing out of here and cut up for parts." She turns back to Diane. "We do so need fresh organs. Every medical ship does. You wouldn't have had to find that out firsthand if you had been reasonable and considered your crew. But I'm getting the feeling you're trying to delay me, madam director. So, the offer, what little it was, is off the table."

A loud metallic buzz sounds just outside the hatch, followed almost immediately by the shriek of metal on metal. Nia's promised can opener is unmistakably cutting through to us. One of the analysts from Accounts Receivable leaps to her feet. We all turn to look at her. She seems ready to shout or do something, something memorable. Her eyes are darting around the room and finally settle on a stapler on the conference table. It's probably the heaviest thing in here, and the closest thing we have to a weapon.

The analyst snatches it up and turned to face the bulkhead.

"We have to fight, don't we? We have to do something, don't we?"

The room fills with unnatural, high-pitched snickering. The skin-wrappers have not cut the feed, looking forward to watching whatever was about to happen to us next.

Another analyst, in a severe brown suit rises and holds her hand out, palm upward, to the first. They had been sitting near each other. Perhaps she is the other one's supervisor.

"Izzy," the supervisor whispers, but in such close quarters and with such frayed senses we can all hear every word, "We're not going to be able to fight back against plasma torches. Not with a stapler. All that's left for us is...our dignity."

The supervisor looks up at Diane. Diane doesn't say a word, but with her silence tacitly agrees. Izzy looks like she has something else to say, but sheepishly places the makeshift weapon in her supervisor's hand. They share a look that suggested they have either worked together a very long time, or are close friends. The look becomes an embrace.

"Oh, no, no, please fight," Nia says with a snigger, "Please fight back. We have so little entertainment out here."

"Gash," Izzy's supervisor hisses as she leads her friend back to her seat.

The shriek of the can opener continues, unabated. I look in Zanib's eyes. She puts her arm around my shoulders with a sigh. We haven't known each other long, but are reduced to cold comforts. I never thought before I would just wait, resigned to my end.

The can opener fizzles and stops. On the vidscreen, Nia looked around her command center hastily.

"What? What happened?"

The screen mutes for a moment and I dare to let my heart soar. Has someone come to our aid? Have the diseased pirates simply decided we aren't worth the effort after all? Nia's grotesque, dripping visage belies that hope before she even turns the volume back on.

"Oh, sorry about all the theatrics. I guess we hacked your system sooner than expected. We'll be in directly."

The hatch shudders and shakes. I gasp, along with everyone else, though we knew the end was coming eventually. Whatever damage the can opener has done to the outside of the hatch is clearly clogging it up now, so they are just trying to open it the standard hydraulic way. The hatch moans in agony, and then, finally, at about a quarter normal speed, it opens.

A skin-wrapper stands in the hatchway, wrapped from head to toe in gauze and then that surrounded by a second layer of plastic boom suit, like a bubble. She holds in her hands a dangerous, toothy plasma torch, a weapon more like a flamethrower than a soldering iron. Plasma torches have long been the favored weapons of space combatants. Plasma was necessary to cut through bulkheads, because unlike projectile weapons or lasers a plasma torch can't accidentally punch a hole in the bulkhead and lead to explosive decompression.

Judging by the size of the nozzle and the amount of admixture in the tank strapped to her back, the skin-wrapper could instantly vaporize the entire complement of the meeting room. The question is how many of us will voluntarily go with her for dissection – or, even the thought makes me shudder, vivisection – for the value our organs would go towards prolonging the lives of the disease-riddled corsairs.

"Madam director," the skin-wrapper says, her voice muffled behind layers of gauze, though sounding distinctly un-croaky, like the other skin-wrappers.

"Helena," Diane replies.

I realize with a start that we have all turned away from the vidscreen and the leering voyeurs that the skin-wrappers have made of themselves. Clearly the distraction was not solely for our sake. The skin-wrappers on the other boat had been so fixated on our hatch, they hadn't noticed the arrival of Helena's people outside their own bridge.

Two goons in boom suits, affixed to the skin-wrapper ship with what I assume are mag boots, level beam rifles at the transparent dome that serves as the skin-wrapper command center. I gasp as they begin firing in what I at first assume to be a willy-nilly manner, but as the skin-wrappers' heads snap back and chests explode I realize the goons are actually aiming with deadly and deliberate precision.

"No, you fucks!" Nia shrieks, her voice rising to an octave I hadn't believed her capable of.

As the far side of the dome turns to Swiss cheese, explosive decompression is almost instantaneous. The goal of Helena's goons is not to board the enemy vessel and plunder their goods, as the plasma-torch-armed skin-wrappers had intended for us. No, their goal is murder, judicious and expert. I'm surprised but weirdly relieved that we have two such hardcore professionals on board.

The bodies of her crew tumbling backward around her, Nia scrabbles at the camera feed and manages to grab it. We see her, hanging on to us for dear life, as her morphia bag is sucked back towards the increasing rows of holes. In that instant, I feel for her as a fellow human being, forgetting that she is a grotesque minister of death who would have happily watched me burn me alive moments ago. All I see is a sick woman, scrabbling to keep her medbag from coming loose, and clinging with another hand for dear life.

In the end, the camera gives out, pulling loose and tumbling off to bounce against the various surfaces of the dome.

"...And I think that's about enough of that," the director says, as though cutting off a particularly chatty subordinate.

She reaches out and switches off the feed. We all groan like a class full of kindergartners. It strikes me that we all just cried out in protest of having our view of a bloodsport cut off. That worries something deep inside of me.

Diane raises herself from her seat, halfway pushing and halfway pulling on the heavy conference table. She reaches for her crutches, which two people grab and practically shove under her armpits unbidden.

"Ladies," she states flatly, "I apologize for the ruse. As some of you have probably guessed, it was necessary."

The director then explains what we have just witnessed.

Helena and the director had been in control of the situation the entire time. Helena and her people had no trouble sniffing out our infiltrators. Then, disguising herself as one, Helena began communicating with the skin-wrapper vessel. Then the problem was the plasteel dome atop the skin-wrapper ship. Pointing in every direction, the skin-wrappers would have been able to spot anyone approaching, and presumably raise a blast shield.

The entire business of pretending to cut into the meeting room and then capturing the codes was all solely to keep the attention of every skin-wrapper in the command center locked on the vidscreen, watching us squirm. Diane had played along, trying to draw Nia into conversation, but when that hadn't worked they had switched over to plan B: the play acting. And with all of the skin-wrappers focused like lasers on us, the two goons had been able to crawl around the far side of the enemy vessel and get the drop on them without raising suspicion.

The conventional telephone rings and Helena picks it up.

"This is security. I see. Well done. Yeah...I don't think that's up to me. I'll ask." She proffers the phone towards Diane, without actually seeming to want her to take it. "Madame director, Prosser and Tampa have the corsair leader alive. Shall we... rectify that situation?"

Diane turns with some difficulty to look at Helena standing behind her.

"I'm hardly a subject matter expert on security, but if I recall my supervision class correctly, corporate regulation state we're to take and hold any corsair captains for intelligence-gathering purposes."

Helena's costume is beginning to unravel. Her face, damaged mouth and all, is a mask of bafflement, as though Diane had just told her to go take a flying fuck. Her lips work as though trying to gum up some words.

"Has the regulation changed?" the director asks acidly.

"Well, no."

"Then why the sudden confusion?"

I suddenly feel awkward. This is a dressing-down, and it shouldn't take place in front of us. But Helena has brought it on herself.

"You're... you're going to waste food on her? And oxygen? After she came into our workplace? Threatened our lives?"

The way Helena says it, she's clearly far more aggrieved by the violation of her sacred office than by the threat to her wellbeing. Life's an afterthought for a deep ink security specialist. The sanctity of the workplace is everything.

"It's not your decision, Helena. Nor, frankly, is it mine. The food and oxygen on this boat is not mine to distribute as I see fit. It belongs to the corporation and we are merely its stewards."

She glances around the room, as if remembering for the first time that she has an audience.

"That's a lesson each of you can take to heart. It's been a tough day. We'll reconvene in six hours to complete our briefing. That'll put us one hour out from the objective."

# EIGHT

I hold in the yawn as long as humanly possible, but can't wait for the entire corridor to clear before letting it out. The important thing is the director didn't see me.

"You getting tired, virgin? Better go rack out for a while."

I'm exhausted. Beyond exhausted. All the adrenaline has fled from my body like rats from a demolition site. But something else tingles further forward on the front burner of my anatomical messages.

As if on cue, my tummy rumbles. I haven't had a speck since we last ate together. I'm not sure if she hears it (in a way, I hope she can't, because nothing can spike a friendship quite as quickly as an unwanted exchange of bodily noises) but I pat my belly anyway.

"I will, but I need to grab something to nosh first. Up for your eighth ribeye of the day?"

"Nah, I've got to bow out this time, or else catch up with you later. But make sure you grab some human fuel this time, though, and not just the flash-fried noodle garbage."

I may not know Zanib intimately yet, but turning down food does not sound like her at all.

"What have you got to do that's so important?"

She smiles.

"I've got to visit my babies."

She pronounces "babies" like "beh-bies." She must be headed for the superluminal phone bank. Frankly, I'm a little stunned. Ink surfers aren't famous for being family types, and Zanib in particular seems too young. Not to mention her figure doesn't suggest a single pregnancy, let alone multiple. Then again, she must have the metabolism of a camel to eat the way she does and look like that.

"I didn't realize you had kids."

She turns her head back and barks out laughter so long and hard she has to grab herself to stop.

"Kids? Like actual kids? Hell, no, virgin, I ain't dead yet. I've got years of surfing the ink left in me. What, did you think I was calling home?"

Well, this is cryptic. My mouth quirks, halfway of its own accord.

"Well, yeah."

"Jeez, virgin, don't you know anything? We don't have free comms out here. The only thing that goes in or out superluminally is certified, notarized business with HQ. You weren't planning on checking in with home, were you?"

"Well, not now, I guess. So, what are these, ah, babies of yours then?"

"Walk this way," she says, affecting a spooky accent and a villainous laugh.

She leads me down into the working area of the *Borgwardt*. Being stuck in research mode, I haven't really had a chance to explore the ship this far. It's about what I expected from a corporate vessel. Each department has an assigned bay, packed with desks separated from each other by felt-lined cubicles. Across from each open bay are two or three individual offices for first line supervisors, and most of those bear actual name and position placards.

The attack by the skin-wrappers has sent staplers, personal photos, and phones tumbling to the deck, but many of the workers are already back at their desks, fastidiously re-arranging things. In Accounts Payable, one woman is having a very animated conversation on her jotter with someone who, based on what Zanib just told me, must be elsewhere on the ship. Hoping not to miss it, I stop to peer into the Accounts Receivable bay, and, as expected, the angry woman's conversation partner is there, seemingly just as upset.

Zanib grabs me.

"All the places you could be interested in, and it's accounting that's caught your eye. Come on, we're almost there."

Once we're past the departmental bays we get to some bays that are designated for technical work, packed with lab equipment and researchers in white coats. I don't recognize what any of them are working on, but I can notice certain differences between their disciplines, based on the names listed on the bays. The xenoclimatologists all wear flip-flops and short sleeves, like they're used to hanging out on alien beaches. The pure mathematicians are all wearing the fat, fist-sized, short-hanging neck cravats that are all the rage on Broatoa. They also seem to favor old-fashioned slate chalkboards, whereas the engineers have a bulkhead-sized computer screen they are scribbling on and constantly crossing out and writing over one another's ideas.

This time I pass Zanib by, missing the fact that she's stopped to begin jimmying open a hatch to a smaller, almost closet-sized bay.

"What's this?" I ask, perplexed. The hatch is not marked, except by biohazard signs and cautions not to enter ranging in urgency from frantic to quite frantic.

"This is where I keep my beh-bies. My beh-bie shack."

Finally, something gives and the hatch lifts on its hydraulic hinges. If I didn't know better, I'd suspect she doesn't even have a key. But she's probably simply putting on airs of being mysterious to amuse herself/shock me and she could have easily gotten it open any old time.

The room is small, but only for two people. For its inhabitants, it is perfectly well suited. She flips on a light and the grotesque feeling of unease I had in the darkness abates, but only slightly. The darkness was full of monsters, but only very mundane ones. Small, furry, scaly, and occasionally slimy, blood-drinking ones.

"Hematophages," I whisper.

"Ding-ding-ding," she says, as though I've won a prize at a fair.

Here are the creatures she alluded to at the meeting. A pair of leeches in a small, murky brown aquarium. Two vampire bats, hanging from a perch in their cave-like enclosure. There are ticks, birds, butterflies, a number of worms, and almost a whole bulkhead of various mosquito species.

"Two of each?

She nods.

"Breeding pairs. A regular Zanib's ark."

"You don't prefer just keeping frozen seed on hand?"

"You ever try to inseminate a mosquito by hand, virgin?"

I grin.

"No, I suppose I haven't."

"Well, then. Trust me on this one."

I'm not normally squeamish – and I've never considered myself to be superstitious – but as I approach the furthest bulkhead of Zanib's little menagerie, I can't keep from feeling that someone has stepped on my grave. The hairs on the back of my neck stand up and I feel a chill run through my spinal column.

The water is murky, murkier even than the brackish enclosures for the leeches. I approach with trepidation, transfixed, waiting for something to show itself, when suddenly something slams against the glass, so alien in appearance and visage that I nearly drop to the deck, clutching at my heart.

A circlet of teeth presses against the glass, the teeth pointing in all the directions of the compass and then some. And in the center of this jawless monstrosity's throat is what appears to be a toothed tongue. This must be one of Zanib's lampreys, the creature most like what she expects to find on the fleshworld below.

"I see the stonelickers have caught your attention."

I nod, hoping I'm not looking too pale, but all the blood seems to be rushing away from my face, as if avoiding its natural enemy in the tank there.

"Is this every species of lamprey?"

"I have them all here. The saltwater ones are in a separate enclosure. Would you like to meet Crassus here? He seems eager to meet you."

"Oh, no..." I start to protest, but it's already too late.

With the deftness and rough-and-ready nature of a born zookeeper, Zanib reaches into the tank, and barely seems to be rifling around before she latches onto the lamprey and drags him out of his little freshwater home. I shudder as a loud, audible pop accompanies his mouth being pulled off the glass.

She approaches me with confidence, as though wrangling a long, eel-like fish is the most natural thing in the world to her.

"This is Crassus," she repeats, "He's a river lamprey. *Lampetra fluviatilis*. From Earth. And very rarely exported offworld. For some reason."

I swallow a lump that has suddenly appeared in my throat.

"Is it safe to have him out of the water like that?"

"Oh, sure," she says, as though fish being out of water is the most natural thing in the universe, "just for a second. Go ahead, pet him. He's not so bad. He's just a big baby, aren't you, Crassus?"

She reaches out with her semi-free hand to stroke Crassus under what would be his chin. He makes a definite attempt to latch onto her arm and begin sucking the blood from it, his sharp tongue pounding like a piston. I can only stare in horror. I know this creature is no more or no less than as evolution and nature made it, and it can't control its appearance any better than I can, but something deep and reptilian inside of me rejects the notion that this is anything but a monstrosity, an aberration, the greatest crime or joke the universe ever played on us.

"Go on," she says again. "Now he is probably starting to drown in the air. Just run the back of your hand along his spine."

My hand is shaking as I reach out to do as she says, and I have no doubt she is enjoying my discomfort, but ultimately, whether because of peer pressure or some deep need inside to prove myself, I stroke the blood-drinking fish. I shiver at the slimy consistency of his skin as she wrangles him back into his tank.

I watch in grotesque fascination as Crassus begins to undulate in his tank, wrapping around his life-mate and they show some kind of distant, piscine version of affection to one another. Zanib doesn't even wash or disinfect her hands before putting one of her hamhocks on my shoulder.

"Now how many people do you know who can say they've petted a lamprey?"

"Just you and me, to my knowledge."

She waggles a finger in my face.

"I know you didn't want to. I know it was uncomfortable. But if you want to make it out here, you've got to get comfortable doing the uncomfortable, if that makes sense."

In a perverse way, it does.

"Well, now it's feeding time. I'm going to go out on a limb and guess you won't want to stay for this. It'll definitely make you lose your appetite."

I raise an eyebrow.

"Shouldn't I get comfortable being uncomfortable?"

She grins.

"One step at a time, virgin. Just..."

She trails off.

"What?" I finally prompt her.

"I don't know what we're going to be dealing with tomorrow. Or, really, in a few hours, I should say. You know, Paige, some people aren't made for this."

It might be the first time she's called me by my given name. I take quiet note.

"I know."

"Are you one of them?"

I think about it a moment. Then, before Zanib can stop me, I barge over to Crassus's tank and snatch him out of the grasp of his lady love. I'm no expert animal wrangler as she is. It takes both hands and all my concentration to even keep him from slithering out of my grasp. But then I have him, in front of me, just his tail dangling down in the murky water, and he is stuck in my grasp, fixed in place, waiting. I'm staring into his eyes.

I press my lips to his swelling, puckering, jawless mouth, and give him a kiss. I feel him latch onto me, his dozens of teeth piercing my lips and chin. He suckles at me and I feel the blood draining away from my face.

"Paige!"

With a yank, I rip the stonelicker away from my face. But I don't fail to make the loudest lip-smack I can. With the gentleness of a lover, I let Crassus slip back into his tank. I look at Zanib. She's staring at me in horror, which is gradually giving way to respect, and finally to amusement.

"Your face is a mess. And who knows what he's carrying. You should report to the infirmary."

I shake my head, and walk over to the bottle of disinfectant she keeps at the front of the room. I press down on the head of the bottle, squeezing a fat blob into my hand, and rub it all over my lips and chin. I feel the sting from the dozens of penetrations, but I glance at myself in the mirror and it really looks no worse than a bad case of razor burn. Or maybe herpes.

"Nah, I'll be fine. Got to toughen up if I'm going to surf the ink."

"All right," she says, "Don't say I didn't warn you."

"So maybe I get diarrhea. Wouldn't be the first time."

I walk toward the hatch, which obligingly opens for me. I stop, something striking me that hadn't occurred to me until just then.

"Zanib?"

"Yeah, virgin?"

"When you go to feed these hematophages... what exactly does that entail?"

She smiles.

"Don't believe the hype."

I don't know what that means, but I don't press. My stomach is grumbling.

●●●

The director is lingering at the register. A few of us have already picked up our meals and are ready to check out, but we hang back by the salad bar, pretending to be pondering adding croutons or cheese to our meals. One of the security goons is dutifully ladling one of the soup bins, as though she may discover some hidden ingredient down in the depths that will suddenly change it from cream of mushroom to white clam chowder. Honestly, I've never seen a label on any of the soups, so it could be twat juice for all I know, but no amount of fussing and stirring will ever change it into anything other than twat juice.

The truth is our prevaricating is all horseshit, of course. Aside from the fact that you can't add salad bar condiments to sandwiches or other food (as countless signs proclaim and countless slapped wrists recall) we really just don't want to queue up behind Diane. Perhaps we don't want her to feel rushed (not that I think she'd ever give a shit and certainly wouldn't show it if she did) or perhaps we just don't want to be near her. It hardly matters. We can hear every word she's saying to the cashier anyway.

"This is a big opportunity for you, Rebecca," the director is saying.

"Thanks, boss," the cashier replies, her Broatoan brogue making her sound even more disrespectful than her baseline level of disdain could.

"I can't promise you anything, but with Delilah off the payroll, that may free up some chits for you and your staff. I'll talk to the bursar about it, anyway."

"Well, that's the important thing, is chits. Oh, but ain't you forgetting about one thing, madam director?"

Diane cocks her head.

"What's that?"

"Them two pennies what go on Lilah's eyes. Guess we won't be getting those."

The director's face hardens and not the swizzle of a spoon or the drip of a tureen can be heard in the whole galley.

"Well, you're grieving. I can understand that, Rebecca. We have a counselor available, any time, day or night, for you or your people. I suggest you make an appointment."

"I surely won't."

Diane either pretends not to hear or ignores it. She starts to limp away on her crutches.

"Good. I'm counting on you, Rebecca."

"No worries, Diane, everyone's still going to eat."

Diane turns her back and Rebecca makes the customary Broatoan kiss-off gesture of shitting in her hand and popping the turd in her mouth. A number of the other galley patrons turn away in embarrassment, but I can't take my eyes off the little fireplug of a woman.

She's so short she can't work the register without a stool, and has to clamber up to get on the stool and jump to get down from it. Her hair is clipped close, as most of the food service workers wear it, though hers seems to retain the muscle memory of once having been a mullet.

"Hey! Yo! Ambroziak! Those fixings are only for salads."

"Yeah, I know I was just deciding whether I wanted chunked salami or, um..."

I look around. My erstwhile friends and allies have abandoned me, shifting their focus to the drink stations and condiment islands. I feel like a character in an old comedy sketch when the boss asks for volunteers and instead of anyone stepping forward everyone else steps back.

Fuck it.

I put my tray down on the register.

"Why lie? I was watching you fight with the director."

Her right eye otherwise locked on the screen as she punches in the codes for each of my lunch items, the cashier glances briefly at me with her left.

"Oh, yeah? How'd it go?"

I shrug, though she's deliberately not watching me.

"I'd say you won."

"Won what?"

"Uh... it's a moral victory anyway."

The cashier snorts, so loudly she might be a bear coming out of hibernation. She finally looks me in the eyes.

"Thing you got to remember about the director is, she just don't give a shit about people. It's like she knows human people got emotions, but it just don't click in her head or something."

"You're upset about the old chef getting killed."

The cashier's face explodes in exaggerated delight, as though I've just won a Kewpie doll at a fair. She rings an imaginary bell.

"Ding-ding-ding! And you don't even know me. That's sixteen chits, Ambroziak. You want it out of your account or you carrying it on you?"

"Account, please."

I glance back to see that a line has finally formed behind me. Fucking cowards. I stick a finger in my Ramen. Cold, of course. Not that it was ever particularly more than lukewarm.

"Hey, Ambroziak?"

I look back at the cashier, surprised.

"Account, please. I'm not carrying any cash."

"Yeah, I know. Are you eating alone?"

Zanib's busy feeding her little coterie of blood-drinking animals. I could glance around the galley looking for some vague acquaintance whose name I can coax from my semi-ambulatory memory, but why bother?

"I am..." I say, trailing off.

"I'll join you."

The cashier sticks her fingers in her mouth and whistles loudly, the sort of whistle I didn't think people could really make but seems to happen all the time in old movies.

"Yo, Urs! Take over for me here, will you? I'm going to take lunch."

The tiny woman jumps down from her weirdly low perch and accompanies me, clapping her hands against one another as if clapping off chalk or debris. A white-clad, hair-netted woman emerges from the bowels of the galley in no great hurry to take her place.

"So, Rebecca..." I start to say as I take a seat.

Unlike Zanib, the cashier sits down in the correct position, across from me. In fact, she takes it a step further and sits across and diagonally opposed from me. Perfect.

"Flying fuckballs," she replies, "nobody calls me that. Becs. Please."

"Becs. Becs from Broatoa."

She grins.

"That obvious, huh?"

I shovel a spoonful of noodles into my mouth, and speak again when I've slurped a bit more than a spoonful down.

"You could say that," I answer. "You know, it's not going to be much of a lunch break for you if you don't go get something to eat."

She eyes me as though I've sprouted a unicorn horn from my forehead.

"Serve myself? In my galley? I don't think so."

As if to prove her point, one of the white-clad cooks waddles out of the back and sets down a tray in front of her. Everything about the tray of food is ordinary – same cutlery, same alloy cup, same everything that everybody else gets – except that the plate is covered with a metal cover and a single flower in a tiny vase adorns the tray.

"Weekday special, Becs."

"Thanks, Andi," she replies, stuffing a napkin halfway down the throat hole of her shirt.

Becs lifts the cover from her plate and steam rises from the still-hot meal. I gape in astonishment as the steam clears.

Zanib can pack down food like there's no tomorrow, but they still just serve her ordinary cafeteria food. I don't get anything fancy, and nothing fancy is all I expect. But here, the newly christened boss of the kitchen has a gourmet meal laid out in front of her.

The meat is a tiny, elegant filet. The potatoes are a delicate, braised affair, and the sprinkle of Hollandaise over the artichokes is almost poetic in its artistry. Becs cuts her meat as though she is teaching an etiquette class to a roomful of petty bourgeoisie. She takes her first taste and nods appreciatively, as though it is completely unnecessary to say, "Perfect." She takes a sip from her alloy mug as though pairing some expensive wine with her course – Hell, for all I know, she is – and suddenly she notices me staring at her. I must be turning red in the face like a fat kid caught with her hand in the cookie jar.

"What? You surprised Broatoans know how to eat with a fork and knife?"

I shake my head and almost snort cola out of my nose.

"No. Sorry. I didn't..."

"Oh," she realizes, stretching the single syllable out over the course of a few seconds, "you thought we wasn't capable of making a decent meal back here. That we're just knuckle-draggers who don't know kiwi from quinoa."

I eye her with mock-scorn over my mug.

"You're shoveling the words in my mouth as fast as you can. I didn't say anything even remotely like that."

She sizes me up.

"Yeah, I guess you didn't. Sorry, Ambroziak. I get it coming and going. It's not easy feeding a shipful of skinny Gashes. But I do it. And I do it on time. And I do it on budget.

And I do it with no fucking staff. And now we're even one less."

She stops as though she hadn't fully thought out what she had been saying.

"I'm sorry, Becs. Did you know Lilah well?"

"Lilah," she repeats, her head a million light-years away. The second time she says it, she's halfway cognizant again. "Lilah. Yeah, I knew her pretty good. Half a dozen tours on this tub, her and I. I wasn't going to come this time, you know. I really wasn't. I could've used some time on Yloft for R&R. It never hurts being off a boat for five minutes, you know? I definitely was not planning on hopping the next light-hearse out of there."

She seems a million light-years away.

"What changed your mind?"

She fixes me with a gaze.

"Lilah. She begged me. This weird emergency thing came down. I'd reckon you got caught up in it, too. Fat bonuses and overtime?"

"A bonus, yeah."

She stretches back like a cat that's been napping too long but wants to nap just a little bit longer.

"Yeah, well, Madam Severity promised even us lowly potato-peelers bonuses and time-and-a-half for actual overtime worked. We was understaffed but we was going to get paid, you feel me? Even so, I wouldn't have set foot in the ink again for at least six months if Lilah hadn't begged me to. And now I'm understaffed, and in charge."

"I'm sorry about your friend. I didn't know her, but..."

"Well, no need to blow smoke up my ass, then. I know exactly what kind of metal plated her ass. She was worth more than the whole damn lot of them. The board of directors, the investors, Madam Gash Queen Director, all of them. I'd trade the whole lot of them to have Lilah back."

"Was you..." I stop myself. I'm picking up her speech patterns. It's subconscious, but I don't want her to think I'm making fun. Broatoans always have that effect on me. I dated one once when I was an undergrad. Her tongue was to die for, and not just that sexy accent. I start over. "Were you lovers?"

Becs shakes her head.

"No. I've got a girl back in port. Not Yloft. Back home. No idea if she's being loyal to me. I wouldn't be loyal to me either. Maybe she is."

She shrugs, like it makes no nevermind... damn it. I'm even doing it in my own head now. She shrugs, like it doesn't matter to her one way or the other. Maybe it doesn't.

"That's neither hin nor hair, though. Lilah was just good people. Too bad. Stuck her head in the lion's mouth one too many times."

"Risk-taker?"

"Nah. Not especially. Lilah was button-down, if anything. Straight-laced. It's being out here, doing this. Surfing the ink. No matter what you're doing, no matter how safe you think you are – you can be peeling potatoes, Ambroziak – every time you set foot on a tub, you're sticking your head in a sleeping lion's mouth and tugging on her tail. If she never bites down, well, that's just luck."

She pushes her plate away, even the tiny portion her people had made especially for her unfinished. I try to say something like, "Nice talking to you, Becs," but I can't bring myself to do it.

# NINE

I've been laying in my bunk for an hour, not sleeping, just staring at the bottom of Zanib's bunk. She's snoring like a pig, and her arm is hanging down practically in my face, but neither of those are keeping me awake. It's the reality of the attack eating away at me. The possibility that I just could have died. That's never struck me before.

Becs talked about sticking her head in the lion's mouth every time she went into the ink. This is my first time, aside from the barely-remembered, doesn't-even-really-count trip with my parents from Horizant to Yloft when I was eight.

At eight, your choices aren't on you. The universe isn't out to get you. Your parents are a buffer between you and all the cosmic rays and skin-wrappers and supply problems and who knows what else. I hadn't stuck my head in the lion's mouth when I was eight. My parents had. If I had died then, it would've been on them, not me. No one would have said, "Oh, that kid should have made better choices with her life." They would have said, "What awful, awful parents."

I roll over, putting my back to Zanib's dangling fingers and my nose practically to the bulkhead. I don't have kids. Never wanted them. Never planned on having them. Being a mother means throwing yourself on the grenade of responsibility for your kid. No wonder urban myth is rife with stories of mothers saving their babies instead of themselves in a ship crash or having ultimate strength to lift a fallen mine processor off their child or shit like that. Who wants to be remembered as the mother who couldn't take care of her kid? It's a fate worse than dying yourself.

I don't know why mothers and babies are on my mind. Maybe I'm just finally understanding that my neck belongs to me for pretty much the first time. There's no more blaming Ma. My stupid choices are now my own. I stuck my head in the lion's mouth and somehow, improbably, pulled it out. Even that was more luck than anything else. That was Helena's victory, and Diane's, and Prosser's and Tampa's. I didn't have anything to do with it. I was a completely passive audience to my own possible death.

Sighing, I shove my second pillow between my legs. Whenever I have trouble sleeping on my side sometimes (but not always) a pillow between my legs helps. I lay there, restless, for what seems like an impossibly long time, but I must have drifted off at some point because the next thing I know Zanib is jabbing me in the back.

"A few more minutes and you're going to be derelict."

I groan. My exhaustion is utter and complete. If anything, the bowl of Ramen and tureen of coffee I downed with Becs has made matters worse. I shouldn't have eaten before trying to nap. I feel bloated.

"Is there time to shower?"

"How much do you love me, virgin?"

I look into her eyes. Joy shines there, fellowship. For a second I wonder if she's attracted to me, too. "Fast friends" perhaps we are, but I've heard too many stories about ink surfers to think this is more than that. It's too soon to let my heart be broken by another spacer just looking for a warm snatch.

But I'm putting the cart before the horse, aren't I? This is all projection.

"I love you more than anything. More than life itself."

"Keep going," she says with a nod, making the "stretching out pizza dough" gesture with her hands.

"More than a glass of wine on a white, sandy beach. More than Ramen noodles. More than my bonus."

Zanib quirks her Cupid's bow smile and shrugs.

"Okay. Well, then, I woke you with just about enough time. As long as you're taking an ink surfer shower and not a fucking Yloft fucking station bunny fucking grad student shower. And I even saved you a little lukewarm water."

I snatch my towel and jump to my feet. She kisses me on the cheek as I hurry into the stall, which does nothing to help me sort out my Byzantine labyrinth of annoying feelings.

I don't really have the option of taking a horseshit station bunny shower after all, as the stall begins not-so-gently nudging me that my daily water ration is being used up, before finally starting a countdown in red blinking numbers. The "lukewarm" bit was a joke, though. The water reclamation system is an integral part of the *Borgwardt*'s cooling system, and in a workplace the *Borgwardt*'s size there's no lack of heating coils to choose from, so hot water is never an issue. In fact, whenever we need cold water, the pipes run through space for brief periods to cool it down.

We head back to the conference room expecting (or I was expecting, at least, there's no telling what Zanib thought based on her years of experience) a ruined hatch. Helena had either been very surgically precise with the can opener or else had been faking a lot more of the little Kabuki play than I had guessed, because a custodian is crouched over, just finishing oiling up the hatch's hinges. It looks like it's back to 100%.

"Sorry, ladies," the custodian says, crabwalking out of our way, "didn't mean to be in your way."

"You're not," I laugh, glancing at the nametag sewn to her overalls which proclaimed her to be Eden, "besides, we're nobody important."

Zanib shoves my head playfully into the jamb. If she had me off guard I might have been knocked unconscious, but she pulls her punch immediately. I just bang my head lightly. A love tap?

"What, do you have a mouse in your pocket? Who's 'we?'"

"We. You and me."

"Speak for yourself, virgin. I'm the importantest motherfucker in this place."

Eden snorts in appreciation, then quickly covers her mouth so I won't see her laughing at me. All the custodians I know on Yloft are either like that: respectful to a fault, as though somebody like me is a member of an entirely different and possibly better species, or else so surly and grumpy that saying "Good morning" to them is like a personal affront. I'm glad Eden is of the former category.

"See you, Eden," Zanib says, without looking at her nametag, "Keep up the good work."

"You, too, Ms. Zanib."

"You know her?" I ask as we settle into the exact same two seats we had been in earlier.

She shrugs.

"I know everybody. I told you, virgin, I'm the importantest motherfucker in this place."

That elicits a snort from the woman to Zanib's right, this time not of appreciation. Zanib turns and glares.

"What are you laughing at, head-case?"

The other woman is smiling.

"How are your vampire bats doing, Zanib? You feeding them good?"

The other woman reaches out and rolls up Zanib's sleeve halfway before she can snatch her arm away. I look over, too, to see if there are any perforations from fangs or leech-gullets or... what was the other word? Proboscis? Prosbosces?

Anything else about to transpire between my roommate and her opposite-side seatmate is clipped off by Diane's appearance in the hatchway. As she enters, everyone rises out of respect. Instead of gesturing for us to sit, the director glances around the room.

"As long as I've got you all on your feet, how about a round of applause for Helena Marsters and our entire security section?"

Though her crutches made it difficult for the director to clap personally, she sidesteps the issue by gesturing with both hands towards Helena and her crew, who are standing, seemingly embarrassed, in one corner. I recognized Tampa and Prosser, whose faces are etched indelibly into my mind, and there is one other goon who had presumably been aiding Helena shipside or manning posts somewhere during the intrusion.

Myrna, the secretary, sneaks in and presses a piece of paper into the director's hand.

"Oh, no," she says, "not another memo!"

Work humor. Maybe a little in bad taste just at this moment. Nonetheless, there are chuckles, if out of nervousness than nothing else.

"Thanks, Myrna. Okay, come on up here, Helena and everybody."

Sheepishly, Helena, Tampa, and Prosser step forward, and the goon I don't know by name remains notably behind. The others gesture for her to join them, and finally Prosser goes back, grabs her by the shoulder, and forces her to come forward with the rest.

"Yes, everybody," the director said with a chuckle. "Don't be shy, Quinn."

I watch Quinn's face as the humiliation set in. If I had to wager, she must have been working the communications lines during the brief skirmish, or else hadn't reported for duty at all.

"All right," Diane says, clearing her throat theatrically, "I have here a certificate which reads: 'To the security department of the *RV Borgwardt*, This Certificate of Appreciation is issued to honor your fine actions on the date of...'" the director rattles off yesterday's date in the confusing, non-arithmetic system which only Hestle corporate seems to use while everybody else just refers to local time. She continues: "'Your actions are a tribute to your dedication to your jobs and your fellow employees. Continue to remain Hestle Strong.' And then it's signed by the CEO herself."

This elicits some impressed clucking of tongues and oohing and aahing, although even I can see from here that the electronic signature and even the language of the COA are stock. The CEO probably never saw it, and her secretary probably rubber-stamped a hundred of these a day. Still, it's a nice, if likely horseshit gesture.

"I've been on the horn with corporate for four hours, and they didn't want to do it, but I insisted. I insisted they do it right now. And you all probably thought I was just sleeping during the break." More work humor. More unwarranted chuckles. "Care to say a few words, Helena?"

"Oh, no," Helena says, waving off the idea as though it were supremely unpalatable. "I'm not much for words and that sort of thing. Besides, I didn't do anything but make sure my crew was well-trained. They're the real heroes here."

"Well, you claim not to be much for words, but that was very well said. How about another round of applause, everyone?"

We cheer again, though unlike the first time I'm more doing it mechanically than out of real vigor. Scarce though tree pulp may be in the ink, I can't help but think that the women who risked their lives to save the rest of us deserve a little more than lip service on a slip of paper. Still, Helena takes the certificate and quickly passes it to Quinn, the one who had been so reluctant to join the group on stage. She must be the administrator or something.

Diane struggles into her chair.

"All right, ladies, sorry to bring us back here to the scene of the crime, so to speak, but it's time for me to issue my guidance. Can we bring up a real-time image, please?"

The vidscreen hums and the blank screen is replaced by an almost identical image of monotone black, with the exception of a single, tiny red blemish at its center.

"Magnify, please."

Neither the director nor the computer operator plays around with zooming in 10x, backing out, zooming in 100x, or any other such nonsense. She merely zooms in until the tiny dot of a planet fills the entire screen.

Even after listening to Zanib and the xenoclimatologists opine about what, theoretically, such a planet would look like and behave like, seeing the real thing is still a revelation. The planet is red, but not with dust like Mars in the Solar System. The planet's surface is red verging on black, a soupy pudding that bubbles in spots, great tectonic shifts that resemble the explosion of a pimple on the skin. And the atmosphere is dense with bright red clouds. Does blood really rain from the skies on a fleshworld?

Perhaps most disturbing of all, the world seems to have a visage. I know it's probably my imagination, but I can almost see the great darkling spots which made up the eyeholes, noseholes, and grinning outline of a jaw, as though the planet itself is a grim chapless skull. The living planet has the look of a moribund one, and I can't help but take it as an ill omen.

"Ladies, I give you the semi-legendary planet of Vilameen. As many of you have guessed or intuited, though, by regulation, I was not allowed to confirm until now, we are attempting to salvage the wreck of *The Manifest Destiny*.

"First of all, I don't want anyone to get sloppy or starry-eyed. And I won't apologize for the deception, because everything I've done is according to regulation. You should be treating this mission like any other. By the numbers. The fact that we all love an old movie about it shouldn't even come into play. I don't need anyone being distracted saying, 'Oh, this is where the love scene happened in Pod 7' and then bashing her head into an overhang and, bam, suddenly we have a worker's comp case on our hands."

"The love scene was in Pod 6!" someone cries out.

I was thinking the exact same thing.

"Yes, well. Distractions, distractions, distractions. This isn't a Hollywood set. This is a dangerous fleshworld. The xenoclimatologists have briefed you on some of the dangers to expect just from being here. What lies inside, I don't even want to guess. And I don't want any of you guessing, either. This is why we have protocol. This is why we have regulations. This is why we don't just throw caution to the wind and do whatever our hearts tell us. And this is why you are all paid to be exceptionally expert in your chosen fields.

"Here's the good news. In spite of the delay caused by our run-in with the corsairs, we have managed to reach the planet before any other corporation. Our agents on Yloft have informed me that we have at least an eighteen-hour head start on all of our competition. Our agents are working to expand that window, but we cannot rely on that happening."

She's talking about espionage. Corporate shadows hacking systems, bribing docking officials, maybe even blowing up airlocks and more active sabotage. Yloft (and every deep space station like it) is a hotbed for that sort of activity and every administrator who ever ran the place had sworn to stamp it out. But espionage is far too lucrative, and inevitably the administrators became complicit or get hoodwinked by subordinates who don't mind making a quick buck.

"Now to answer your last question. How has this gone unnoticed for so long? Paige."

Didn't expecting that. I fight back the urge to sit bolt upright in my chair.

"Madam director?"

"If I had asked you last week the odds that the story of *The Manifest Destiny* was true, what would you have said?"

I want to hesitate but I mustn't. Form your answer as you speak.

"Ah, around 50/50. Scholars differ. But kind of about the same as you might treat the events of *The Iliad*. There probably was some kind of war between Greeks and Trojans, but, you know, no gods and golden apples."

I hold my breath. Is my answer what she was fishing for? I can't read her at all.

"And that's about the length and breadth of it. Up until last week, most reasonable adults to include corporate information services believed that *The Manifest Destiny* was a great movie about a ship that had probably really been lost in a debris field or by an instrumentation error or something. And Vilameen? About as factual as, say, Brigadoon.

"I bring up the story of Brigadoon on purpose. Every hundred years the town appeared on the map, and then it disappeared. Well, Vilameen appears to be in a similar situation. Not that it ever actually disappears. But take a look at this. Show us the simulation."

The fleshworld disappears from the screen, replaced by an animation of a solar system. The star is a white dwarf. Four planetary bodies and an asteroid field lie nestled uncomfortably close to the sun and each other.

"Here's a fun little gravitational anomaly. This is the Endirii System. Endirii-4 and the Endirii Debris Field are locked in orbit around each other."

On the screen, the fourth planet and the asteroid nest begin circling around an imaginary point in between the two, essentially switching position over and over again. The asteroids, which start in the fifth position, keep taking over the fourth position and rotating back again.

"The Endirii Debris Field is probably the result of a planetary crackup of the former either Endirii-4 or Endirii-5. In either case, it's surprisingly compact, and so close to such a huge sun that there's not a whole lot of shift. It functions, for all intents and purposes, as a single planetary body, only smashed into pieces.

"What we didn't know – what no one knew until last week – was that Endirii-4 also has a small satellite, internal to its own orbit."

The screen focuses in on the fourth planet from an "overhead" view (although of course, such nomenclature has no meaning in space.) A small red pimple rotates around the fourth planet.

"Any satellite is obscured from view from any given direction roughly fifty percent of the time. Coming at Endirii from a terrestrial perspective, the moon of Endirii-4 is obscured by its own planet half the time. And the other half of the time, it's obscured by the geosynchronous orbit of its sister asteroid field. The only time the moon is visible is roughly every one hundred and thirty terrestrial years. This moon is our own little Brigadoon. It also happens to be Vilameen. The USA must have discovered it on one of the rare occasions when it was visible.

"This is two-dimensional thinking of the worst kind, ladies. If anyone had ever taken a pass at Endirii from another perspective - the so-called 'overhead' at a minimum

— we could have discovered this gem years ago. But common wisdom said that Endirii was a useless chain of rocks, not even worth a second look. And yet it hides not just the biological and scientific find of a lifetime — a real fleshworld — but an archaeological treasure whose true value is beyond measure.

"So. My first standing guidance: no two-dimensional thinking. And no bowing to common wisdom,"

The same words appear on the screen.

"Now, because Vilameen is outside any corporate jurisdiction, we have no salvage rights, implied or otherwise, by showing up first. Showing up first is just as good as showing up last if someone with more firepower arrives. I don't know who will be arriving in pursuit of us, but I am certain that they will outgun us. The *Borgwardt* is designed for speed. Not stealth, and not a brute fight. If we are challenged, we have essentially no choice but to back down."

Helena shifts in her chair uncomfortably, causing a squeak that may or may not have been intentional.

"And this is no reflection on our brave security staff, as you've already seen. But opportunistic skin-wrappers are not going to be the same issue as the AginCorp super-dreadnaught that was docking at Yloft as we were leaving."

There is some grumbling and at least one audible gasp. I never knew AginCorp had that kind of firepower arrayed against us. I certainly would've reconsidered taking this job if I had.

"But rest assured, ladies, I have no intention of having this prize stolen out from under us. That means we have to have this salvage complete — soup to nuts — in eighteen hours. If we receive word that we can extend, we will. Otherwise, I intend to depart at hour eighteen, regard of salvage status, well in advance of our competitors. That means we get what we can and we blow the rest."

I look at Zanib. Her mouth is puckered as though she had just sucked on a lemon, but she doesn't seem especially shocked. It seems that despite all of Diane's high-minded speak about archaeological treasures, as a director her biggest concern is still the bottom line.

"Future generations may not look kindly on us for that. But my duty is not to posterity; it is to our shareholders. As is yours. Knowing my intention are any of you unable or unwilling to comply with an order to destroy *The Manifest Destiny* should the need arise?"

Seats shift and chair legs scrape against the deck. I never understood in old movies when the great hero drew a line in the sand and asked for volunteers why everyone always stepped across. Some high-minded ideal, or perhaps the implicit shame of friends, brethren, and onlookers always seemed to drive them to choose the hard right rather than the easy wrong. I always expected that encountering such a situation in real life, at least a few people would walk away, content to be live cowards rather than martyrs.

It seems some reversal of that supposed altruistic impulse is weaving its spell on those of us in this room. I have no doubt that every one of us here feels somehow in the pit of her stomach that destroying something that belongs to the ages is wrong, terribly wrong, in a way that few things are. And being asked to, shouldn't we all stand up as one and pronounce, "Not I, and not her, either?"

But none of us do. Perhaps since it was posed to us as a test of loyalty, we all consider our greater honor on the line.

Or perhaps that's a load of horseshit, because that's sure how I justify it to myself, but I really don't see how loyalty to bad ideals is any kind of a moral good at all. I think the truth is we're all scared, and maybe just waiting for one person to oppose, because if one, just one, said no, then we all could. But no one does so we all go along.

And for all that's running through my head, it's just the blink of an eye before Diane starts speaking again.

"Good. I'm glad to hear it. Now we're going to have three six-hour phases. In the first phase, we'll be exploring the ship and determining safety requirements. I'm going to want Paige, Zanib, and Helena on this trip. Helena, do you want any backup?"

Helena shakes her head.

"Not for the initial exploration. The fewer the better."

I whisper in Zanib's ear, "Don't we get to request backup?"

"Quiet, virgin."

"What was that?"

All eyes are riveted on us. Zanib clears her throat and rises, as though she intended to raise this question all along and had simply been waiting to be acknowledged.

"I was wondering what our exact parameters for safety were."

"Well, that's up to you to determine, Zanib. That's your job after all, isn't it? If any of the local fauna has infiltrated the seed ship, you let us know what we need to be safe in proceeding."

"And what if it's not safe?"

Diane doesn't strike me as the type to grind her teeth, but she seems on the verge of it now.

"I've got a hold full of very expensive pesticides and poisons for almost every known biochemistry in the galaxy. We're making this ship safe for salvage."

Zanib seems to have something else to say, but wisely sits down.

"Ladies, any time you three can save us during the first pass will be worth your weight in gold. Literally, I suspect, if the promises the accountants have been making to me about bonuses are to be believed. But I can't promise anyone anything right now that's not in their contracts.

"That being said: if the first phase only takes two hours, we'll be doing quite well. If it takes nine... I'm going to be very peevish. Which is not to say cut corners. Safety first, as always.

"In the second phase, Paige will be leading everyone except support staff and those with reasonable accommodations aboard the vessel. We will be stripping out everything that we can physically move as individuals. Now remember to wear back braces and gloves and boots and any other safety equipment that your team leads have indicated you should. During this same phase, you should be marking anything you can't physically move but that is valuable and can be moved with the equipment we have on board."

Diane motions for one of her flunkies, who brings over a non-aerosol paint splatter gun. Much to everyone's delight, hers included, the director fires her gun across the room and a green X appears on Helena's shoulder.

"Our security director is, of course, exceedingly valuable. Don't worry, Helena, that'll flake off in a few hours by itself."

"I know, madam director."

"Good, well try not to look so cross then." Chuckles. "Now, in the final phase, Paige will be leading our heavy equipment crews in to remove whatever's got a green X. I know my pushers and pullers, you love to look at everything as a challenge, but please, if you've spent more than a few minutes on a marked object, move on. We don't want to get into any battles of wills with ancient terrestrial technology. The point is to get as much as possible, so when we blow it, we don't all feel like Visigoths savaging ancient Rome.

"Now, then, are there any questions?"

Diane has covered everything so extensively that at this point, a question would've been nothing more than a nervous tic, or else you'd had to have your head so far up your own ass that...

"Yes?"

A woman from what I guessed from her appearance to be one of the heavy equipment crews, rises.

"Yes, I've been asking HR for a few weeks now to update my local taxes on my..."

The woman begins blathering on about a personal issue that affects literally no one other than her, while we all sit there in agonized silence. I have a sinking suspicion that it will not be the last stupid question of the day. Yes, they say no questions are stupid, but this is still a damn stupid question to be asking. Zanib leans in and whispers in my ear.

"Notice anything?"

I look her in the eye.

"The fact I'm on all three chalks?"

She punches me in the shoulder, and I nearly yell out, which would've interrupted Diane's vain attempt to mollify the heavy lifter who should really have just gone to HR or talked to her supervisor.

# TEN

The *Borgwardt* hangs suspended in mid-air, an improbably huge metal office complex in the sky. A hundred meters below, the suspensors which keep us hovering as though we're lighter than air churn up the sticky red soup which makes up the surface of the planet. Doubtless we're flying at hundreds of kilometers an hour through the atmosphere, but it feels like we're standing still.

"How you feeling, virgin?"

I'm breathing into a paper bag, so I suspect the question is rhetorical. Zanib is fiddling with what has to be about a dozen different-sized cages, ranging from about a half-meter square to something big enough to hold a wildebeest. She brings her hand down heavily on my back, a sisterly gesture, but it doesn't help my nausea.

"Here, I know what'll help. A little honest work. Give me a hand with these rat traps."

I gesture at the behemoth of the twelve.

"I'd hate to see the 'rat' you catch with that one."

"Well, you know what they say, you want to catch a bigger rat, you've got to build a bigger rat trap."

"Isn't the saying 'better'?"

"Eh, whatever. Help me toss these over the side."

"That's all? Just over the side? We don't have to prime them or anything first?"

"Already primed."

She hands me the one that's no bigger than a breadbox. The cage is open and a chunk of some kind of rancid meat is attached to a simple device in the back.

"This bait reeks," I say, tossing the first one over the side.

I watch as the cage plummets into the sticky red soup below with a satisfying squelch. It, and all of what Zanib calls the "rat traps" are attached to the undercarriage of the *Borgwardt* by lengths of hyper-strong, tensile elastic rope. Judging by how long the ropes are, I guess that the rattraps are not going to reach the floor of the blood ocean. They'll bob along in it.

Zanib begins tossing hers over the side and I throw a few more. Together we force the biggest one over the side and it drops into the red gunk, which seems to devour it like a greedy beast. I glance down at my heavy rubber boots and bounce up and down a few times, making sure they stay on my feet.

"Are these going to get sucked off?"

"Relax. You're never setting foot in that slush. We're walking straight across this nice pretty umbilical and right into *The Manifest Destiny.*"

I pull up a real-time silhouette of *The Manifest Destiny* on my jotter. The seed ship had actually crashed in a relatively favorable position for a salvage operation. The sea of blood-like protoplasm is about thirty meters deep, before giving way to a spongy, flesh-like ocean bottom, the "cherry pit" of Zanib's presentation. The central shaft of the seed ship is about eighty meters in length, and it had plunged in at about a sixty-degree angle.

None of the pods are entirely untouched by the ocean of blood, and the ones at four, five, and six o'clock are almost completely submerged, but the flip side of that mess is that the pods at eleven, twelve, and one are almost completely out of the goop. As long as the crew didn't lock off any of the pods, they should all still be connected, so we can make ingress at the twelve o'clock pod and be able to salvage everything, even down to six o'clock. The only issue, of course, is if any of the pods had been breached, and were full of the organic gunk. The question of whether we should safely evacuate any breached pods was probably one that was up to Zanib.

"There she blows," Helena mutters under her breath, as if not really caring whether we hear or not.

She lowers the binoculars from her eyes. I catch a glint on the horizon, the reflected sunlight of a shaft which has managed to sneak between the storms of blood which our operations section is now (rather adroitly, I have to admit) navigating us through.

I check the carabiner attached to the metal hook on my salvaging outfit. A length of rope which Zanib assured me was stronger than alloy is threaded through the carabiner and attached to the ship. The carabiner itself has a screwing mechanism which turns it into essentially a solid hoop. The weakest portion of the whole setup seems to be my overalls, however Zanib assured me they're made of the same super-strong fibrous material as the rope. It's all supposed to be foolproof, which just makes me worry how big of a fool I can make of myself.

In the seconds between me spotting the glint and checking my harness, the seed ship has grown into a recognizable shape, reinforcing to me the astonishing speed at which we were traveling. Repulsor technology is baffling and terrifying all at once.

We come to a genuine halt, though (I can tell because the seed ship has seemingly frozen in place) about a hundred kilometers from our destination. I look to the veterans.

"Now what?"

"Now we find out if the operations section is worth a damn," Helena responds.

I turn to Zanib.

"Are they?"

She shrugs.

"They're not the worst I've ever seen."

"You know I can hear you," a voice says through our jotters.

I nearly jump out of my skin, but from the looks on Zanib's and Helena's faces I can see they were expecting this.

"Hi, Kelly," Helena says in the most playful tone I've yet heard from her.

"Hi, Helena," Kelly, the operator on the other end says back. "Are you girls ready?"

"Ready as we'll ever be," Zanib responds.

"And Paige?"

"Yes? Um, yes?" I reply to the disembodied voice.

"Don't worry. I'm the best."

The *Borgwardt* becomes a partner in an intricate dance, played out over a tempestuous sea of blood rather than a faux wood tile-covered deck. *The Manifest Destiny* is stationary, true, but all around it the atmosphere and the ocean's surface roils, as if defying us to approach. The length of bridge we stand on, which Zanib and the other vets called "the umbilicus," isn't straight, per se, but rather is made up of dozens of interlocking deck panels, so that it can weave in the air like a snake.

I understand why they can't have a single, straight length of connecting tube. It would be so rigid it would snap in a storm like a twig, throwing any poor suckers like us who happen to be standing on it off into oblivion. But watching as Kelly attempts to control the trajectory of the *Borgwardt* and the spastic shimmies of the umbilicus so that it will connect with the seed ship we were attempting to salvage just about makes me sick.

Zanib pounds on my back to get my attention.

"Oh! They're in love. They're in love."

I look out between my greenening gills and see what she meant. The umbilicus is waggling and brushing lightly against the bulkheads of the *Manifest Destiny*'s various pods and the dance resembles nothing so much as a pair of chaste, tentative lovers cooing and caressing. Then, almost as suddenly as it had begun, the cuddling ends as the far end of the umbilicus slams hard against the hull of the twelve o'clock pod, locking into place as the electromagnets ringing the far end of the umbilicus activate.

"You're the best, Kelly," Zanib says, "I've always said that."

"Think nothing of it."

Helena grabs ahold of the can opener and turns to us.

"Come on, let's go!"

Zanib already has her hand on the other handle of the can opener and starts running. I know I'm also supposed to help with the huge, circular device, but the two veterans manage to outpace me before I even start stumbling over my rubber overboots.

The can opener resembles a massive metal teacup, turned sideways. I finally catch up and grab hold of my handle when we're about halfway across the umbilicus. I realize that I'm not really contributing much. The device is heavy, and Zanib and Helena were carrying it perfectly fine without me. I'm not even sure if I'm carrying my share of the load when we slam the rim of the "saucer" into the hull of the twelve o'clock pod. Like the end of the umbilicus, the can opener locks into place magnetically.

I crouch over, breathing heavily, hands on my thighs.

"Move, virgin!" Helena shouts, shoving me out of the way.

A loud shrieking sounds and sparks begin to fly from the back of the can opener, which are then replaced by a flame of exhaust. Had I remained crouched where I was, my face would've been melted off.

"Don't tell me this stupid nickname is catching on," I say, glaring at Zanib.

"That's all right. Helena just knows what's up."

Zanib raises her fist over the can opener, but Helena just stares at the two of us rather than bumping it back.

"You two had better get your fucking game faces on. And you are lucky you didn't just get a plasma blast to the face."

I nod, the reality of the fact that this glowering woman had actually just saved my life, and not from anything exciting or unpredictable, but from my own stupidity, dawns on me.

The plasma exhaust begins sputtering and returning to fumes. When it finally stops, the can opener dings like a microwave going off. All three of us grab hold of our handles. There is no chatter or joking this time.

"Ready?" Helena asks.

We nod.

"On three. One. Two. Three."

Helena flips the switch for the electromagnet and the full weight of the can opener drops into our grasp. We slowly lower it to the ground, rim downward, and Helena turns on the safety mechanism so that it won't accidentally go off and burn a hole through the deck of the umbilicus bridge. A perfect hole, the exact diameter of the can opener, now offers us ingress to the twelve o'clock facing pod. Its edges still gleam white-hot from the plasma which had carved it, and the missing piece of hull clatters inward into the seed ship, its edges similarly glowing.

"We're go for cold juice," Helena says, pointing at me.

I reach into the pocket of my jumpsuit and pull out an aerosol can of coolant. Most station bunnies like me are well trained in cold juice procedures, which go hand-in-hand with welding procedures. Certified welders and coolers are about as commonplace stationside as commodes. Everybody stationside has to be on call in case of an emergency decompression. I had never used a can opener before, obviously, but cleaning up afterwards is as natural to me as wiping my ass after a shit.

I spray the outer ring once clockwise, once counterclockwise, then once more for spots. I pulled out my thermal gauge and run it quickly around the hole. Just the fact that it's no longer visibly glowing doesn't make it safe to crawl through yet, but my gauge tells me it's well within tolerances. I stick my head and torso through the hole and repeat the procedure with the severed disc.

"We're good," I say.

"Nice job, virgin," Zanib says, clapping me on the back and crawling through the hole.

"Yeah, well done, Ambroziak," Helena says, poking me in the chest with her finger, "That's what I expect from you now, not those monkeyshines back there with the can opener."

I nod. It's like being lectured by my Ma (well, my Ma if she were much younger and had a facial deformity.) Helena barrels through the hole next and I realize for the first time, with no barriers left between us, how truly terrifying the idea of boarding an ancient ghost ship is.

It's not only terrifying, it's exhilarating, too. The director promised me a place in history. Now I'm about to take it. With trepidation, I lift my leg and stick it through the hole.

# ELEVEN

Helena grabs me by my scruff so I don't fall. Outside of the tiny circle of light that we cut in the hull, all I can see of the interior of the seed ship is a deep, seemingly impenetrable darkness. I fumble for my floating glow-globe.

"Hang on there, speedy," Helena says, pressing her hand over mine.

She's starting to get awfully handsy, and I'm not sure how I feel about it. Now, if Zanib wanted to start getting handsy with me that would be a different story. But Helena isn't my type.

"Speedy, virgin, you're getting all kinds of new monikers today," Zanib says with a laugh.

She's waving a glowing green wand through the air, which is attached to her jotter, and she periodically checks the jotter.

"Well, shit. Air's good. Temperature's good. No unknown toxins. I'd say we're safe for globes, ladies."

Helena takes her hands off mine, and I shake my globe, which immediately takes up a position over my head to illuminate as much around me as possible without shining in my, or anybody else's, eyes. It just follows a simple algorithmic program. It could hardly even be considered AI, but everyone always thinks of their globes as little pets. I call mine Millie. Millie remains tethered to me by a short length of rope, probably the same supposedly unbreakable kind that currently keeps us tethered to the *Borgwardt*.

The other two do likewise.

"Did you say the air's breathable?" I ask, "Can we ditch our breathers?"

"Not unless you want to forfeit your insurance policy, you won't," Helena replies.

I look to Zanib for succor. The breathing mask is uncomfortable. It's slightly better than a boom suit, I suppose, but still not that great. Zanib shrugs.

A few custodians – I only recognized Eden – hurry after us to retrieve the can opener from where we left it.

"What now?" I ask.

"What now?" Helena repeats. "Now you earn whatever we're paying you."

Two pairs of eyes focus on me and the whole reality of how in over my head I am sinks in. A brick of ice settles over the exit from my stomach into my intestines. I pull out my jotter and immediately fumble it. It clatters end over end to the deck, shattering the still and quiet silence of the dark pod, though, thankfully, not its screen.

No. This is not you. This is who they think you are. Get a grip on yourself. Retrieve the jotter. Don't say something self-deprecating like, "Oops, butterfingers." Just retrieve it and don't even acknowledge the mistake. They won't focus any more on it than you do.

I pick up the jotter and punch up an internal schematic of *The Manifest Destiny* based on my research. I overlay it with real-time data streaming from the *Borgwardt*. This is something anyone could do, though, anyone with a jotter. Prove you're worth a damn. Prove you know something they don't.

I walk up to a girder holding up the ceiling. Here's something they don't know. Here's something only an elite researcher could find.

"All right," I say, "we're in Pod Eight. Pod Eight is facing twelve o'clock, which means that Two is facing six o'clock, and so forth. Adjust your jotters accordingly."

Helena and Zanib exchange a look of confusion.

"How do you know that? I thought all the pods were identical."

"They are. And they were constructed simultaneously to cut down on fabrication costs. Which meant that all the building materials were earmarked for their individual construction sites. On most of this stuff the earmark would be invisible, but on a girder like this..."

I tap the girder. It's embossed with a numeral eight.

"I didn't even notice."

I shrug.

"Not your job to. Now that we know which side is up... literally... we can make some progress."

I tap on my jotter to go into edit mode. I adjust Pod One from the twelve o'clock position to the five o'clock and press confirm. The image flashes briefly. My jotter pings and a trumpet announcing a new communiqué appears on the screen. I click on it.

"Ambroziak."

"Hey, Paige, this is Kelly Overland down in operations. How are you doing?"

"Oh, fine, fine, how are you, Kelly?"

"Good, good. Listen, we just got an update from you showing that you're in Pod Eight, but we were anticipating that being Pod One. Have you got anything to confirm your location?"

I roll my eyes. They must not have been basing their assumption on anything beyond the blueprint of the ship, which always showed Pod One at the nominal top. There's certainly no easy way to identify the pods from the outside.

"I'm sending you a photo, Kelly. You ready?"

"Yep, send it."

I raise my jotter and snap a picture of the "eight" mark. Send. There's a brief pause while Kelly either collects her thoughts or puts me on mute and confers with a supervisor or team lead or maybe just someone smarter sitting near her.

"Okay, confirmed, Paige. Let me know if you need anything."

I won't.

"Sounds good. Have a good one, Kelly."

"You —"

I cut the transmission. Zanib and Helena are looking around, already a bit further afield than I am. Helena being the designated grouch of the group, I walk up to my roommate.

"Oh, there you are!" she says, seeming excited that I'm done with my brief phone call. "Take a look at this."

She walks over to the bulkhead and taps on a panel of what appears to be an obtuse artistic decoration behind a primitive plasteel screen. In fact, the transparent substance may even be a thick layer of glass. I'm not 100% sure how advanced the technology was at the time. I should probably be more familiar with these sorts of things, but my modern eyes can't help but translate what I'm seeing into what I'm used to seeing.

"What is this weirdness?"

The "weirdness" she's referring to is the art piece itself. I wonder if it's carved from wood. It seems to just be random shapes, circles and leaf-like patterns, forming a long panel of wood. I don't remember reading anything about this, and it seems strange that cosmonauts and pioneers would give themselves over to an extensive artistic display when every square centimeter of space aboard this vessel was at an absolute premium.

"I don't remember reading about anything like this. Why would they have some kind of woodcutting on board anyway?"

"Sentimentality?"

"Based on what I know about the USA from that time period it's less likely to sentimentality than almost anything else."

Helena approaches us, done with whatever had captured her interest as a possible security hazard.

"Perhaps we can contemplate the mystery of the weird art installment on our own time, ladies? We've only got eighteen hours to salvage this wreck, and worrying about whatever this is..."

She taps the glass. One of the brown circular whorls comes loose, disappears, and suddenly I realized what I was looking at.

"This isn't an art installation. And it's not wood. It's not even solid."

I slam my entire forearm against the glass, and bits and chunks of the brown stuff begin to shimmy away from the glass. Helena and Zanib gasp, realizing what had occurred to me first. The glass is actually a window onto the combined sewage/hydroponics/fuel system which runs throughout the ship and throughout each pod, all interconnected.

What is pressed against the glass is vegetables — countless, countless radishes and beans and corn and vegetables. With a few more taps to the glass, we knock much more of it loose, exposing what looks like a cross between a swamp and an underwater jungle. The hydroponics gardens aren't just functional, they're blooming. The waterlines which are supposed to flow freely throughout the ship are veritably clogged with vegetables.

"I can't believe this system is still working," Zanib says, "Shouldn't this all be tainted with effluvia from the fleshworld?"

"Probably in the lower pods there are breaches. Four, five, and six o'clock which are Pods...One, Two, and Three. But just think, every pod can lock itself off from the greater system. Someone when they realized the lower pods were breached must have locked off Pod Eight. If not more."

"But if the hydroponics are still functioning, couldn't that mean..."

A loud crack sounds and Zanib and I both rip our attention away from the hydroponic garden. Blood gushes from a hole in Helena's shoulder.

# TWELVE

Helena looks stunned, like the reality of being shot has not yet reached her brainstem. Her mouth works, as though trying to bring words to her twisted lips. Then something clicks inside her. She growls, a subhuman, animalistic sound, claps her hand over her wound, and shouts, "Get down!"

Shielding us from the invisible shooter down in the depths of the ship, Helena shepherds us back toward the ingress hole we carved with the can opener. With one hand over her shoulder, she holds her beam rifle at her hip. Not the best way to return fire, I think, but, then, Helena is a professional and has a lot more experience than I did. Maybe it's just fine for her.

Another shot rings out and I heard several ricochets, but it doesn't damage either anyone in our party or an obvious spot of the glass to the hydroponic garden.

Zanib, finally getting her wits about her, grabs a pack of gauze from her medkit and begins hastily binding Helena's shoulder, even as the other woman tries to brush off her ministrations.

"Out! Out!" Helena shouts, "Don't stop."

I scramble through the hole, then help Zanib through. We both tried to help Helena through, but she angrily brushes off our outstretched hands and clambers through herself, hardly letting her beam rifle quiver.

"Should we replace the..."

Helena practically palms my entire head and shoves me half a meter across the walkway of the umbilicus. I might decide to sue for whiplash later, but I know my pride isn't as important as my life in the heat of the moment.

"I said not to stop!"

Walking backwards, using her back to shield as much of the umbilicus as she can, Helena practically sweeps us back towards the *Borgwardt* faster than we can scramble ahead of her. With Zanib's hasty patch over her shoulder, she's now leveling the beam rifle with two hands. She must be in pain that would debilitate someone like me, but the only sign of it is a foul expression and clenched teeth.

"Medical assistance Airlock 3, medical assistance Airlock 3," Zanib keeps repeating, over and over again into her jotter, as though repeating it will make them come faster. Kelly is just as emphatically assuring her that it's on its way.

It's only when the airlock closes on all three of us that Helena finally gasps in pain, drops her weapon to the ground with a clatter, falls to her knees, and vomits right on the deck. I want to rush to help her, and I think Zanib did, too, but we've both seen enough of Helena's personality to know not to. A nurse in lilac scrubs with a black leather bag comes pounding down the hall and immediately begins laying Helena down to look at her. The nurse's name is Tina, I think.

I glance out the airlock porthole and nearly have a heart attack as a solid slug bullet flies straight at my face. Of course, it flattens like a can against the plasteel and slides down the outer airlock hatch like a cartoon character after slamming into a cliff. Only beam rifles of the sort Tampa and Prosser had used earlier can burn through plasteel. Even knowing this, I clutch at my heart. Centimeters of impenetrable alloy notwithstanding, I've never felt so close to death.

I try to spot Helena's (and now my) assailant, but all I can really see are some eyes glinting in the shadows through the hole we had cut with the can opener.

"They're still out there," I announce. "Should we retract the bridge?"

"No!" Helena shouts.

She recoils in pain, having either just pulled a stitch or just overexerted herself. All the fight has definitely fled from her, and she's turning white. The nurse is muttering dozens of instructions, all promptly forgotten or ignored by the pig-headed patient. I motion as deftly as I can for Zanib to step to the side with me.

"Is she right?" I whisper, "Or delirious?"

"I'm still the security director here!" Helena barks loudly, "And I know what I'm talking about. You don't break that umbilicus!"

"All right," I agree. I look at Zanib. "We'd better go see Diane."

"Don't you go over my fucking head!"

I look down at Helena. She's completely prostrate, on her back. Sweat is pouring off of her. She still sounds dangerous but I can tell she's been reduced to the strength of a kitten. I'm not sure what the right thing to do is. I want to put my hand on her head and soothe her, but that doesn't seem right. Just being a clinical, professional automaton doesn't seem right either.

I sit down and cross my legs and take Helena's hand in my own, squeezing hard, making her squeeze back. She looks at me. All right. We're not much. But we were comrades in arms for a minute back there. At least, we came under fire, anyway.

"We're not going over your head. We have to report. The boss has to know. Don't tell me it's not what you would do."

"Don't tell us it's not the reg, either," Zanib says.

Helena looks up at her, then at me, then at her. She has a panicked look on her face, like we're trying to get one over on her, but she desperately wants to believe us.

"All right," she agrees.

I pat her fist one last time then rise. We're both double-timing it down the corridor. It's not often that I find myself struggling to keep up, but Zanib is a farm girl, used to getting from place to place with a quickness. I'm practically running, though, by the time we reach the anteroom to Diane's office.

Myrna looks up from her jotter as we enter. As she lowers her jotter I see she is reading one of those sex advice sites which poses as a fashion guide. Not exactly high literature. Or, now that I think about it, work.

"Can I help you?"

"We need to see the director," Zanib says, practically walking past the secretary and into the boss's office.

I'm astonished at the speed with which Myrna places herself in between us and the hatch.

"Do you have an appointment?"

Zanib and I exchange a glance.

"No," we both say practically at the same time.

Zanib is shaking her head. Myrna shrugs as though that's pretty much the end of the matter.

"Well, I can't just let you in then."

She returns to her desk and pulls up some calendar software on her work screen. I notice that's after she minimizes a few more fashion-cum-sex guides and what seems to be research on a trip to Lahiniti.

"Okay, now let's see," she says, staring intently at her screen as though the longer she stares the more days will appear in a standard solar week, "I can get you in at eleven o'clock on Wednesday. Are you both free then?"

She looks up at us. I can only guess what sort of expressions we're wearing based on her next sentence.

"Can you make yourselves free, then?"

"This is a damned eighteen-hour mission!" Zanib shouts.

"There's no need to swear," Myrna says testily, her face puckering up. "Look, I may keep the director's schedule but I'm not really in control of it. There's no point in getting mad at me. I'm just the messenger."

I start knocking on the director's hatch.

"Diane! Hello?"

Myrna jumps up.

"Hey! Stop that! If you two can't behave, I'll get security in here. You have no right to act this way."

"Look, you bubblehead, the security director is bleeding out on the deck of Airlock 1. Have you got two fucking brain cells to..."

The hatch opens. Diane is standing there on her crutches, looking between me, Zanib, and Myrna.

"What the hell are you two doing here?" Preemptively, she looks at the secretary. "I apologize for the salty language, Myrna. I know you don't like it."

"Madam director," I say, not really sure exactly how to go about this, "we have an issue."

She glances between the two of us.

"We really don't have time for issues, ladies."

"That's what I tried to tell them, madam director. I told them I might keep your schedule, but I'm not like, the queen of time, you know."

"Thank you, Myrna. You haven't forgotten about those pay stubs that are due by noon, have you?"

By the blanching of her face, it's pretty obvious that Myrna had forgotten. Entirely.

"Oh, uh... no, madam director."

"Good, good. I won't give it another thought, then. You two, in here, now."

Zanib and I scuttle in and the hatch closes with a click. Without sitting, Diane takes our measure.

"All right, tell me what happened."

I swallow a lump in my throat and try to speak, but Zanib is already halfway through the story. By the time she finishes, Diane's face is ashen gray.

"This whole mission has been cursed from the beginning. I halfway wonder if we don't have a saboteur on board." She presses a button on her jotter. "Note. Urgency: high. Review all staff files for possible insider threat. Cannot believe multiple instances of delay and violence are due to coincidence or even outside espionage. Look within. Deliver to security. Not just director. Wide blast. Deliver now."

The jotter dings once, twice, thrice, then makes a sound like a swoosh, and the message is away. She turns her attention back to us.

"Who was it that shot at you?"

"I don't know," I reply, "I didn't get a good look at them."

"Zanib? What about you?"

She shakes her head. The director sighs.

"I don't suppose Helena will be able to shed any more light on this. And if I know her she's probably raging against everything within arm's reach."

"You can say that again," Zanib says. "I mean, er...yes, madam director."

Diane nods.

"Now the question is, ladies, who could possibly have gotten here before us? Who knew we were coming? And who would have the resources..."

Diane doesn't need to say another word. Apparently we all come to the same conclusion at the same instant.

# THIRTEEN

"Morning, Quinn."

The least noteworthy of Helena's security crew members tumbles backwards out of her seat. She had been asleep (or all but) leaning all the way back and Diane's words shocked her so much she had tumbled right out.

"Good... good morning, madam director," Quinn replies shakily, dragging herself up by the desk, "I was just... I just read your priority message. We've been working on reviewing files and..."

"Well, we'll have to let Prosser and Tampa see to that right this second. Can you possibly let us speak to the corsair?"

Quinn does a double take.

"The... the corsair? Yes. Yes, of course."

There really isn't a whole lot to the *Borgwardt*'s brig. It isn't really meant to be much of a ship for transporting prisoners. Now and then employees get drunk and obnoxious and get into fights, so there are two separate holding pens, but that's about the extent of it. Right now, Nia occupies one of them. She's lying on the deck, but it seems like she's more than just lying prostrate, nose to the bulkhead. It's as though an elephant or some great ghostly force is depressing her back, holding her down. The full weight of ordinary shipboard gravity is crushing her, which, when you consider how long she had lived in zero G, makes sense.

Quinn clangs on the bars of the pen with her billy club.

"Wakey, wakey, eggs and bakey!"

Nia groans.

"Just kill me."

"Don't tempt me, skin-wrapper."

Diane, struggling slightly with her crutches, places a hand on Quinn's shoulder.

"That, ah, that's all for now, Quinn. Is it all right if we have the room?"

Quinn glances around, a bit peevish.

"Well, I'm not really... I mean, I guess that's against regs. But you are the director. What you say goes, I guess."

"What I say goes, very much so. Thanks, Quinn."

Diane favors Quinn with a warm smile, or at least a simulacrum of one. Sporting a look like someone is getting one over on her, but unable to come up with an escape hatch, Quinn leaves the pens and returns to the antechamber, nodding all the way. Diane taps on one of the bars with her crutch.

"You there. Get up."

Nia slowly lifts her face from the blood-speckled deck of the pen. I never considered how different seeing the flayed woman over the vidfeed would be as opposed to seeing her up close and in person. Her exposed meat is revolting. I must have gasped or made some small subconscious move because Zanib reaches out and takes my hand, squeezing it gently for support.

"I can't get up, you stupid gash," Nia growls.

Zanib and I both take a step back, as though trying to get out of the circle of the director's oncoming fury. But it fails to materialize.

"Oh," Diane says instead, "is that all? And here I thought you were worth a damn."

A low, unpleasant, rasping laugh chortles out of Nia's voice box. It's nothing like her gleeful cackles at our suffering before.

"Why didn't you just kill me? They always just kill us. Like we're not even people. Like we're fleas. Why'd you bring me here? You love watching me suffer? You get off on torturing me?"

"Torture? Now that, I can assure you, is a falsehood. We've had verified video recording of every second of your stay here since you were brought onboard. We've never stopped taping you. We can account for every second. And the reason I ordered that – the express reason – is so that you wouldn't be mistreated by any of my employees, who, let's be frank, have every reason in the world to want to torture you."

"You did it so you'll have something to show Hestle when you turn me in for your bounty. They don't take damaged goods."

"Regardless, no one's hurt you."

Nia's lidless eyes turn wild and she fairly roars.

"Can't you see this gravity is killing me?"

It's hard to deny. She isn't just grotesque. She's pathetic. Her lungs wheeze and she's barely able to move. Every centimeter of her is crushed flat against the deck, as though someone is flattening her out.

"You know, when I lost my leg all the doctors said I'd never walk again. The nerve damage was too extensive. They would give me a fancy prosthetic if I wanted it, but it would be more for aesthetic purposes than anything else. I was never supposed to get up out of my chair again. But you know what I did?"

"Gave a long, pointless speech to someone who doesn't give a shit?"

"I said fuck the doctors. I said fuck that chair. I don't even have a chair anymore. It's all me. Me-powered ambulation and you know why?"

"Because you're a stupid gash who doesn't know when to give up?"

"Exactly. Now get up and look me in the face because I have a question for you."

It's hard to read the skin-wrapper's expression. Without a face, I can't tell which parts are softening and which are hardening. But after a moment, she seems to make a decision. Her right leg begins to pull forward until her thigh is perpendicular to her waist. Then she begins to push off with her foot, emitting a low grunt. She leaves chunks of her body and a long slug's trail of blood behind her.

For what must be two solid grueling minutes we watch as she throws her arms forward, drags herself as far as she can go, then pushes off with one of her legs before she repeats the process all over again until finally she puts her hands on the bars of the pen. Once she catches hold of the bars she pulls herself up until she's standing, finally face-to-face with Diane, separated only by the air between their noses. Nia jams her head between two bars.

After her long, short journey she is practically naked – I mean, naked even for a skin-wrapper. Most of her bandages have come unwound and lay on the deck behind her, soaked in fresh blood.

"Happy?" Nia whispers.

"No. But at least now I know you're worth a damn."

"What's your question?"

"How do I call off your people?"

"You killed them all. There's none left to call off."

"I don't mean them. I mean the ones on the planet. The ones you tipped off. If they're not yours, they're your confederates."

"Confederates? Like there's a great big skin-wrapper community out here? How stupid are you?"

"You don't exchange information? Call for reinforcements?"

Nia shakes her head as much as possible while nestled between two bars. It's like watching someone polish a bruised apple.

"Other skin-wrappers are as likely to shoot you in the back as help you. I hate to ruin all your fancy notions of honor among thieves, but we don't help each other out. Every captain's a CEO, every ship's its own company. There's no skin-wrapper corporate headquarters."

"Assuming I believe that you didn't tip anyone off, who else could possibly be out here?"

"Depends. Where's here?"

Diane pauses for a moment. She seems reluctant to tell her enemy information, any information, that might aid her in some kind of negotiation or escape attempt later. Or perhaps it's that this is some kind of breach of protocol and it's all being recorded.

"The Endirii System."

"Endirii? There's nothing there. No ore, no minerals. A crap sun. It's not on the way anywhere. It's not on the way back from anywhere."

"Rebels? Iconoclasts? Religious zealots?"

Nia shakes her head.

"There's no point. You'd have to have self-sustaining hydroponic gardens anyway. You may as well live in space like us. So, what is here? What did I miss?"

"Nothing," Zanib says. "The corporation asked us to take a pass to update stellar cartography."

"No, they didn't. There's no profit in that. To outfit a ship of this size with payroll, supplies, and everything else would cost a small fortune. They wouldn't do it to map rocks nobody uses."

"Thank you for your insight," Diane mutters, "I'll make sure to annotate on our records that you were cooperative."

Diane starts to limp away.

"There was a wreck."

Diane pauses, apparently just long enough to confirm Nia's suspicions, before continuing on.

"That's it, isn't it? There's a hulk in The Endirii System. But who would go there? They would've been ridiculously off course. No. No one could have gotten there. On ordinary trade routes if you had an issue and you were floating, wayward, it'd take thirty years to float to Endirii. And you'd have to be pointed in that direction, which who would be? And how would you get there first before hitting something more important? Or without being scrapped? A wreck would have to be two hundred years old."

She pauses, just long enough for recognition to enter her eyes. She's never looked so human.

"*The Manifest Destiny*! You've found *The Manifest Destiny*?"

Nia continues yelling, taunting us, certain that she is right. The fact that she is, is simply aggravating, but there's nothing we can do now. Perhaps this is why Diane was so reluctant to give her even a scrap of information. She won't escape, though, will she? She can't escape.

Quinn scuttles to her feet as we enter the antechamber. Her jotter is open and pointed in our direction, humming with a dozen proprietary computing programs, all security-specific. She's desperate to show us she's awake and working.

"Get everything you need, madam director?"

"Yes, I'm done with that corsair scum. But Quinn?"

"Yes, madam director?"

"Bring up a boom suit for her."

A look of deeper confusion than usual dampens Quinn's face.

"A boom suit? For a prisoner? Isn't that..."

She trails off, so Diane finishes for her.

"Against regulations? Technically, yes. But reasonable accommodations trump most regulations."

I glance at Zanib, my eyes furrowed in confusion. She points at her chest and makes a twirling motion, as though twisting a knob. Now I get it. Hestle-issue boom suits have independent gravity systems. Nobody ever uses them that I've heard of except in high-grav mining operations. But in theory it could even the skin-wrapper out.

"Yes, ma'am."

"And make sure you contact Equal Opportunity to get the prisoner's RA on file."

"Yes, ma'am."

Diane's jotter beeps. An emergency message, judging by the red flashing light and the fact that as director she probably receives hundreds of communiqués a day and none have been worthy of beeping at her so far today. It's Tina, the nurse.

"Airlock 1. It seems your attackers have shown themselves."

# FOURTEEN

Diane orders us to hurry on ahead so she won't slow us down. Helena is asleep on a cot in a corner. Tina is wiping her bloody hands with a rag.

"Is she going to be all right?" Zanib asks.

Tina nods.

"She'll be fit to fight in a few. But I had to sedate her. She needs a little rest so this can heal."

She gestures at Helena's shoulder. The wound is sealed over with a small pouch of saline and alcohol, keeping the area clean. The wound itself bubbles as bones knit, ligaments reconnect, and flesh and skin gradually encroaches to seal the whole thing up. Helena's own body is doing all the work.

Well, not all the work. A simple neurostim pack attached to the side of her head orders the brain to heal itself at a hundred or maybe a thousand times its natural rate. The main training of modern medics is knowing how much stimulation is too much and where the sweet spot lies between overloading the brain's synapses, which could kill the patient, and letting the wound fester.

A second pack attached to Helena's heart is in constant communication with the neurostim pack. It delivers small doses of various hormones and chemicals, mostly as dictated by the neurostim. Tina makes small adjustments to both as she monitors Helena's condition. I've seen each of these medical devices before, and almost all of them the time I broke my femur, but I've never seen them all used at once. I'm truly intrigued, but I can't waste much time lingering over it. The important thing is that Helena's going to be fine. She'll wake up in a few hours hungry as a horse, but otherwise healthy.

"And take a look at this."

The nurse holds up a deformed chunk of copper-colored metal.

"What is that?"

"That's what I dug out of her. A solid slug projectile. Very old-school stuff."

I have a strange, sinking feeling about who, exactly, we're dealing with, but I'm not ready to vocalize anything, or, really, perhaps even admit it to myself. Prosser and Tampa stand, beam rifles at the ready, covering the hatch, essentially protecting their boss. Prosser, the shorter, more muscular goon, motions for Zanib and I to come hither. We oblige. She points through the porthole.

"What do you two make of that?"

A woman stands at the other end of the umbilicus, holding up a shirt. She waves it when she sees us.

"Well, she's no skin-wrapper, so I guess the corsair was telling the truth," Zanib says, "But who the hell is she? Who's she with?

"Who cares?" Tampa replies. She's stouter than Prosser, with long, curly hair. "She's some schizoid nut."

"No," I say, "she's not crazy. I think she wants to parley."

Prosser slaps her forehead.

"A white shirt. She could have at least stuck it on a pole so we knew what she was doing. I'll go talk to her. Tampa, cover me."

"You?" Tampa replies, "You've got the diplomatic finesse of a Gore-Fa. And this isn't goon work, either."

Both of the security officers turned to look at me. I nod. "I'll go."

"The hell you will, virgin!"

"Zanib, what else are we going to do? Who else are we going to send? The director can't go out there, you know that. Look, it's my job to pioneer a path for us through that ship. This is just... an unanticipated obstacle."

Zanib scowls, but doesn't seem to want to fight me on it. She's a biologist, after all, and talking to creatures that don't suck blood to stay alive isn't exactly in her wheelhouse. I would fight her on it. This is going to make me look like a team player. This is going to prove my value to the corporation. I just have to dawdle until the director can arrive to see it. Luckily, I don't have to come up with an excuse, because the goons have some preparation in store for me.

Without preamble, Prosser and Tampa unzip my jumpsuit and bear my breasts and everything above my hips to the world. I grit my teeth, hoping Zanib likes what she's seeing (if not necessarily the circumstances of seeing it.) The two goons lower bulletproof plates over my front and back. The plates are bulky and a bit uncomfortable, but not especially heavy. When they zip me back up, you can hardly tell through my loose-fitting jumpsuit that there's anything on underneath.

"What's going on?" Diane asks, entering the airlock.

Good. Now she's here. Now she'll know I volunteered. Start signing that bonus check now, madam director. And you might as well have that worthless Myrna start getting my long-term contract ready.

"We're sending Ambroziak out to parley with the... whoever they are."

"The shooters."

"Yeah."

"And you're all right with that, Paige?"

I shrug, affecting nonchalance as best I can with all these layers of stuff weighing me down.

"Such as I can be."

Diane nods in approval.

"Now, look," Prosser says, "in this armor they're not going to be able to kill you if they hit you center mass. You're not going to like it – it's going to knock the wind out of you, probably throw you on your ass – but you'll survive one of those horseshit solid slug things they're shooting at you."

"Prosser and I are going to be covering you. If she makes a funny move, we can take her out. We're going to get some height here so that we can shoot at a downward angle. Ideally, we'll be able to take her out without hitting you. The only issue is what happens if she grabs you, throws you over the side, stabs you, something like that."

"Keep at least a meter between you," Tampa adds.

"A meter. Okay. All right."

I reach into my pocket and pull out my paint gun. The goons exchange a look, but say nothing. I nod for them to open the airlock. They press a few buttons and the hydraulics open. They clamber up onto stepping stools on either side of the airlock exit to get their height advantage, and nod at me that I'm okay to go.

The woman with the shirt disappears, back into her pod, as I step forward. I raise my paint gun and fire one green X about a half meter past the centerpoint of the umbilicus, then another green X about a half meter before it. To show I'm not being aggressive, I place the paint gun down on the ground and step out, arms up.

As soon as I set foot on the umbilicus I brace myself, eyes clenched shut and teeth clenched closed, ready to catch a bullet. In the head if necessary, but I sort of hope if they are going to shoot they'll hit me – what did Tampa call it? – center mass so I'll just be knocked out of my socks.

Thankfully, the shot doesn't come.

"I'm an unarmed civilian!" I shout. "I work for Hestle Corporation. We're on a mission of exploration." Okay, so that's a lie. "We don't want to hurt you." That's not. Not really.

I walk forward slowly, one foot in front of the other, and stop when I reach the green X nearest me. The wind is howling and red droplets from a not-too-distant blood storm is spraying sideways in my face. My hands are still up, but I start to feel silly, so I slowly lower them. The wait is eternal, tense, agonizing. I feel like a fool out here. Not just a fool, but a damn exposed fool ready to get shot any old minute for my foolishness.

I'm just about to turn back and bag it when the shirt woman re-appears. She has a very distinct appearance, quite unlike anyone I know, and I try to place it. Her skin tone is lighter than the usual brownish, and her look is different.

Then it strikes me. I've seen photographs of people who look like her in the actual histories of *The Manifest Destiny*, and how different they looked from the actors who portrayed them in the movie. We had even discussed it in class one day, and our professor had quite a time explaining to us how we were all members of *La Raza Cósmica*, a blending of various ethnic groups which had once been deeply segregated on Old

Earth. They were usually identified by colors – black, white, green, blue, things like that. In space, the old prejudices had simply become unfeasible. We had, to put it simply, fucked until we were all one color.

The shirt woman, though, must have represented one of the colors before they had all blended. My earlier sinking feeling now seems prescient. We've gravely misjudged the situation. *The Manifest Destiny* hadn't wrecked, killing all aboard. It had continued to function as a seed ship, exactly as it was designed to, for the better part of two hundred years. We had already seen that the hydroponics arrays were still functional. This woman is the offspring of the original colonists.

"Come, come," I say gesturing towards her and pointing at the green X I made about a meter away from my current spot.

The shirt woman says something, and I only understand about a quarter of it. Of course. Just as our ethnic makeup blended over time, so, too, has our language. I remember reading that Cosmic was a blend of primarily the languages of the original spacefarers: Old English, Old Russian, Old Hindi, and Old Mandarin.

"Just... just one minute," I say, hoping that she, too, understands about a quarter of what I'm saying. "I'm going to reach for a device to help us communicate. It's not a weapon. No weapon."

The woman stops and watches as I slowly reached into my pocket and draw out my jotter. I press a few buttons and pull up some translation software. The translator is actually extremely elegant. It silences the area around the ears of both users, and translates in almost real time, "throwing" the voice where it should be coming from like a ventriloquist. Over time it even cobbles together a rough approximation of the speaker's voice based on fundamental phonemes, morphemes, and syllables. The effect is similar to watching a film that has been dubbed rather than subtitled – you hear what you're supposed to hear, though it may not match the moving lips of the person you're talking to.

I order it to translate from Cosmic to Old English and then pocket the device. It will do the rest, gradually ironing out any kinks.

"You can come closer," I say, "Step on the green marker."

Slowly she advances toward the green X I planted for her. Theoretically I was safe from her a meter away, as the security goons had demanded.

"I hear you word better. No perfection, but much betterer than now."

In the space of those two short sentences her voice is already starting to transform from the initial robotic tones of the translating software's default voice into her "real" voice. But I'm confused why it doesn't seem to be translating correctly. That should come instantaneously. I check my jotter.

"Troubleshoot translation software."

She cocks her head.

"I no have... you speak at device?"

"Yes," I say. "Hold on just a moment, I think there's something wrong with my machine."

"Good, yes," she agrees. "You talk strange."

I nod. At least she's having the same issues on her end. The jotter dings after a moment. I read the error message. The translation software is functioning correctly. The problem is that the shirt woman is speaking something that only matches Old English by about 73%.

I shouldn't be surprised. After two hundred years there's bound to be some drift. She's speaking a new dialect: *The Manifest Destiny* dialect.

I do something I've never done before. At least, I'm not 100% sure how to do it. I ask the translator to uncouple from its usual vocabulary logs and attempt to develop a new linguistic database based on context clues. The more we talk the better it's going to get, if everything goes right.

"My translator is going to attempt to learn your dialect. It's different from the one it knows."

She nods.

"How long it take?"

"I'm not sure. A few hours. The more we talk, though, the better it will get at understanding you."

She nods again.

"Why did you shoot at my friend?"

She pauses and makes a fist, as though she doesn't know how to answer the question.

"I take responsibility for miscommunication. Assume my people did that you were infested. I argued against this. Here I am now to apologize."

The translator is definitely improving, but that can't be right. She must have meant "infected."

"Infected? With some kind of disease? Is there a plague on board?"

Her face darkens.

"You really are from outside?"

I nod.

"Where?"

I point upward.

"From the stars. Distant places you never would have heard of."

"Not from Earth?"

"No."

"But your people... they're Brazilian, right?"

"Brazilian? I'm not familiar with the term. Let me just check my machine."

She nods. I pull out my jotter and attempt to type in the word phonetically. I butcher it, but the archive understands what I'm trying to say, and tells me about Brazil, another ancient terrestrial nation-state. A contemporary of the USA. I flip through some pictures, then I realize where her assumption stems from.

"It's because of my appearance you think that?"

She nods.

"Everyone looks like me today. Your people... I mean... all people have intermingled. There aren't really..."

"There are no more Caucasians? No more like me?"

I shake my head.

"Maybe in isolated enclaves. Maybe back on Earth. But for the most part, no."

"Earth is not..." she pauses, searching for the right word, though I'm sure the translator mangles it anyway, "important anymore?"

I clench my jaws.

"No. Not really. It's still our homeworld. Some people still live there. Sometimes people vacation there to visit the ruins or study archaeology. But, no. We've moved on."

She turns and stares off into the distance at a billowing storm of blood. The human in me makes me want to reach out and put my hand on her shoulder. But I know Prosser and Tampa are watching, their beam rifles leveled, and the only thing protecting her from instant death is the meter of space between us. She turns back to me.

"I am called Jaime."

"Paige," I reply.

"Well, where do we go from here, Paige?"

# FIFTEEN

"Go on, Grace."

The woman sitting next to Jaime is seething. The hue of her skin is not like Jaime's, but neither is it as dark as *La Raza Cósmica's*. She is of a different terrestrial ethnicity. She is also tall, broadly muscled, arrogant and angry. She is their Helena.

As though it is painful beyond all reasoning, Grace stands. She is trying, genuinely trying. They are trying.

"I sincerely apologize for firing my weapon at you. We did not realize who you were. We thought you were infested."

There's that word again. "Infested." The translator has mostly reached the point where there aren't even any hiccups in translating the odd *Manifest Destiny* dialect of English anymore. It seems that they really are concerned with some kind of infestation. I have to inquire more about that.

Helena is stony-faced. Her wound has entirely healed and though she looks pale and drawn, overall she seems no worse for wear.

"What I did, I did thinking I was protecting my family and my home. This is not an excuse. This is an explanation. And a sincere apology. I hope you will offer understanding. And... forgiveness."

Diane turns in her seat to fix a weary eye on Helena. She's barely been able to take her eyes off the meeting room's chronometer, which is still counting down from our original eighteen-hour deadline. At this point we have about sixteen hours remaining. The discovery of living colonists aboard *The*

*Manifest Destiny* and the associated shenanigans isn't just eating into our schedule, it's devouring it. The way forward now is up to Helena, but really, it's clear the director is not prepared to tolerate any more delays.

Helena, for her part, seems to sense all of this in Diane's gaze the same way I have. With a barely perceptible sigh, she rises to her feet.

"I am the director of security for this office. My career and my sworn task and I guess you might say my calling is the safety and protection of the employees under my charge. I would be lying if I said I appreciate being shot, but I would equally be lying if I said I wouldn't have done the same thing were our roles reversed."

She looks to Diane, who gives no response. She holds out her hand toward Grace.

"May I offer our friendship? And that we bury the hatchet?"

Grace looks to Jaime, who nods. Tentatively, *The Manifest Destiny*'s Helena steps forward and clasps the real Helena's hand. For a moment, I fear they might test each other's strength in a crushing contest the way adolescents sometimes do, but it seems that Grace is as eager to escape Helena's grasp as much as Helena seems to want the whole matter to be over. They both return to their seats, and I half-expect something like embarrassment to color their faces, but far be it for embarrassment to show on such rugged individuals.

"Fine, fine work, all around," Diane says. She's eager to get on with the business at hand. "Now, to get down to the root of the matter. Your people. What do you want? Do you want to be taken off of this planet? Returned to civilization? Do you want to be left alone? What are you hoping for?"

Jaime pauses, and I know every second of it is agony for Diane, even if she doesn't let it show. This simple salvage mission is quickly spiraling out of control.

"All we want is to survive," Jaime says finally. "If that means spiriting us away, so be it. But I think the more important question here is what do you want? The more I see of your *Borgwardt*, the less I believe you came here for an exploratory mission."

The director actually smiles, and for a moment seems less distracted by the ticking clock than by her adversary across the meeting room table. If Grace is the *Manifest Destiny's* version of Helena, then surely Jaime is their version of Diane herself.

"Very perceptive. We came here on a salvage mission. We were not expecting the seed ship to be occupied."

"Then none of our distress calls have been received?"

"No, I'm afraid not."

"You see," Grace growls. "I told you it was a waste of time to continue to hope for aid. Two hundred years and they never bothered to look for our ancestors. Why should they care about us or our petty struggles?"

"My friends, it's not a matter of not caring. It's a matter of simple ignorance. Paige? I hate to constantly make you the bearer of bad news, but..."

"It's quite all right, madam director," I say, rising from my own seat. This time I'm seated at the conference table rather than on the periphery. My star is rising as I've hoped it might. "It's what I'm paid for. Grace. Jaime. What you have to understand is that the world your ancestors left behind is very much gone. Your country of origin, the nation-state called America collapsed very shortly after you were presumed lost in space. In fact, all nation-states are gone now. There is nothing of the world you knew left. It's not that your people were ignoring you, it's that there was no one left to listen. The great stellar listening posts of the old USA have gone untended for years. The transmissions you were sending, well the technology is...it's what we'd call quaint."

"It's antiquated, you mean," Jaime says. "Two hundred years old. I'm under no illusions about that. What you're saying is we may as well not even have been broadcasting."

"That's correct. And for quite a long time we thought *The Manifest Destiny* was lost with all hands killed. There was a very famous movie made about it."

Grace seems livid.

"A movie? About our struggles? You knew that much and you still didn't send a rescue mission?"

Jaime puts a hand on her partner's.

"No, Grace. I think she means about the glorious death of our progenitors. That's what they think happened. Isn't that right, Paige?"

I nod.

"I'm afraid so."

A smile flitters across Jaime's face.

"I think I might like to see this movie. But that is a matter for a decidedly later time. I do not wish, madam director, for you to think of us as throwbacks. We are not Neanderthals who need to be patronized. We want to help you and be a part of society again. Would it be fair to say that if we assisted you in your salvage operation you would grant us passage back to what you call civilized space?"

Diane's eyebrow rise. Now Jaime has not only caught her attention but dangled a carrot in front of her. They truly do think alike.

"There are certain logistical considerations. Prosser, run and grab Rebecca from the galley." The security goon nods and disappears. "How many of your people are there?"

Jaime leans in while Grace whispered in her ear. She whispers something back under her breath. What about... somebody. Grace shakes her head.

"There are thirty-two of us left."

"Only thirty-two?" I repeat.

All eyes in the room lock on me. Shit. Shouldn't have spoken out of turn.

"How many were you expecting?" Jaime asks evenly.

I look to Diane and Zanib and Helena, but there's no help from any of them. I put my foot in it and now I have to take care of it myself.

"Well, to be frank, we weren't expecting any. Our assumption was that all hands were lost. But if even a single pod survived and your ancestors were following generational protocols there should be hundreds... maybe thousands."

"I can't feed no thousands," Becs announces loudly, entering the room.

"Ah, thank you for coming, Rebecca," Diane says, "How about thirty-two?"

"Thirty-two?" Becs rubs her chin for a moment. "We'll have to go on rations. No more ordering what you want. But, yeah, we can make it back to Yloft with thirty-two additional souls on board." Becs looks the two guests up and down. "What's wrong with you two?"

"We haven't fucked until we all look like Brazilians yet," Grace replies.

There's a moment of silence before Becs begins howling and slapping her thigh.

"Hey, you shipwrecked weirdoes are all right."

She takes a seat. I also sit back down, hoping that my impolitic outburst has been wallpapered over by the appearance of the loud Broatoan. No such luck. Jaime turns to me.

"As for your question, Paige, or... your implied question I suppose I should say, our ancestors did follow the original plan. Our people held out hope for quite some time that a rescue would be mounted, or at a minimum that we could figure out a way to terraform this planet to some extent. But the lower pods became infested and we've lost many, many people in the battles that followed."

Zanib leans forward.

"What are the lower pods infested with?"

Grace rises, agitated.

"This is unwise," she says.

Jaime pats her compatriot, and gestures for her to sit down.

"I know we must seem like savages to you..."

"Not at all," Diane says.

"Please, there's no need to patronize me. I know we must appear. Isolated. Cut-off. Barely scraping by with what to you must seem like primitive technology. We don't even look like people do anymore. I'm under no illusions that we'll be anything other than an oddity when we get back to civilization. But it's the hope that my children and perhaps my children's children can be reintegrated with society that drives me now.

"I hope you'll forgive us our superstitious ways. Amongst us it is considered a terrible taboo to speak of our enemy directly. This is why Grace is so...agitated right now. There is a creature or perhaps a vector or perhaps a disease...we're not entirely certain what it is and much of what we know is passed down by oral tradition and not entirely reliable. Our people are in Pod Eight, which landed pointing up when *The Manifest Destiny* went down. Our diametric opposite is Pod Two."

Grace hisses.

"You'll doom us all with your loose tongue."

Grace tosses her chair backwards and storms out of the conference room. Helena rises to follow.

"Please. Let her go. She just needs to cool off."

Helena jams a thumb towards the hatch.

"Tell Shit-For-Brains to keep an eye on her through the monitors. Corral her back in if you have to. But don't put a tail on her for now."

Prosser nods and ducks out the hatch. I suppose Shit-For-Brains is Helena's not-so-playful nickname for Quinn. I suppose she really doesn't fit in with the rest of the security staff.

"Please continue," Diane says, now apparently more absorbed with what we are learning than concerned about the time it is taking up.

Jaime nods and sighs.

"It's bad luck to even talk about Pod Two. I'm trying... I'm trying not to be the superstitious savage you must take me to be. But it's like fighting generations of inherited knowledge, if you know what I mean."

"I do."

Becs jumps to her feet and strides over to a hospitality tray. She pours a tall glass of water and puts it down in front of Jaime.

"Thank you."

"Any time."

She claps Jaime heartily on the back. After taking a sip our guest continues.

"Pod Two was breached upon impact when our ancestors crashed here. It began to fill up with that foul muck outside. It's like blood. The pods were all open to each other at the time, and Pod Two remains open to the ocean. Our ancestors had to evacuate the two adjacent pods, One and Three, and seal them off. The ocean water got in but they're entirely sealed off now.

"Our people distributed the evacuees from the lower three pods evenly among the remaining nine. About three hundred people were divided among nine pods, so we each took on about thirty-three. There were a few that didn't survive the crash and the subsequent challenges, so the numbers aren't exact.

"What we didn't realize was that an enemy had been brought into our midst. There is something sentient and I can only call it... evil... living in the depths. I hope you don't think me mad."

Diane shakes her head slightly but the rest of us are focused raptly on Jaime's story. She clears her throat and takes another sip of water.

"People began dying. Our ancestors suspected there was a plague, but it was revealed to be foul play. Among the twelve hundred survivors, all hand-picked the best of the best, astronauts specially trained for this mission — there seemed to have developed overnight a rash of murderers. But it wasn't mere human weakness or even the psychosis that had developed from the desperation of crashing. No, our ancestors lived well at the time, they still had their hydroponic gardens and their chicken farms and quarters weren't even terribly crowded. They were still planning to make a go of forming a colony here, even if it never amounted to more than a few sunken pods from the wreck of *The Destiny*. They were convinced that, given time, they would be able to populate the planet as they had been meant to, or else to hold out for a rescue mission they considered inevitable. *The Destiny* was far too valuable to simply be written off, we thought.

"The rash of murders, though, caused a witch hunt. And it wasn't very long before we had proven that survivors of Pods One through Three were responsible. The rest were treated as pariahs and in the darkest day in the short history of our colony here, the others conspired to kill them all. Three hundred people we'd been living with and fighting with and building a future with... rooted out like enemies of the state."

"But that wasn't the end of it."

I look up, startled. Grace stands in the jamb, shadowed not far behind by Prosser, who had been sent to watch her. She looks haunted, like she had been there.

"No," Jaime agrees, "It wasn't. In fact, it was just the beginning. Imagine slaughtering a quarter of your crew. Friends, lovers, comrades-in-arms. Fear, I think, motivated our ancestors. Fear drove us to near madness. But the infestation... we couldn't root it out. It had already taken hold, spread beyond the original carriers. Instead of cauterizing a weeping wound we had simply burned innocents at the stake."

"This infestation," Zanib says, "Are you able to identify the carriers?"

Ruefully, Jaime shakes her head.

"Not through any medical science we have access to. We can only identify the infested through detective work. When they attempt to sabotage us and we can trace it back to the saboteur... assuming it's not simply a disgruntled person."

"The result's the same in any case," Grace growls.

Jaime holds up her hands placatingly.

"Please... I don't know how you look on capital punishment. I know it's not... civilized. But for us it's a necessary way of life."

"Our corporation's not usually in the habit of judging other cultures," Diane says. "Ladies, thank you for your honesty. Would you please excuse us? I need to have a brief discussion with my staff."

Nodding, Jaime rises and joins Grace at the jamb. Both exit and the hydraulics close the hatch behind them.

"They need to die," Helena says, "Every last one of them."

# SIXTEEN

"Much as I value your input, Helena, doesn't it seem a bit premature to jump to genocide?"

Helena snorts.

"Genocide. There's thirty-two of them."

"Mass murder, then," Diane "corrects" herself icily.

Helena rises and slaps both of her palms down on the conference table opposite the director.

"Madam director, we've worked together for twelve years. Since long before you were 'madam director' and I was a goon who didn't know which end of a nightstick to hold."

"Kill 'em all, Diane, for old time's sake, is that what you're trying to sell me?"

Helena shakes her head slowly.

"I'm not selling anything and I'm not being sentimental."

"That's evident," I mutter.

"Watch yourself," Helena says, waggling a finger at me before turning back to Diane. "I've known you a long time and I've never known you to choose the easy out. Tough choices, that's how you became a director. Not the easy wrong, the hard right. Now you tell me, Diane, those people, they have some kind of disease. We could all already be infected. We have no way of knowing. Bringing them onboard, it's worse than leaving the barn door open, it's letting the fox in the henhouse. I couldn't swear right now that they'll let us through quarantine. With thirty-two potential plague vectors on board? Yloft or any other station would be fully justified in blasting us out of the sky. Hell, don't listen to me. Ask the station bunny. She'll tell you."

My mind's racing. Unfortunately, she's not just right, she's damn right. And there aren't a whole lot of ways around it. We departed from Yloft with our complement registered and verified. We can't just show up with thirty-two new bodies and not expect to trigger every warning bell on the station.

Not to mention we would have to falsify countless logs to keep the station goons from figuring out there was a disease amongst the new people. And no matter their loyalty, there will always be crew members who will sell out a ship trying to avoid quarantine in exchange for special consideration. I've seen it happen like clockwork. Freighters, even cruise ships where the whole crew from the captain on down insist they're clean, but there's always one cook or janitor or somebody who sells them out in exchange for being quarantined in a suite in the lap of luxury.

Not to mention the corporation would torch all of our paystubs, bonuses and all, and might just dismiss us for falsifying records in a plague protocol.

Long story short, Helena's right. Yloft or any other halfway legitimate outpost will put us in indefinite quarantine if not destroy us outright.

"I'm familiar with quarantine protocol, thank you," Diane says, thankfully not forcing me to weigh in with an opinion I don't like myself for having. She presses a button on the intercom. "Tina, would you come to the conference room, please?"

"On my way, madam director."

"Thank you."

Diane sighs and leans back in her chair. She glances over at Zanib and I, then back at Becs.

"Your thoughts, Rebecca?"

Becs holds up her hands.

"You asked me if I could feed 'em. I can if we ration. That's the extents of my thoughts on this matter, in total and in perpetuity."

Diane turns to us.

"What about you two?"

Zanib doesn't seem to be in a hurry to say anything. I clear my throat.

"Well, aside from the moral implications of any action we take..."

"Our moral duty is to the company," Helena says. "Our moral duty is to ourselves. Morally, we don't owe these people a damn thing."

"That would be ethics, not morals, Helena. And I can assure the both of you that my personal morals have never interfered with the performance of my duties. Continue your thought, Paige."

Shit. I've already lost my train of thought. Do I even have one? Am I just going to flounder? Luckily, at that moment, Tina appears at the hatch, distracting us all for a moment.

"Thanks for coming, Tina. Close the hatch behind you, please."

I can see Grace and Jaime out in the hall. They have Prosser laughing. I'm reminded that these are human beings we're talking about, not cockroaches or rats or any other "plague vectors." People with hopes and dreams and parents and possibly kids. Shit, how many kids are on that damn seed ship right now?

"Paige was about to say something, but then we'll bring you up to speed."

I swallow the lump in my throat. A thought occurs to me. One that's not sentimental at all.

"I know our decisions are supposed to be based on what's best for the company, and I'm new here so I'm not great at that."

"You seem to be doing fine so far, in my estimation."

Is that a compliment? From the director? I only nod.

"Still, I have to look at the bigger picture here. These people, whatever else they are, they're a find, for lack of a better word. They're like a society out of time. Their value in the fields of history, anthropology, archaeology…they're priceless. I don't know what it profits the company, but I know what it profits humanity."

Diane nods but doesn't respond. She turns and briefly brings Tina up to speed.

"Oh my," the nurse says.

"'Oh my,' indeed. First things first. A disease that makes you act as a saboteur against your own best interests. Is there such a thing?"

Tina sucks air through her teeth.

"It's not unprecedented. There are illnesses that make you act… for lack of a better word… crazy. But this could also be a case of mass hysteria. Or even something as simple as cabin fever posing under the aegis of an urban legend."

"In other words, it only happens because they believe it happens?"

"Possibly. There are lots of examples of psychosomatic diseases. Witch doctors in ancient cultures seemingly capable of the magic ascribed to them."

"Hope is not a planning method," Helena says, "We have to treat this disease as though it were real."

"True enough," Diane concedes. "Would you be able to determine if these people are infected or not?"

"I don't know. Our diagnostic equipment on board isn't terrible, but if I don't know what I'm looking for, how will I know if I've found it?"

"And just because you've identified one disease doesn't mean we're not bringing on other, unidentified ones," Helena says.

"Well, that could be the case anyway," Tina says. "That could always be the case. That's one of the dangers of ink surfing, isn't it? That was the case as soon as you three set foot into this atmosphere."

"We didn't have reports of a disease then."

"Thank you, Helena, I think you've made your point."

"Apologies, madam director, but I don't think I have. I feel the need to state my case one more time, for the record, as director of security in this office."

Diane folds her arms and leans back in her chair.

"Oh, by all means. As always, the camera is running."

Helena looks up at the roving eye above the hatch. Perhaps she had forgotten she was being recorded. I never realized, but it seems in keeping with everything I've seen on the *Borgwardt* so far. There's probably even a clause in my contract saying I'm open to constant surveillance. I make a mental note to re-read it more carefully and possibly see if I can negotiate that clause when I re-up.

"These people are not our people. That's a fact. They are hostile strangers. That's also a fact. I have the soft spot right here to prove it."

Helena jabs a thumb into her recently-healed shoulder. I've never been nursed back to health from a gunshot wound, but I suspect it must be tender. Helena doesn't act as though she feels it at all.

"And you don't think your anger at being shot is influencing your decision making process here?"

"No, I don't, madam director. I'm capable of separating my ego from what's best for the ship."

"You're on thin ice."

"So be it. I won't have this go down as dereliction. Maybe it'll go down as insubordination. But it won't go down as dereliction. The fact is company regulations state that we have no responsibility towards hostile strangers. When they open hostilities, we are free to respond with any measures deemed necessary by security to protect the company's assets and, to a lesser extent, the company's human resources. That is regulation. I say we toss those two silver-tongued bleeding hearts off this office, and we fill that seed ship to capacity with white-hot plasma."

"You're talking about committing a war crime in response to being shot in the arm," I say. "Where's your sense of proportionality?"

"Don't forget I took that bullet for you, Ambroziak. Was proportionality on your mind when I was saving your ass?"

"Ladies," Diane says simply, a full sentence in a single word before continuing. "Has everyone had their say?" She glances around the room. Even Helena seems mollified at last. "I've made my decision."

# SEVENTEEN

"Helena is right, of course, to be cautious. That's her job. Caution. In all matters. It's security's watchword. However, though she didn't mount an especially strong defense, I'm swayed by Paige's input. Ultimately, our highest concern is the company. They pay us. It's our job to draw a profit for them. Otherwise what's the point of all this?

"It's impossible for me to say right now what value these people with have to Hestle. But it's also impossible to deny that it will be immense. Science will be better, yes. That's a fair assessment. But we're also talking about stories. Multi-million chit stories. Rethinking what we know about *The Manifest Destiny*. I don't work for the studio arm, but I have to think the movie rights for that would be astronomical. Book deals, personal tours, the list goes on and on. These people, every one of them, has the potential to become a multi-million chit asset to Hestle. Burning them up? That eliminates the risk but it also eliminates the reward. And make no mistake, ladies, we are here to find the company its reward. It may not even matter what we can haul off of that hulk in terms of junk when we have these people.

"That being said, Tina, I need you to find out what you can. Screen them. Figure out what the disease is, if it exists, get us some hard data for when we return to Yloft. We may have to rely on the company's influence before we can dock, yes. We may even need to wait for a company tug to bring us back to friendly space. But if we have solid medical evidence for them that there is no disease or that we've quarantined the diseased colonists, or, heck, let's just shoot the moon, that we've cured the disease before returning, that'll go a long way towards getting us through quarantine protocols.

"In the meantime, Helena your top priority is making sure I can execute your plan with the push of a button. I will burn them out in a second if it becomes necessary. Don't think I've ignored you, old friend, and don't think I've taken your professional opinion for granted or taken it personally. I know you're a straight talker. And I know what you've suggested may become necessary at the drop of a pin. So, make us ready to burn that place to the ground. But right now, I'm not throwing out the baby with the bathwater. When I'm convinced you're right, we'll burn it out together and I'll owe you a coffee. But until then I have to act as though these human resources are invaluable to the company.

"As for the rest of you: the plan stays in place. If we get nothing else out of this rotten trip, we will get what we came for. Strip that ship. And bear in mind, we've lost time. Put those colonists to work. Remind them what we're offering them as often as necessary. And use the carrot, not the stick, ladies. No need to bring up the possibility of burning them out."

Or burning ourselves out. She doesn't say it, but it's self-evident. If any of us happen to be aboard *The Manifest Destiny* when whatever imaginary red line is crossed that necessitates firebombing an occupied seed ship, it's impossible to imagine a scenario where our people would be recalled. Necessary losses, we'd be called. Insurance write-offs. Cost of doing business.

"Any questions?"

The silence is deafening.

"All right then."

We all shuffle out of the conference room except for Diane. Out in the corridor, Tina walks up to Grace and Jaime with a smile.

"Excuse me, ladies, would one of you mind coming with me? We're going to run some tests. See if we can't find out more about this disease that's been plaguing you."

Prosser glances at Helena for confirmation. Helena nods.

"Of course," Jaime agrees.

Zanib's jotter beeps. She glances at it and begins patting my side wildly.

"What?" I whisper.

She holds up her jotter, which is displaying a dozen lights. Eleven are blinking red but one is solid green.

"Caught a rat. Too bad you can't come see."

"I'll go," Grace says, sounding so much like she's replying to Zanib's statement that it jars me out of our sidebar. "You should head back and speak to the others."

"All right." Jaime looks up at Helena. "Would it be all right if I went to speak to my people alone at first? I'll have to ease them into this."

Helena's glance ping-pongs between the two colonists.

"That's fine," she says, "but let's reverse it. You go and you stay. A little bit of an insurance policy, you know?"

"A hostage, you mean," Grace corrects her. "No offense intended. I would've insisted on the same thing in your shoes. I'd have been insulted if you hadn't."

"Ah, excuse me. How long do you think this will take?" Zanib interrupts, raising her hand like a schoolchild.

Grace shrugs.

"Twenty, thirty minutes. I'm generally brief. Why?"

"Perfect. We'll meet you at the umbilicus. Right now, I have to check on a local specimen we caught. Make sure we didn't just catch a boot. And I need Paige's assistance."

She grabs me and started dragging me back toward the bowels of the ship.

"Patel," Helena says sharply, not needing to say another word to get her point across.

"I know!" Zanib shouts, putting out her hands as though there's nothing she can do. "We're in a time crunch. Burn the candle at both ends. I've still got to get this done."

That seems to placate the goon. I can't believe how fast Zanib is moving. She's practically flying along the corridors, like she's wearing hover boots. I've never seen her so excited. This is her life's work, I suppose. She's in her element now.

It seems like only a minute before we're back in her secretive menagerie. As soon as the hatch closes behind me she grabs me and slams me against it, crushing her lips against mine.

# EIGHTEEN

"Zanib…"

"What? Don't tell me you're not into it. I don't think I could handle that rejection right now."

"No, it's not that," I reply, "It's not that at all. I'm interested. Very interested."

"Then what?"

"There isn't time for this."

"There's always time for this."

I feel my zipper coming down on my jumpsuit, almost magically, as if of its own volition. I'm concentrating so hard on her tongue gently caressing the inside of my mouth. A tiny impulse in me says to fight back, but a vastly stronger feeling urges me to let it go. Zanib is stroking my stomach, the sweaty area under my breasts, and then, with almost no further deliberation, she slides right down to my crotch.

I'm embarrassed. I haven't shaved in ages. My only lover has been the university on Yloft for so long that such niceties seem a waste. She slips a lone digit into me and I gasp. My heart is racing like a hummingbird. It really has been a long time. I break away from her lips and smile, coquettishly, I hope.

"Aren't we forward?" I whisper.

"Well, I thought we didn't have much time. What's changed your mind?"

"Zanib."

"Yes, virgin," she mutters, nuzzling my neck and continuing to finger me.

"Is there a camera in here?"

She looks up, startled.

"I... I don't know."

"Didn't Diane say the cameras are always running?"

Zanib's lips purse and she slams a fist against the bulkhead she's pressing me against, hammer-style.

"Dammit! This is so frustrating!"

I take her face in my hands.

"You think you're frustrated? I'm halfway over the moon and we have to stop."

"No," she says, cutting me a sly glance, "Just from that?"

"It's been a long time, roomie."

Reluctantly I zip my jumpsuit back up, and we both sigh almost simultaneously.

"Fuck it. What the hell do we do now?

"We could slip back to our room. No cameras there. Against company policy."

She smiles and slips a hand under my shoulder. Even she must know it's not going to happen. Our quarters are about as far away from her lab as you can get. Even if we give in to our lust here it would have to be a quickie for us to get back in any kind of reasonable timeframe.

"Aren't we supposed to be looking at one of your rat traps?"

"Ohhhh," she says, "You're right."

I've managed to switch her from her one great passion to the other. In the center of the room lies a circular indentation in the deck next to a small pedestal. Zanib attaches her jotter to the pedestal and punches the green light. The circular indentation opens and Zanib places her hand on my chest to press me back. The rope begins to wind and we stare down waiting in anticipation for the cage to break the surface of the blood ocean. After a few tense seconds, it finally does and I squint down trying to see what we've caught.

"Watch the edge," Zanib warns.

I can tell there is something moving in the cage, flipping and flopping around, but it remains indistinct at this distance. The cage winds up the full distance and enters a small conveyor device which brings it up through the hole in the deck of Zanib's lab.

"Looks like a new friend for Crassus," I say.

It's not the largest cage. Neither is it the smallest. The creature we've captured bears a distinct and unsettling resemblance to the lampreys which Zanib has briefed us on and I kissed earlier. It's not quite identical. It's longer and appears to have backward-facing spines running in three seams lengthwise across each third of its body. It doesn't appear to have Crassus's distinctive toothed tongue, either. It is also blind, lacking the eyes the stonelickers have on the side of their heads.

Its jaw, though, is unsettlingly similar. A distended, jawless mouth, with teeth pointing inward at all angles, it clenches its mouth and attempts to suckle at the empty air even as it flops about.

"Shh, shh, baby," Zanib whispers, and I think if it wasn't in a cage she would started stroking its body. "We'll get you back into a nice habitat in a minute."

Zanib begins punching all kinds of buttons on her pedestaled jotter. Lights of varying colors run over the creature, blue, orange, yellow, and finally red, from projectors in the ceiling. When the various scans stop, Zanib sits, rapt, staring at her jotter and flipping through readings. I'm beginning to worry – if "worry" is the right feeling to have toward such a grotesque thing – for the creature's life.

"Zanib?"

"You should check out these preliminary scans, virgin. They're amazing."

"What about the creature, Zanib? It's suffocating."

"What? Oh, shit, you're right. Where's my head at?"

"It used to be on me. Then this fishie came along."

She grins.

"Come on, give me a hand with this."

Together we maneuver the cage up and into a tank Zanib has prepared for the occasion, filled with the disgusting brine from the surface, or else a facsimile thereof she has concocted herself. Not knowing the procedures of xenobiology, I can't swear which. She unlocks the cage and lets the eel-like thing wriggle out into its new habitat before we retrieve the cage and lower it back through the hole in the deck before sealing it up.

"You're reusing the rat trap?" I ask.

"I've only done this a few times before, but I've noticed that the rat traps seem to work best by size. If old Number Seven here is what caught this little fella, it's the right size to catch other little fellas like him."

"How many samples do we need?"

"Ideally? At least a breeding pair. Although after your little speech about population controls, I'm sort of interested in whether we need to start breeding until we have a stable population."

I reach out and run my hand along her side and grasp her tight little ass through the fabric of her suit.

"I knew you still had breeding on the mind."

"Oh, you know just the lingo to turn a xenobiologist on."

She brushes her lips against mine again, and a spark of electricity crackles through me.

"Buuuut..." she says, dragging out the single, abbreviated syllable, "we have to get back."

I can't help pouting. We've gone from being friendly to low-level flirting to actively teasing each other in such a short period of time, but I really can't be letting this take up space in my head when I have a mission to do, and lives (not to mention a big fat bonus) are on the line.

Zanib seals the tank containing the new arrival.

"It's a shame," she says. "We really ought to name him."

"Him?" I say, mildly surprised. Of course, I'm aware of the concept of males. It's just strange to think of them outside the context of xenobiology, which I've never really studied.

"Oh, yes. Our little friend here is a member of the dead gender."

"Huh," I grunt, "well, what would you want to name him?"

"That's the thing," she says, running a finger under my chin. "I'd want to name him after you. But he's a boy. Is there a male form of Paige?"

I shrug. A question for academia, if there ever was one, though not, unfortunately, my area of expertise.

"What would you call him?"

I smile, the only male profession I can think of springing to mind.

"King."

"King Paige. I like it. All right, K.P. it is."

# NINETEEN

We arrive in the airlock only two minutes later than we were supposed to. I half expect Helena to start yelling at us, but she's pacing the airlock like a caged dog and clearly doesn't wish to be disturbed. She doesn't even look up when we came in.

My heart is fluttering. I wouldn't say I'm excited at the idea that we might have been caught on tape – we never spotted a camera in Zanib's lab – but I feel like a kid who snuck a cookie from the cookie jar. My mind's already racing with thoughts of how to escape what sounds like an interminable fourteen remaining hours of scavenging ops – all on duty for me – to sneak a guilty twenty-minute romp with my roommate. No way immediately jumps to mind, and, strangely, the next fourteen hours loom ahead like far more of an insurmountable obstacle than the last three years or so I've gone without a lover.

I can't tell what Zanib's thinking – well, not exactly what she's thinking – but the way her eyes keep roving over my body and her tongue keeps seeming to involuntarily flick out like a lizard's to coat her lips with saliva, I can certainly guess.

We go to the porthole to look out, but the umbilicus remains resolutely empty. Grace is either still talking to her people or dead. We settle down, slouching against the bulkhead and not far from each other, and as the seconds tick by I begin to gravely regret not letting Zanib talk me into being a few minutes late.

I don't know how, considering how horny I still am, but somehow I doze off. Next thing I know, Tina and Jaime are standing in the shipside entrance of the airlock. Zanib snorts awake next to me and Helena, I note, has abandoned pacing the room to take up a position looming in the corner like a gargoyle.

"Where's Grace?" Jaime asks.

I shrug.

"What does that mean?"

"Not back yet," Helena snarls. "Is this a declaration of war? Should I say a second declaration of war?"

She steps deep into the smaller woman's personal space, obviously trying to intimidate her, but Jaime doesn't even tense a muscle. It occurs to me that she has been so calm and well-mannered her entire time aboard the *Borgwardt,* that I had somehow forgotten she has risen to apparent leadership over a gang of presumably undisciplined survivors on a merciless deathworld. Helena, I think, senses the same thing: restraint and discipline rather than weakness and softness. She backs out of Jaime's small circle of air.

"My people can be... difficult to rally. But I have faith in Grace. She's ever been my trusted right hand."

"What about you?" Helena asks, jutting her chin towards Tina. "What'd you learn?"

"Don't speak to me like I'm one of your little goons, Helena," the nurse replies. "I don't work for you. And I'm not the reason you're in a mood. I'm the reason you're not in a body bag."

Tina pokes the security director in the shoulder, and Helena actually flinches. I'm holding my breath. But instead of storming into a rage, Helena actually seems to calm down.

"Sorry, doc. Did you learn anything? Pretty please with a cherry on top tell me?"

"Well... I wasn't going to, but since you put the cherry on top..."

Tina holds up her jotter so that we all can see. We all gather around except Jaime, who presumably has already been told about her medical condition. It occurs to me that it's probably a violation of medical ethics to show a bunch of strangers a patient's chart, but Jaime either has no concept of privacy codes or else simply doesn't care.

I can't make heads or tails of what I'm looking at. Luckily, I'm not the only one, so I don't have to be the first to voice my ignorance.

"What the hell does that mean?" Helena asks.

Tina grins. It's a joke – she knows none of us, with the possible exception of Zanib, know what the jotter is saying.

"It means she has a clean bill of health. At least as far as I can tell. No known mutagens or pathogens. I even tried extrapolating based on everything we know about the fleshworld, based on all the passive readings and active research we've been doing since we got here. Science marches on, but I can't find a thing."

"Then there is no disease?"

"I'm not infested," Jaime says, "which I already knew. The trouble is: can you identify anyone at all who is?"

"I don't know," Tina admits.

"So then we've accomplished nothing," Helena growls. "We still don't know if there is a disease or if she has it."

"No," Tina agrees, "but now we have a baseline. We can do this thirty-one more times and compare the results. I mean, we can never know with certitude what we don't know

– there's no way to disprove a negative – but maybe we'll get lucky."

"Luck: the ultimate planning method."

"It's called science, Helena."

Zanib nods.

"That is kind of the long and short of science. Keep trying until you get lucky."

"What about you?" Tina asks.

"What about me?"

"Your specimen?"

"Ohhhhh," Zanib says, stretching it out, "you mean K.P. He is a handsome little guy. Wouldn't you say, Paige?"

"Charming," I agree, rolling my eyes.

"Excuse me," Jaime says, "is this some sort of animal you're talking about? A local specimen?"

"It is," Zanib replies. "Are you familiar with the local fauna?"

Jaime shakes her head.

"After the infestation took hold in the lower decks we remained sealed off. But we weren't aware there was local life above the germ and viral level, or possibly fungi. That is to say, except for the planet itself."

"The fleshworld is a fascinating ecosystem," Zanib says, "but that bit's above my paygrade. It's really the climatologists and the chaos theorists who are trying to make sense of that. But I've always suspected that a fleshworld had the potential to be home to essentially an ecosystem of parasites. And it seems I'm right."

Zanib plugs her jotter into the bulkhead adapter and presses a few buttons. A shimmering, three-dimensional image of K.P. shimmers into existence in the middle of the room, so photorealistic I feel sure I can reach out and touch his slimy flesh. It's the same technology we used to watch "The Manifest Destiny," adapted for business use. The hologram bucks and slithers through the naked air, mimicking the parasite's movements in the tank Zanib had relocated it to.

"Grotesque," Helena states simply.

"Oh, I think they're beautiful," Zanib counters, approaching the hologram and petting it. "These are going to be named after me one day, you know?"

"Are they edible?" Jaime asks.

Zanib reflexively tucks the projected K.P. under her armpit and hides him from Jaime's view. Apparently, it is an interactive hologram. I've only ever seen such things at children's parties. The projectors at the university are very much pragmatic.

"You wouldn't dare eat my little beh-bie!"

Jaime smiles wanly, and for the first time I felt that she is truly forcing herself to act pleasant. Zanib must have struck a real nerve to cut through the Vilameenian's steely reserve.

"There have been times – many times – even in my own lifetime when we have suffered from famine. Even been forced to resort to..."

She pauses.

"Cannibalism?" Helena asks, more intrigued than repulsed.

Jaime doesn't respond, but I get the jangly feeling in my nerves that Helena has guessed correctly.

"It's taken massive efforts and the better part of my lifetime to get the hydroponics gardens secured and producing enough food for even our small population. It's by far the most popular target of sabotage for the infested."

"The hydroponics we saw were clogged with produce," I say.

Jaime nods.

"My legacy to the next generation. Never to go hungry. I suppose it doesn't matter anymore. To think, though, that we had this food source available to us all along if only we'd opened up our windows, and perhaps our minds. Many lives could have been saved."

"Or lost if additional people had been exposed to the infection," Helena states flatly.

"Well, I won't lie to you, K.P. here is fat with protein and fatty fish oils, but I don't think you would've had much luck fishing for his kind. My initial brain-scans show that they are surprisingly intelligent. I'll have to do a lot more investigation, but I think they might even be puzzle-solving, which is fairly rare in nature. I have eleven other traps out and so far this is the only parasite I've caught. And I think I only caught him because he was curious. You might have gotten a meal or two out of them, but after that they probably would have stayed away."

"Who wants to eat space lamprey anyway?" Tina asks.

"When you're starving," Jaime says quietly, "frivolities like disgust and morality slip away very quickly. Desperation is an awful, awful thing. I hope you never experience it."

We all fall silent, but the awkwardness is short-lived. Grace is knocking on the airlock hatch.

# TWENTY

I think each of us jump, though I can't swear about Helena, and I don't think it's in her nature. Prosser and Tampa quickly open the airlock, and as Grace steps through they each click something on their beam rifles that makes an intimidating noise. Grace eyes them both up. I'm not very knowledgeable about weapons, but I do know that a beam rifle works just as well whether you make it click or not. The clicker is a vestigial device from ancient times. Just something that every gun is supposed to have, I suppose, for intimidating people.

"What did..." Jaime starts to say.

"Excuse me," Helena says, making it clear by her tone that she means less than zero per cent of the generally agreed upon definition of "excuse me" and steps in between Jaime and Grace. "What's going on? What did your people say?"

Grace glances at Jaime, who nods for her to continue. She quickly glances at each of the rest of us in turn and I sense a calculating mind. Perhaps she's considering whether she can fight her way through us, or how hard it would be to get back to *The Manifest Destiny* before us, something like that. Whatever Grace's evaluation of the situation, her demeanor doesn't change.

"There was a lot to discuss," Grace says, "but in the end, no one wants to stay. Or be left behind. They'll come."

"Excellent," Tina says. "Can we start having them come down to the infirmary? I have a lot of work ahead of me and I'll need to see each of your people."

"Didn't the director say to put the colonists to work?" That was Helena.

"I'm not putting anyone to work until they've got a clean bill of health," Tina replies, "which so far means only her."

Tina jerks a thumb in Jaime's direction.

"Bring everyone over," Helena says to Grace. She turns to her crew. "You two are going to lay down roots in the infirmary, you get me?"

"We get you," Tampa and Prosser mutter in the exact opposite of excitement.

"Now you three are coming with me to get started," she says, pointing at me, Zanib, and Jaime in turn.

●●●

"What's this?" Zanib asks the empty room.

I double check my manifest a third time before firing my paint gun at what I suspect is a primitive subluminal communications array. This is the device (at least partially) responsible for Jaime and her ancestors being marooned on Vilameen for so long. As a squawker it's useless, but as a historical relic the accountants have deemed it as valuable.

My duty (and paint pellet) discharged, I turn to look at whatever Zanib is talking about. She is standing before three metal slabs, apparently taken from other parts of the pod and welded together to form a sort of table with two supports. Jaime is blushing and not moving to answer. Her skin is so remarkably pale she's turning a shade of red I've never seen a human being turn before. I glance at Helena, who is standing by the exit, weapon at the ready, apparently completely disinterested in the salvage operation and only concerned with safety.

I check my jotter. The colonists have definitely made modifications to the original design. Areas are littered with gear that they had fashioned or jury-rigged, and, as such, some of our attempts at finding the manifest items will be hopeless.

"This area used to house the chicken coops," I say, looking deliberately at our guide.

Looking around, I find that hard to believe. There are zero signs of feathers, excrement, blood, or even cages. None of the tell-tale marks of animal husbandry.

"Chickens?" Jaime says. "Oh, yes, that was a long time ago. My grandmother used to tell me about them. The little... animals. 'Ee-caw, ee-caw,' they'd say, and sometimes flap their arms just like this."

She flutters her arms, a mimicry of a long-forgotten children's tale. Even Helena can't suppress a smile at the profoundly silly act. Everyone knows what a chicken acts like, or is supposed to act like. Except Jaime. She has no idea. No first-hand experience.

I suddenly feel profoundly sad for her. This is a person who has never seen an animal, or even a free-growing plant. We are the first humans outside of a tiny, incestuous community that she or any of her kind has ever met. Her entire life took place within the claustrophobic confines of a crashed ship. It's impossible not to bring to mind a prison sentence, brought on due to no sin or crime of her own.

"What happened?" Zanib asks. "Your ancestors over-ate them?"

"No," she replies. "Supposedly they were very good stewards of the livestock. Our people are trained from birth in math and breeding science. Our ancestors took very good care of the chickens, in fact, and according to my grandmother there was a time when this entire hold was packed with them, and eggs were so plentiful they grew sick of eating them. But as with all good things, the infested got to them. Poisoned their food supply, because it was less well guarded than the corn that went directly to the crew members. In the space of a single day, all the chickens were wiped out, and one of the worst famines in our history set in."

It suddenly occurs to me what the large metal slab would have been used for after such a tragedy. I stare into Zanib's face, willing her to drop the matter, but she either cannot read my expression or doesn't care.

"What's this table for, then?"

I can tell by Jaime's pained expression that I have guessed correctly.

"Prayer," she replies after a prolonged moment, "at first. Our ancestors were not a religious people by nature. They were scientists. Most were irreligious if not outright atheistic. But after the loss of the chickens, some element of superstition rose to the surface, gaining currency among our people. Then the sacrifices began."

"Sacrifices?" Zanib asks, before understanding finally dawns on her. "Oh."

"There was a power struggle after that. Many of the religious zealots were exiled down into the lower pods. But this thing remains. A monument to our shame."

"All right, all right," Helena announces with an intolerable edge in her voice, "Enough with the chit-chat. You're on company time now."

"Company time," Jaime repeats, with a wan smile. "Yes, of course."

Jaime leads the way into the next major area, Helena trailing just behind. Zanib grabs my hand and holds me fast in the chamber with the sacrificial altar. She plants a kiss on my nose.

"This place gives me the heebie-jeebies."

"Then why are you lingering here?"

"Just to get two seconds alone with you."

"Two seconds is all we've got."

Helena's loud voice underwrites my statement.

"Ambroziak! Patel! Quit lollygagging!"

We squeeze hands tightly before breaking our miniature embrace and following after.

"Are you worried about the other pods?"

"What do you mean?" I ask.

"Well," she says, checking her jotter, "at the rate we're moving, we should have this whole place scrapped inside of two, three hours. You really think Diane's going to let us depart with eleven unexplored treasure troves?"

"Two is filled with ocean plasma, which, last I checked, we have no way of navigating. One and Three are also compromised."

"Which leaves eight pods full of priceless artifacts. Diane has her flaws, but she can count."

"We made a deal with Jaime's people," I say. "We don't even know what's down there."

"Cannibals. Cultists. Some kind of infestation that turns people against their own kind. Which we may already be exposed to. It all sounds very scary for the salvage team, but not like anything that's going to deter madam director from pressing further."

My eyes shift to Helena, who is meditating darkly on something.

"I suspect our intrepid security director will insist on not pushing out luck."

"Diane gives Helena's word a lot of weight. But not all the weight. She listens to you, too. Remember that last meeting we had."

"What do you want me to say, Zanib?"

"I want you to say you're aware of the danger and you're going to be careful, virgin."

"I'm aware of the danger and I'm going to be careful. But you already knew that."

"I just want you to come back to me in one piece. And hopefully I won't have to call you 'virgin' anymore after that."

She smiles a bit too broadly and I elbow her in the side.

"Hold up," Helena snaps, holding up her fist in a gesture I take to mean, "halt."

She pulls out her blinking jotter and clicks a few buttons. She glances at Jaime.

"The infirmary's done with your people."

Jaime manages to look simultaneously agitated and relieved in equal measure.

"What's the result?"

"They're all clean."

Jaime furrows her brow.

"How is that possible?"

"Maybe it was all in your heads."

Jaime's expression darkens.

"You're saying I made it all up? My grandmother's death? My mother's? Countless people I'd come to rely on and call friends and lovers?"

"She's saying," I interrupt, stepping between them, "that it could be space madness. Not a physical disease. A mental one. From being trapped up here. Not that you're making anything up."

I don't know if I should go on, but Jaime doesn't seem mollified.

"No one's accusing you of lying. But mental illness in a place like this..."

I shrug.

"Generations? Generations going crazy, all in the same way? There's a physical infestation. Your science is just not good enough to discover it."

I want to be kind, but maybe ripping off the bandage is the best way to be kind.

"Jaime, space madness in a place like this... it can metastasize into an urban legend. And an urban legend can work its powers on generations and generations and..."

The little woman steps toward me and I'm so surprised I nearly drop my paint gun. Her eyes crackle with a fire I've never seen before.

"I know what is real and what is false. Now I can't speak for your people but I know what I've seen. Not folklore. Not urban legend. I've seen it. You want to see it, too? Drill through that bulkhead over there."

She points at a bulkhead which I don't even have to check my jotter to know leads to Pod Nine.

"What's in the other pods?"

A thump against the bulkhead seems born of a dark impulse, some imp of the perverse taunting and threatening me.

"You can deal with me. Negotiate with me. Them? You'll never be able to handle."

# TWENTY-ONE

I wait patiently, eyeing the corridor. The last of Jaime's people have disappeared for the moment, redirected in a move that fooled no one to the south end of the pod. I look to Helena for permission. She nods.

I hook the jotter into the comm system of *The Manifest Destiny*. Primitive though it is, it doesn't take much jury-rigging to get the holography working. A moment later, Diane is in the room with us, propped up on her crutches.

"Madam director," we both say, stepping out of the way of the hologram as though it's really our boss.

"All right, bring me up to speed," the Diane-gram says.

I look to Helena. She gestures right back at me to continue. Never before have I missed my roommate quite so much, but having declared the pod free from xenoforms she is now busying herself back in the lab with the specimen. Le sigh.

Only thirteen more hours, give or take, I remind myself. Then we'll know whether we're actually interested in each other, or if the attraction is just the result of prolonged close quarters. Either way is fine with me, honestly.

"Jaime's people," I begin with barely a pause.

"The hostile strangers," Helena interjects nevertheless.

"The... colonists, yes," I agree, "have stripped every nut and bolt of even marginal value from the ship. They've... earned their passage, I'd say."

"Their existence earns their passage," Diane intones ominously.

I understand what she means. They didn't have to be hauling comms arrays and all that other horseshit to earn their keep. Each of them was worth a fortune on the open market. The least of them could make a living on the lecture circuit. The smartest among them would be self-made billionaires within years. Some would be taken advantage of, but all would be wealthy, essentially carnival curiosities who had made good. Instead of dancing for quarter chits they'd be doing talk shows for quarter million chits.

If they had any kind of business sense – and some would have that sort of low cunning, even having never been exposed to the greater, darker world of show business and politics – they would be able to leverage their time as prisoners marooned on a distant planet into vast fortunes. Still, for now we were treating them like slave labor, and that was how they were acting.

"We've stripped everything of value from Pod Eight," I continue. "I recommend we pull up stakes and return to Yloft."

As quickly as she can on her crutches, Diane turns around and fixes me with a withering glare.

"Oh, really?"

"Yes, ma'am."

"Tell me, on Yloft are you accustomed to leaving jobs half-done? Or, in this case, one-twelfth-done?"

I take a deep breath. Zanib's face is front and center in my mind's eye.

"Diane, you have to understand that the risk involved in this operation is off the charts. We're talking about a plague vector that we know nothing about, that we can't even detect with modern science. We're talking about an unknown enemy with unknown resources on the other side of that hatch. If we go in there, we will die. And I don't mean just me and Helena, though that's a given. I mean we open that up and that is a Pandora's Box that will swallow up this mission. It'll kill you. It'll kill everyone on the *Borgwardt*. The company's going to follow up and there will be more death. It's going to turn this planet from the tomb of *The Manifest Destiny* into a graveyard. We're all at risk. The corporation's at risk. We need to leave now with what we've got and be satisfied. Leave the table while we're ahead. I don't see any other alternative."

Except... I don't say any of that. I stand there, silent, zoned out, until finally Diane's voice snaps me back to myself.

"Paige? Paige!"

"Yes?"

"Bring me up to speed, please."

I run my hands through my hair.

"Sorry, madam director. I'm just getting tired."

The Diane-gram eyes me askance.

"Do you need..."

"No, ma'am."

I slap the crank dispenser on my arm. In an instant I feel a cool rush of fluids hit my veins. My heart begins beating faster until it disappears again into my chest, and I feel even-keeled and level-headed. A perfect dose of juice specially designed for my biochemistry – ambrosia, I sometimes call it.

I look to Helena. She nods for me to continue, just as in the daydream. I sigh. I don't want to do this. But I must.

Act confident. Act so confident, you even fool yourself. Lie. Tell a little lie and convince everyone. That'll be the start.

"This room," I lie, gesturing around me, "is referred to as the shed."

In fact, no record has ever described this room as anything other than a prophylactic chamber, similar to the one I stood on exiting the *Borgwardt* during my brief return to Yloft. If the colonists have a nickname for the room, I've never heard them say it. I try not to make it clear that I'm glancing at Helena and the hologram of Diane to gauge whether they've believed me.

Okay. You've lied once. Now everything's based on a foundation of lies. Juice them with a little truth first, then the whopper.

"That hydraulic," I say, pointing at the hatch behind Helena, "will close and seal off the shed from the rest of Pod Eight. Then that one," I point at the hatch behind me, the way Diane is facing, "will open into Pod Nine. It's been sealed for over a century, since the witch hunts began. If there are people on that side of the hatch they may as well be from a different planet for all the similarity they'll bear to Jaime and her group."

"Are there people there?"

Downplay it. Give her the answer she wants to hear, by telling the truth through vague platitudes.

"Well, what we know is that the hydroponics *could* be working. Pod Eight's system is independent and sealed off from Nine's, so it could also be not working. The colonists report noises, but that could be anything, couldn't it? The ship settling, local wildlife. Zanib's already proven that such parasites exist under the planet's skin."

"Yes," Diane agrees. "The Patel eel. She was rather quick in claiming that one."

All right. Go in for the kill. Give her your one flimsy piece of evidence and give it last, and give it so hard that it sounds like it's the only important fact, and it'll stick in her head.

"Yes, so, without having any certitude on almost anything else, we do know that if there was a physical malady that afflicted the colonists, it's now confined to those pods. Jaime's people are clean, but they're convinced that something afflicted their ancestors. I think their occasional flare-ups have been psychosomatic. And Helena agrees with me."

Diane looks at Helena.

"Do you?"

The conflict is clear on the goon's face, but she doesn't lie.

"I do."

Diane sighs, long and loud, a product of staying on her crutches for a lengthy period of time.

"Then in your estimation, the witch hunt that ravaged *The Manifest Destiny*'s population a hundred years ago or so... was successful?"

It's her idea now. She's suggested it. Drive it home now with skepticism.

"Well, anything is possible, madam director. I guess what you say could've happened." I shrug. "I certainly can't come up with a more reasonable explanation."

She nods. Excellent. You've got her on the hook. Reel her in.

"In my estimation, madam director, it would be contrary to the company's best interests if we didn't at least attempt to find out what's in Pod Nine."

Now the cards are all on the table. *Alea iacta est*. Helena won't take it sitting down, but I've already trumped her.

"I think this is an unnecessary risk, madam director," Helena growls.

The Diane-o-gram eyes her suspiciously.

"How so?"

"We have been fortunate so far. And I cannot emphasize how much luck is not a planning method. But so far we haven't been exposed to this infestation that the colonists insist is down in the bowels of the ship."

"That's a very conservative argument," I say. "Of course, you might also say that whatever there is to be exposed to, we've already been exposed to it. In for a penny, in for a pound, as they used to say, don't you think, madam director?"

"Personnel have value to the company, too. Insurance policies are expensive. And retraining is expensive, too. Like I said, we have had good fortune. Why test it?"

Why, indeed? Every instinct, every spark of intuition I have in me is screaming at me to agree with Helena, to give in, to, in fact, throw my full-throated agreement into the ring. Not only is Helena right, she's damn right.

But there's a monster in me. There's a little nugget of ambition in me so strong it powers me like the singularity powering the *Borgwardt*.

"It seems to me," I find myself saying, "that failing to at least attempt to complete our mission is the bigger risk."

Helena stares at me. The Diane-o-gram nods.

"I'm inclined to agree. Let's take a shot at it. You know, Paige, I wasn't sure if you had what it took to do this job. Academics aren't always made of the right stuff for field work. But right now I think I made the right choice in hiring you. I think you'll go far in Hestle."

The hologram flickers and vanishes. In the now dim light Helena is still staring at me. Her mood is unmistakable.

"You're a real mercenary, you know that?"

"Just thinking about what's best for the company," I lie.

"Mm hmm."

A clattering from inside Pod Eight interrupts our staredown.

# TWENTY-TWO

Becs, in her galley whites, is wheeling a mobile food cart towards the prophylactic airlock.

"There you two are!"

She pats her hands down on her apron, then, thinking better of it, holds her hands under a small disinfectant ray on the side of the cart. When the ray has finished its business, the top of the cart opens up hydraulically.

"All right," she says, "I know you two are busy, so it's finger food all around for all the salvagers. I fed up the colonists on rolls and fiber bars, but for you girls I've got sandwiches. Turkey, roast beef..."

"I'm not hungry," Helena states flatly.

Becs scowls.

"Don't be that way, Big H. I know you. I've watched you. You don't mess around in my galley. Listen, I'll make you your favorite: roast beef and mozzarella, how's that sound?"

Helena bites her lower lip. Becs looks between the two of us. She's not dumb. She realizes she's interrupted a fight or showdown of some sort. Either she doesn't care, is hoping to defuse it, or is just really, really devoted to her job.

"Look, don't you two worry about being stingy. The company picks up the tab when you're actively working. Zero chits, girls. I know there's no such thing as a free lunch, but, well, this is the free lunch cart."

Helena relents.

"All right, but, just, don't make it so dry this time."

"Ha ha! I knew it." Becs rubs her hands together. "Mayonnaise and horseradish, right? Kind of beats the purpose of finger food when you're slopping it all around, but, hey, I'm just the fucking slop salesman, what do I care what you drip drop in here?"

She slathers two different kinds of white goo onto Helena's pre-made sandwich and hands it over.

"What about you, Ambroziak? No fucking pot noodles this time. Unless you want me to ladle it into your hands."

I can't help but smile. Whatever the Broatoan's intentions, she has, indeed, successfully defused the tenseness.

"I don't know. Do you have egg salad?"

"I got tuna salad."

"Perfect. As long as the company's paying for it."

"Oh, yeah. Wouldn't want you to splurge on 100% albacore. Lettuce, tomato?"

I nod at each of her suggestions. She hands the sandwich over.

"Now what am I looking at here?"

"This?" I say between bites. "This leads into Pod Nine. We're going to open it up and find out what's on the other side."

"I should probably scarper, huh?"

I shrug.

"Unless you want to witness history."

Helena growls, somehow polishing off her massive meat and bread concoction as I've only taken a few bites out of mine.

"Unless you want your ass shot at. Or worse."

"Never had my ass shot at before. Hey, it's not like we can lose two food and beverage chiefs in the same expedition, can we?"

Helena is struck silent, perhaps feeling the sting of being reminded of her failure on Lilah's part.

"You guys really don't mind if I watch?"

"No, I don't mind," I say.

I look to Helena, but she remains stonily silent. Nodding, I put down what's left of my sandwich. Unlike Helena, I don't actually have much of an appetite. Like all those times in the Yloft stacks, I'm working, and when I'm working, all bodily concerns fade away until I nearly piss my pants.

I remove my jotter from the pedestal where it had been generating the hologram of the boss. I press a few buttons.

"Operations," a cheery voice says, "this is Kelly."

"Hey, Kelly," I reply, happy to recognize my favorite ops geek, "this is Paige Ambroziak over on *The Manifest Destiny*."

"Well, howdy there, Miss Explorer Extraordinaire! I just heard from the director about you."

"Am I fired? Already?"

"Right out the next space-facing airlock. Those were her orders."

"Oh, well, can't argue with that. Tell my widow I died a hero."

Kelly giggles.

"What can I do you for, Paige?"

"We're ready down here. Can you close the Pod Eight-facing hatch?"

"You got it."

The hatch slides closed with a loud thump that causes Becs to jump. She rubs her hands together.

"Oh, man, you know, I've been surfing the ink for an age now, but I almost never get to get out of the office. This is some exciting stuff."

"Maybe you should be thankful you've never been exposed to any real danger. It's when people decide to start doing things that aren't really their job, that everyone starts dying."

Maybe that was a dig at me. I don't care. I know what the rest of my career is going to look like, and it's not going to be ending up as a low-level shipboard security chief in middle age like Helena. Hestle is going to remember my name. It's going to be etched on a plaque somewhere, if not in a hallway under a portrait of my face along with all the other people of consequence down through the years.

"Okay, Kelly," I say, "please open the Pod Nine-facing hatch."

Helena levels her beam rifle toward the hatch.

"Your wish is my command," the ops controller responds.

I drop my jotter into my pocket as the hatch opens. The hydraulics grind, and I can tell Kelly is working some magic, making the hatch roll up and down to get it to open all the way. These things always seem straightforward to the end user, but ops always seems to have to canoodle the network to get the supposedly 'automated systems' to do what they're supposed to do. In this case, there seems to be decades' worth of dust and debris on the far side of the hatch, and a great cloud is kicked up as it finally, gradually opens.

Becs is the first to gasp. A Broatoan, her eyes are used to seeing through such pollution. But Helena is quickly swiveling her beam rifle to and fro. She's probably cursing me in her head, but thankfully not out loud just yet.

Eyes gleam in the low light like cats'. I glance left. There are half a dozen down there. I glance right. Maybe even more on the other end of the corridor.

I try to slowly slip my hand into the pocket of my overalls and press the emergency button on my jotter, but even the slight movement causes the others to scrabble forward, hooting and banging on the ceiling, bulkheads, and even the glass of the hydroponics gardens.

They hold makeshift weapons of rebar and tools scavenged from around the ship. And they are dressed not as cosmonauts, but as savages, in loincloths ripped from towels or former pieces of clothing. Many lurid tales dance the spaceways of lost colonies and drift-less wrecks reduced to savagery and cannibalism, but I have always taken them with a grain of salt. Aren't humans in some fundamental way better than this? Wouldn't we weather the difficulties of isolation and deprivation better than being reduced to our Neanderthal or Cro-Magnon roots?

I raise my hands in surrender, and Becs does the same. Helena refuses to lower her weapon, and the savages are staring at her, trying to decided what to do about it.

"What do we do now?" Becs hisses.

"Is operations still monitoring?" Helena growls.

We wait. There is silence, undeniable, seemingly never-ending silence. Something has cut us off. They may even be monitoring the situation and just unable to communicate with us.

"Guess we're on our own," Helena says, stepping forward, in front of me and Becs.

The savages hoot and wave their weapons at us.

"Yeah, I hear you, assholes. Back. The fuck. Off."

Without lowering her beam rifle, Helena kicks Becs's food cart forward, toppling it and sending lettuce, pickles, and a bevy of condiments splattering to the deck. The savages back away from the clattering metal in alarm, and Helena takes the opportunity to plug the nearest one through the shoulder. She begins firing indiscriminately into the crowd, and as quickly as they came, the writhing mass of limbs and hair and muscles retreats back into Pod Nine. Helena holds her rifle leveled at the ingress point.

"Get ops on the fucking phone," she hisses at me.

"Right, right," I say, fumbling into my pocket and pulling out my jotter.

The signal is dead...of course. That alone should probably have triggered something over on the *Borgwardt*, but exactly what I can't even venture to guess. Perhaps a rescue party. Perhaps something more...permanent. In any case, we never get to see what their response is.

Two small clay pots came flying in through the ingress point. When they smash against the bulkhead, a noxious green gas fills the room.

Helena shouting, "Get down!" is the last thing I remember hearing, before falling and cracking my head against the metal deck.

# TWENTY-THREE

I awaken to the sensation of Tina repeatedly slapping my face. Although I've seen this sort of thing in movies, coming from a medical professional I have to question the clinical efficacy of such behavior.

"Back with us?" she asks absently, looking elsewhere.

"Yeah, I think so," I moan.

I reach up and gingerly touch the side of my head. Tiny ribbons of skin dance under my touch, the bizarre feeling of flesh mending at hyper-accelerated speed. A neurostim pack is attached to the other side of my head, and I glance down to see another medkit attached to my heart.

"I was in bad shape?"

"Dead. Clinically. It's no small matter getting concussed. I had to fight for half an hour to get you breathing on your own again. And this did not help matters."

She dangles my armband in front of my face. I blush and reach for it, hissing in pain. She holds it out of my reach. I'm as weak as a kitten from the neurostim, and as hungry as a horse. I'm a kitten-horse.

"You can't just fiddle with your biochemistry like you're mixing a cocktail. You know, every time you dose yourself you make it that much harder for a medical professional to help you when you get hurt. Like you just did. You know that, don't you?"

"I would nod, but my head is killing me."

I doubt there's much defiance in my eyes. Her glare softens.

"By rights, I should take this from you."

"It's not illegal."

I sound like a junkie. Maybe I am.

"No. But I can give you medical orders. So, do I need to take this from you?"

"I'll stop. While I'm shipboard."

She looks me up and down. That's not a junkie's answer. A junkie would've promised to stop forever. I made a much smaller promise. Oh, fuck. Am I playing her? Normally when I'm playing someone I feel like I'm conducting a symphony in my head. Right now, though, it just seems to be flowing. It's become subconscious for me.

Am I a bad person?

"All right," she says, reluctantly rolling up the armband and stuffing it into one of the cargo pockets at the bottom of my pants. Somewhere I'll have to very deliberately go digging to get it back.

I rise up to my elbows. Prosser, Tampa, and Helena are gathered in a corner, quietly not quite stage-whispering. Becs's food cart is unmoved from its position, kicked over on the deck, with bits of slowly rotting vegetables and sauces splattered around the hold.

"Where's Becs?"

Tina looks at me, reluctant to speak, then looks towards the now-closed hatch to Pod 9.

"They took her?"

Tina doesn't respond. The goons are practically shouting now, their attempts at feigning secrecy forgotten.

"We should get Quinn," Tampa is saying.

"Not a chance," Helena replies. "That one's a fucking liability."

"Three's not a great number. Four's better," Prosser points out.

"Quinn's trained, at least. She may not be the sharpest tool in the shed, but…"

Helena cuts Tampa off.

"No. Better three that are competent than a fourth we'll have to carry."

"I'll go," I say, rising from my prone position.

The three security goons glance at me. I struggle to my feet.

"No, really, I want to. I feel responsible for… for Becs."

I'm greeted with three unreadable stares. I glance at Tina.

"Will you tell them I'm okay to go? I'm not an invalid. I'm… I'm good. I want to go. I should go."

Silence.

"They know," Tina replies.

Slowly, Helena lowers her beam rifle so that it's pointing at the ground. She walks towards me.

"I wouldn't take you if everyone else in the company was dead. You're a careerist. Careerists leave bodies in their wake. I hope to Hell we pull the cook out of that lion's den there. But if we don't… as I know we probably won't… I hope you never enjoy another promotion again. You'll get them. Oh, I know you'll get them. You're slimy enough to slither up that corporate ladder. But every time you do, I hope that girl's face haunts you at night."

She shoves me and I'm surprised at how far I don't fly. She didn't mean it. She's an immense ox of a woman, and she didn't mean it. I'm not even worth shoving to the deck.

"Get her out of here, doc."

Tina nods, and not-so-gently urges me out of the airlock. The last thing I hear is Helena contacting ops and asking Kelly to close the Pod Eight-facing hatch. It slams in my face. I look to Tina.

"I didn't know... I didn't want Becs to get hurt."

Tina shrugs.

"Helena takes everything personally. It's what makes her a good goon."

"But you believe me, right? I didn't think anyone was going to get hurt."

"If you say so."

I grab her. I'm surprised at myself. I've gone from the kitten who could barely move to a tiger. Something's running through me, something stronger than the meds in the armband rolled up and stuffed in my lower cargo pocket right now ever were: a crisis of identity.

"Tell me you believe me. Tell me right now. You. You forgive me, right? I'm not... I'm not a slimy careerist or anything like that. I just do what I think is right. You believe me, don't you?"

Tina stares at me for a moment. She pauses before speaking.

"My mother used to tell me that if I was feeling guilty, it was because I had done something I deserved to feel guilty about. Of course, she was an emotionally abusive fuck who could've made a fortune as a travel agent if people paid for guilt trips."

"That's all it is, then? Helena is just guilt-tripping me?"

Tina shrugs.

"Maybe. Or maybe you feel guilty because you did something you deserve to feel guilty about."

"What are you telling me?"

"Look, Ambroziak, I don't really know you. I have an obligation to fix up your fucked-up body. Your fucked-up soul, that's for you and your clergy or your company-assigned grief counselor. Don't look to me for absolution."

"Well, what am I supposed to do now? I'm supposed to be in there. I'm supposed to be helping save Becs. Or at least avenging her."

Tina shrugs and starts to walk off, turning her back on me in more ways than one.

"Go ask for orders. Or, better yet, take a break. And yes, that's medical advice."

# TWENTY-FOUR

I'm famished. I know I should go to the galley and get something, but the specter of me sending Becs off to some shady doom amongst half-clothed savages on some distant world when all she ever wanted to be was a cook is too much for me. That's her place. Even if her people don't know what I did, their every ordinary move will seem like they're eyeballing me, judging me. I can't go near that place.

My stomach howls in objection.

"Yes, yes, my pet," I say, patting my tum-tum, "Maybe we can find a vending machine or something."

I wander in a haze, not even sure where I'm going. Eventually I stumble into a vending machine – literally. I wave my wallet wand in front of the pay dock. Everything, strangely, looks appealing, although I usually eschew vending machines altogether. I choose an exorbitantly priced candy bar, as well as a vacuum-sealed package of cheese and beef jerky that seems appealing, but I can't imagine how it can be after sitting in a vending machine for more than a few days. I peel back the package on my cheesy, meaty treat, and it tastes exactly like wax, as I should have guessed. There's not even an obvious distinction between the cheese and the meat, except for color and (I suppose) consistency. I wolf it down anyway.

The candy bar is tastier, but I'm somehow able to savor it slower. I'm wandering again, wavering as though there is an ill crosswind aboard the weatherless *Borgwardt*. Only a morose musical score would complete the scene. After a few minutes the waxy treat begins to kick in and my eyes begin to focus and suddenly I know not only where I'm going, but where I practically already am. My feet had subconsciously brought me all this way without me even realizing it.

Standing outside the hatch to Zanib's lab, I have a funny, almost indescribable feeling. It's guilt, yes, but also a desire to do wrong. I want to seek comfort in Zanib's arms. That sounds so warm and inviting, even though I should be doing something, almost anything, else. Becs is missing because of my insurmountable ambition. I won't pay any real consequences for it. They're not going to be able to fire me for giving an opinion, even if I knew at the time it was a lie. Diane made the decision, the responsibility is hers...even if it's really mine. It's hers on paper.

I should be doing something. Even just a little bit of work. It would make me feel better. But I don't want to feel better. I want to laze about while people are dying on my behalf. Even more, I want to suck Zanib in, too, stop her from doing anything valuable for the mission. I don't care if the cameras catch us. I want them to. I want to wallow in it.

I press my lips to the seal of the hatch.

"Zanib," I whisper.

I press my ear to the same space, and hear nothing but the whirl of the mechanical winch we used to bring K.P. up into the ship. Another catch. I'm surprised. Zanib said the eels were too clever to get caught twice. Perhaps word hadn't gotten around yet. Or perhaps there were more parasites in the fleshworld than just K.P.'s species.

"Zanib!" I repeat, a little bit louder this time, still glancing up and down the ship. I know it's a small ship and sound travels.

Zanib must be in there, but she must not be hearing me. I'm loath to knock on the hatch. I try to open it, but it's locked, of course. I pull out my jotter.

"Let me in," I type to her personal account.

Supposedly it's secure from the corporation's meddling, but I've also read a hundred different little text blocks telling me the corporation is welcome to view anything sent out over its comms networks, supposedly "private" or not.

There's a pause as I see she's received my message, then the indication that she's writing back.

"Forget your code already, virgin?" she replies with a smile indicator.

Irritating woman. Come fuck me already.

"You never gave me the code."

It seems to take forever for her to write back.

"The company gave you a code when you came onboard."

I'm not in the mood for her nonsense.

"Will you just open the hatch?"

"Fuck. Hang on."

My heart's fluttering. I haven't felt this way in ages. I start to pace a little circle in the deck. Still waiting. Still waiting. What the hell is she doing in there? I'm about to pound on the hatch, finally giving up on discretion in frustration, when I glance back down at my jotter.

"Okay, and why am I standing here looking at an empty hallway?"

Shit. She's in our room.

"I'm an idiot. I'm standing outside your lab. Don't go anywhere."

"I wish I could lock you out. No, just kidding. Hurry."

I do. Our room is practically on the other side of the office. It feels like an eternity crossing the distance. It's made longer by me glancing at every camera I pass in every hallway. I swear each one is following me. That's impossible, of course. None of the security personnel are even on the *Borgwardt*. Well, no, I guess on second thought, Quinn still is. But she can't be angry at me. It's my guilty conscience spying on me through the lenses.

I feel naked, nude, exposed, every centimeter of me out on display like meat in a butcher's shop. What is it? What is this paranoia that is running through me, coursing through my veins like anti-crank? It's like I'm afflicted by a madness and I won't be safe until I pass through the archway of my own room, safe and sound.

When I finally do, it's like diving into a pool. The air even tastes sweeter. I know there's no difference between the office outside these bulkheads and the small haven within, but it feels like I've stepped off the edge of a cliff. Zanib is there to catch me.

Silent, she descends from her bunk. I know she's just clambering down as I've seen her do many times before, but this time tastes different. This time the scent of anticipation is on the wind. She's moving less like a shiphand and more like a goddess.

Now she's on the deck, level with me. Her feet are bare, her toes amazingly dainty for someone her size. She looks at me, into me, through me. I don't know what to do. I'm frozen to the spot like a hare. I've been struck by Medusa's bolt, turned into an effigy of myself.

She reaches up and unzips her jumpsuit. Again, I know in some way it's a pedestrian maneuver, the simplest possible of ways to doff the simplest possible of garments, but it is imbued by my anticipation and, let's just admit it, lust, with the power of a siren's call. She is a glamorous fashion model, strutting down the catwalk just for me, her sultry eyes just for me, her body for my eyes alone.

She doesn't even squirm. The suit just slides off of her. I hope the same rose-tinted colors are affecting her gaze on me, because I know I could never be that smooth and subtle. I have all the grace of a gorilla plowing through a china shop. In fact, as if to prove me right, I reach up and grapple with my own zipper, only to instantly get it caught on the wrong teeth on the wrong side. I'm a hopeless mess.

She strides toward me, her teeth on bold display. She's enjoying my awkwardness, yes, but she's happy to see me. Neither of us has said a word yet. She merely takes my zipper in between her hands and I admire her strength as she gives it a yank and the mechanism recatches the teeth correctly closer to my bosom. She stares down at my cleavage and so I follow suit. When I come up for air she's looking into my eyes.

"Like what you see?" I ask, hoping I'm not grinning too dorkily.

"Shh, shh. You're ruining this, virgin. No talking."

"Yes, ma'am."

"What did I just say?"

I decline to respond this time. She unzips me the rest of the way. As she does, her knuckles brush against my crotch. I flush, worried that I haven't shaved down there in an age, but she doesn't say anything. In fact, the next few strokes of her hands, which it only takes me a few seconds to realize are not accidents, seem to luxuriate in my pubis. She doesn't mind. She starts to stroke me and I look down at her but she stops, takes my chin, and forces me to look into her eyes. Only then does she begin again.

"This is me doing this," she seems to be saying without a word leaving her lips. "This is me up here, the one looking in your eyes, doing this, down there, to you."

I nod. I don't know if she's communicating with her finger-strokes or her eyes or what, but I nod. She slows down and stops again, more organically this time. She reaches up to slip me out of my suit, sliding my sleeves down one at a time, like a snake sloughing its skin. I'm nude now, my jumpsuit pooled around my ankles. We both are. I step out of the puddle of cloth as she takes my hand and leads me back to our bunks.

She lays me back on my own bunk like I'm an empty dress. The lower bunk is easier to get to. We'd both make asses of ourselves trying to clamber up into Zanib's bunk, even Zanib who seems to have a preternatural, cat-like grace in the boudoir that I hadn't noticed previously. I look up into her gleaming, earnest eyes and almost ask her to be gentle, but I've remembered her one rule.

"Are you ready, virgin?"

I giggle.

"What happened to no talking?"

"Plans change."

With a horrifying pop, like the sound of all the air being sucked out of an airlock, Zanib's left eye pops out of its socket. I gasp in shock as it dangles near the corner of her mouth, still attached by a long string of nerve endings.

"Are you...?"

I can't even fully get the question out before the right eye pops out as well. My libido drains away like a tub emptying in fast motion. This is no medical emergency. And Zanib's eye sockets aren't empty. Each one is filled with the distended, tooth-filled jaw of one of the monstrous lampreys from the planet below.

# TWENTY-FIVE

I struggle to escape, but Zanib – or whatever the things that are inhabiting Zanib's body are – holds me fast. I knew she was strong but she feels unnaturally strong, her hands on my shoulders are like iron.

"What-what-what," I'm muttering, out of breath and unable to control my mouth.

The panic's rising, filling me up so that I can practically feel it in the back of my throat. I cringe in horror as the lithe, sinewy body of one of the blood-drinking parasites slithers out of Zanib's right eye socket. It looks like K.P. did. For all I know it is K.P.

If it is, he is rooted somehow in her head. I can't see past his chubby body, at least past the point where he emerges from her eye socket. I shudder to think of what must have happened although it seems pretty obvious: they've devoured her brain and taken up residence in her skull.

The second hematophage emerges from the left eye socket, and this time I can see more, though it is horrifying. The left one is thinner in diameter, which makes me think it may be a female. I can see past her and see that indeed, except for small, ragged chunks still clinging to the inside of her skull, Zanib's brain is missing.

K.P. – if it is K.P. – makes a sudden lunge downward, completely at odds with the hypnotic rhythm with which he has been swaying in the air up until now. I cry out in pain as he latches onto my breast. It feels like a thousand tiny needles piercing my skin. As his teeth dig into my flesh, a sickening feeling washes over me as the blood begins to drain out of me. As he suckles at me in a perverse mockery of nursing, I feel as though someone is swirling the thousand needles around in my skin. His teeth are undulating in time with his suckles.

I feel a wet slap against my cheek and cry out a second time as the female latches onto me. Her teeth pierce straight through my cheek and I can feel her teeth clattering against my own as she drains me. A warm wetness pools under me and I realize I've voided my bladder without noticing.

"Zanib," I finally manage to say.

"Sorry, virgin," she says in a weirdly distant voice, "there's not a whole lot of Zanib left."

She's holding me by the shoulders. My arms aren't free, but they're free enough to struggle. I pound on her belly as best I can with so little leverage. It's a feeble attempt at best. I have to calm down. My heart is fluttering a meter a minute, which just means that my strength is ebbing away faster as the vampiric little monsters drain me.

There's a solution here, Paige. Analyze it. Analyze your surroundings. Tackle it like you would any other problem.

I swoon, the world going completely black and consciousness slipping away from me for the briefest fraction of a second. My impulse is to panic, but my will is stronger. Time is running out, sand is draining out of the hourglass as quickly as my blood is draining out of my body. I have no idea how much time I have. All I know is that it is limited, and precious. I could fall unconscious permanently any second now.

I glance around the room. No weapons spring readily to mind. We don't have much except our clothes. My jumpsuit is in a pile on the deck. Could I strangle Zanib with it? Cut off her oxygen? Does she even need oxygen? Is she dead already, a corpse animated by the strange will of these creatures? Or is she still alive? Are they keeping her alive, using her, driving her like a vehicle?

Table that for now. No time for the theoretical. Working theory: Zanib is alive and I can affect them through her. If that doesn't work...

I'm swooning again. No time for worrying about hypotheticals, either. One chance to do it right, and hope the plan is sound, that's all.

My eyes fall down to the lump in my pile of clothing. What have I got in my pocket? Of course! The armband. Fucking Tina. If she hadn't taken it off me, I could be slapping at it now, either cranking myself up or filling my blood with some kind of poison that would hopefully stop the parasites from their unholy ministrations.

A plan is forming hazily as the seconds tick by, and I feel myself growing paler and more distant.

Step One: get out from under Zanib.

Step Two: slap the armband on her and juice the aliens.

Step Two seems rock solid, although the armband may as well be on Lahiniti for all the good it's doing me over there. Step One is the real hurdle, though.

My mind races. By luck or happenstance, the perfect memory rears its head. I'm a child on Yloft. Fighting with Peavey before she was even Peavey, back when she was still Yadira. Fuck, we've known each other a long time. Peavey punched me, not hard, but I still doubled over in pain because she had struck me directly in the solar plexus. Knocked the wind out of me. For what couldn't have been more than a few seconds I was drowning, drowning in the perfectly controlled air of Yloft station, unable to draw a breath. Up until this very moment it had been the starkest single moment of horror I had ever experienced. The literal inability to draw a breath was terrifying beyond anything I could have ever imagined up until that point.

I might... might... be able to strike Zanib in the sternum from this angle. I make the attempt, even hit the mark, but I'm far too enfeebled from blood loss and from her rock-solid grasp on my shoulders. I try again, again nothing happens. I have one minor advantage: she's not shifted her methodology. She hasn't noticed I'm trying something new. She's just holding me as fast as I had been, when I had merely been wriggling before.

I need something harder to strike her with. Nothing's in reach. The female hematophage gnaws sickeningly at my deformed cheek, a grim mockery of a lover's kiss. The light in the room is bleeding away. I know it's not really. It's exactly the same luminosity it's been the whole time. It's that my eyes are becoming unfocused, unable to even see, my body betraying me in the very grasp of my attacker.

My neck relaxes. I lean back, resigned to the end. They will drain me dry and leave my corpse here, perhaps unnoticed for hours or days or weeks, unmourned, killed by the only person in this part of the galaxy I could even rightly call a friend. Worse things will happen then. Others will be drained. Many will die.

Suddenly I surge forward, but not really as I'm still held fast. I've just felt a new rush of energy. It's not philanthropy. I don't give a shit if all the others die. Perhaps my body had been storing one last burst of adrenaline for this very instant.

No, I don't give a shit about the others. I just refuse to be left here, all my ambitions left unfulfilled. No. Paige Fucking Ambroziak does not go out this way.

And I do have something hard to hit her with. I even have it at my disposal. She's clenching my shoulders so powerfully, I'm completely free to pull my legs up to my chest. I wrap my arms around my shins. Pull back like a rubber band tensing, then release. My right knee strikes her dead center, right in the sternum.

Zanib gasps. I recognize it, the same dry, mucusy cry that I gave that day on the playground with Peavey. I've knocked the wind out of her. That means the hematophages aren't in total control. Some element of Zanib's physiology is still important. She staggers back, the lampreys' suckers ripping horrifically out of the two spots where they had stuck themselves to me. I know all I've done is bought myself a few seconds. When your diaphragm spasms, it feels like an eternity to you, but in the real world it's just a moment.

The hematophages are flailing wildly, as Zanib stumbles away. Which means my guess was right: they are driving her like a car. I just have to get up now and get to the armband. I can't, though. I'm too weak. Like a fucking baby. I surge with all my strength but all I can manage to do is throw myself out of the bunk and down on to the hard metal deck. I brace myself with my elbows and wince in pain as both are struck by the onrushing deck.

Fuck that hurt. My feet scrabble, but they're in no condition to lift me up. No, standing is right out. Shit. I reach out, grab a handhold of the deck, and pull myself forward. This must have been what it was like for the skin-wrapper in our gravity. I fling myself forward.

And, of course, Zanib has already recovered.

"Sorry, virgin," the Zanib-that-is-not-Zanib voice states, "you're not getting away."

"Don't call me that," I growl.

It's a stupid thing, but it infuriates me. That was her nickname for me. Those...things have no right to use it. I flop forward once more, like a seal moving along an ice floe. Zanib is standing, though. My hand touches fabric just as she reaches down, grabs me by my heels, and yanks me back. I manage to hold onto the jumpsuit for an instant, but it flutters out of my reach, closer to the bunk, but no longer in my grasp.

"Why can't you just die like a good little girl? Like Zanib did for us? Can't you tell we're hungry?"

Roaring in mindless rage, I roll onto my back and kick swiftly upwards. My shin connects with Zanib – or what's left of her – right in the box. She doubles over in pain. That was a good shot. I scramble backwards, crabwalking essentially, and reach out to grab my jumpsuit just as she grabs me and yanks me off the deck. She wraps her arms around me in a deadly embrace, clutching me so tightly I can barely breathe.

The only good news is that she hasn't figured out my plan yet. She – or they, perhaps I should say – thought both times that I was making for the hatch. But now I have my jumpsuit in my hands and I'm furiously fondling it, trying to find the armband without being able to look down at it. My hands clasp around my jotter. Great. Useless. Or, more accurately, useful for sending out a distress call and being dead by the time it arrives.

K.P. waggles into view, suddenly taking up my whole field of vision. Zanib's mouth moves and it is her voice – or a somewhat robotic facsimile thereof – that emerges, but for the first time I realize it is him (or them) speaking. She's nothing but a puppet to them, a giant meat puppet.

"Give us a kiss, lover."

K.P. strikes like an asp, shoving his entire body into my mouth and down my throat. I try vainly to bite down, almost not sure I want to bite through him even if I am capable of it, but his scaly, undulating body is far too tough. I can't do more than scratch him even with the full power of my jaws. He wriggles down my throat, and I don't know what he's attempting to do, but it feels like my whole body is being violated. It's so painful I'm in tears, and suddenly his mate snaps forward, covering my entire eye and digging in before I can close it.

Now I'm caught in a vise, one hematophage is burrowing down into my throat, still not stopping, while I'm staring down the other one's throat as it bleeds me from the eye. Maybe I'm finally dead, but my hand finally digs into the right pocket and emerges with the armband. With only one eye to look, I slap it around Zanib's wrist and crank the dials wildly. I don't know what sort of concoction it's pumping into her now, but I know it's far past the safe levels for human consumption.

Suddenly K.P. stops digging around in my esophagus and goes limp. The female stops munching on my eye as well. The female drops from my face, doing a terrible amount of damage as she rips away. I'm now blind in one eye. Zanib groans and begins frothing from the mouth. She collapses and as she does, K.P. wetly slips out of my aching, overstretched throat. Zanib twitches for a few seconds, then stops, finally dead. I don't even reach down to feel her pulse. I don't do anything. I collapse.

I hope in the instant of consciousness I have remaining that I won't crack my head against the bulkhead again, but I really have no choice in the matter. I've never been so exhausted or physically damaged in my entire life. Shock consumes my senses and I fall into a fitful slumber.

# TWENTY-SIX

I'm surprised I wake up at all. I didn't think the hematophages had left me with enough blood to come to. My cheek is on fire. My eye, what's left of it, is swollen shut and the whole area is agony to touch. My breast is comparatively pleasant, only throbbing with pain. My jaws ache and I feel like I have strep throat. I'm dizzy and weak and never in my life have I wished so much just for death. Not sleep. Death.

I'm in too much pain to sleep. The icy grip of unconsciousness didn't offer me much by the way of rest, and I am exhausted. Zanib's crumpled form catches my eye. The hematophages remain still. I guess killing their host has killed the parasites. Perhaps not always. Perhaps I was just lucky and the dose I gave Zanib shot through their bloodstreams, too. Perhaps they can survive losing a host and these two just didn't.

Groaning in agony, I crawl to Zanib and, with some difficulty, flip her onto her back. I reach down and my hands are shaking as I yank the female out of her eye. When she comes loose, a chunk of grey matter comes out with her tail. I shudder, but I'm too curious not to explore further.

"Lights brighten," I moan and the illumination rises from the level of romantic encounter to give me the actual ability to examine things. It is grotesque, but I take my lover's head in my hands and stare into her brainpan. K.P. is still attached to a small lump of undevoured brain matter practically at the neck.

Tiny, clear globules litter the open space where her brain was. Eggs, I realize with a shiver. The hematophages had been copulating in her head, mating and then breeding. They had attached themselves directly to the barest portion of her brain that could still function in an animal sense, and then yanked on her nerves at the tip of her spine like the strings of a marionette.

I grab K.P.'s corpse and angrily yank. He doesn't come loose at first, but after a few long, hard pulls I finally manage to dislodge him from Zanib's skull. I toss his carcass thoughtlessly alongside his lover's. It was time for me to embrace my own lover, one last time.

I cradle her head, which feels disturbingly light, and then lay it in my lap, stroking her hair softly.

"I'm sorry about this, Zanib. Terribly sorry. I think we could have been happy together. At least…we would have had fun together."

I've been too groggy to think of anything but my own sorrows, but now other concerns are beginning to rear their ugly heads in my anxiety-riddle state. Why, for instance, has no one come to investigate? Surely we've both been absent from duty for hours now.

Then the thought of Zanib's lab comes back to me. The winch had been whirring when I had been convinced she was in there. How many hematophages had she brought on board? How many had she brought on board accidentally? If K.P. alone had been able to overpower her, and then bring his lover on board, how many had the parasites deliberately brought on board once they had taken control of Zanib's body? Are the parasites already in control of the office?

I have to get up, but everything seems strangely out of place. My formerly horizontal bunk is now vertical. The right-hand bulkhead is now the deck. The entire office, it seems, has been knocked ninety degrees to the right.

"Oooh," I moan as I struggle to my feet. The world swims around me for a moment before finally settling down into its normal state, give or take a few cigarette burns that keep popping up in my field of vision.

Things are a mess. At least the electronics still seem to be working. I grab my jumpsuit, and with more difficulty than seems strictly necessary, shove myself into it. My throbbing wounds are making me feel hot so I tie my jumpsuit off around the waist and pull on a t-shirt.

Struggling not to let it get away from me, I fish my jotter out of my pocket. The entire screen is blinking red and it displays an announcement that office communications have been shut down due to an emergency. Well, that's helpful.

I head for the hatch, which opens, but I must clamber up to get through it since it is perpendicular to its usual position. I'm not doing very well. I need to get some food, so the galley sounds like a good destination. Maybe there are others in there. Maybe the easiest thing right now is just to find the nearest other person and find out what's going on.

Emergency lighting is the only illumination. In the distance, an alarm is blaring, which seems strange to me. I would think you'd be able to hear an emergency siren anywhere in the office. I hear the distinct sizzling crack of a beam rifle behind me. I turn and see another strand of light zap down the corridor perpendicular to where I am lying, trying to catch my breath. A whiff of ozone strikes me full in the face and I scrabble to my feet.

Almost immediately, a figure comes ripping around the corridor. Seeing me, her eyes widen and she yells, "Run!"

I turn and nearly stumble. The other woman is instantly on top of me. She entwines her fingers in my own and practically yanks me down the hallway. My heart is fluttering and I'm not used to sprinting like this. I fear I may pass out again. As my mind swims, I recognize the runner. It is Eden, the custodian.

"What..." I manage to choke out, "what's going on?"

Suddenly Eden's chest snaps forward and her head snaps back. She claps her free hand to the small of her back and her other hand pulls free of my own as she collapses in a heap. There is a hole about the size of my thumb in Eden's stomach, through which I can see right to the deck. I've never seen the handiwork of a beam rifle up close and personal before. It passed through her back and out her front with clinical precision. The wound is cauterized all the way through, but no less devastating for the damage it caused.

I wince, expecting my own deathblow to follow. There is nothing between me and the gunner now, and I really haven't the strength to run any farther. Or, really, even to stand. I feel like I'm swaying in a hard breeze.

But the hammer doesn't fall. I finally turn to look at my pursuer. Standing at the head of the hallway is a figure in a boom suit. It's not readily apparent to me why. I can breathe the air just fine, and gravity seems normal. It occurs to me that perhaps the survivors are worried about infection – or what I now understand why the *Manifest Destiny* colonists called it infestation – by the hematophages. But as the figure approaches, I see that my guess was wrong.

Her face is a mess of red, exposed muscle, where it's not covered by bandages. Nia, the skin-wrapper captain. So, she's managed to escape, no doubt aided by the chaos of the infestation. Perhaps when the office fell on its side she was thrown free of the brig, and Diane's grudging decision to grant her a boom suit had resulted in her being free to roam the hallways.

I raise my hands in the air as much as my screaming muscles will allow me to. I'm not sure what else to do. Nia levels the beam rifle at me.

"Step away," she says, filtered through the microphone located on the suit at the base of her chin.

I don't move. I'm not sure what she wants, or even why she's not shooting.

"Step away!" she says again, shouting this time and gesturing with her weapon, and I could almost believe there's a note of franticness in her voice.

I'm alarmed, but again I don't move, and suddenly Nia is plowing towards me like a rampaging bull. She shoves me backwards, and I fall hard on my tailbone, wincing in pain. Nia drops a heavy boot on Eden's chest and points the beam rifle at her head.

"She's already dead!" I cry out.

But I'm the one who's been a fool. With a grotesque noise I've heard only twice before, but which remains etched indelibly in my memory, Eden's right eye pops out. A hematophage wriggles up and out of her eye socket, like a snake being charmed in some Tafra-Nell street bazaar. Nia fires the beam rifle again and again, and a smell like overcooked seafood fills the corridor.

She kicks at Eden's head a few times before finally bringing her boot down hard and popping it like a balloon. Chunks of grey matter, bone, and face splatter the deck and bulkheads, and a few drops of blood strike my forehead.

Nia turns her gaze on me. She points the rifle at me again.

"Are you clean?"

"Yes," I reply, although the truth is I have no idea. Would the parasites even let me know if they had taken me over? Do I only think I'm thinking what I'm thinking? How do I know I don't have two eel tails stuck into my brainstem, feeding me thoughts and impulses I think are my own?

"Are you sure?"

"I don't know. How can I know?"

"Oh, you'd know. But I don't think you'd tell me either way. They wouldn't let you."

"Are you going to shoot me?"

She hesitates.

"I probably should, just to be safe." She looks me up and down. "You're the history expert, aren't you?"

I nod.

"The others are looking for you. If you were somebody else, I probably wouldn't take the chance. I'd better let them give you the test."

"What's the test?"

"You're about to find out," she replies, as she gestures for me to get up and start walking.

# TWENTY-SEVEN

When we stop walking, we're practically to the galley. There is a mark on the bulkhead where we stop: a green X from one of our paint guns.

"On your knees. Back against the bulkhead. Hands on your head."

"I'm really weak as a baby right now," I reply, pointing at my ruined cheek and eye, "They bled me white. I couldn't fight back if I wanted to."

In the exact same cadence, Nia repeats: "On your knees. Back against the bulkhead. Hands on your head."

Nodding, I comply. My knees complain sorely about the situation. The skin-wrapper never turns her back on me as she picks up one of the old-fashioned intercom phones the security goons use. She unhooks the handset and plugs the wire into her suit speaker, which has a socket for it.

"Yeah, it's me," Nia says. "The custodian's dead. Nope, no question about it. She was the one. Let's just hope she was the only one. Guess what else I found. Yep, the little one you've all been looking for. The historian. Ambrosey-whatever. Yep, right outside her quarters, like where none of you wanted to check. Yeah, we're in the green room now. All right, I'll keep an eye on her until you get here."

As soon as she reattaches the phone and hangs it up, a ton of weight seems to settle on Nia, and her shoulders slouch. The rifle drifts down to where I'm not even sure it's pointed at me anymore. She's tired – bone tired. She reaches up and flicks a small switch on a panel on the front of her suit. I take it to be a safety lock for the small knob which she immediately turns counterclockwise before flicking the switch again and locking the knob in place. She almost immediately perks up, the same way I do when my armband is pumping ambrosia. Shit. I forgot my armband. It's sitting on Zanib's corpse. I don't want it anymore. I don't want to have to go back for it.

"Crank?" I ask, pointing towards the knob with my nose.

She looks at me. The rifle wobbles a little bit, and now I'm sure it's pointed at me again and not the deck.

"Huh?"

"Drugs? Is that an IV control pack?"

She glances down at her panel. She taps it with her finger.

"Oh. No. This is my internal gravity. You know us skin-wrappers, we like our G low."

I take a closer look. There's a small ring of color around the knob. From twelve o'clock to three o'clock the paint is white. From three to six is green, six to nine is yellow, and nine to twelve is red.

"The white is low G?"

She nods.

"Green is earth-like, yellow is for folks from high-G worlds."

"And I take it red will flatten you like a pancake."

She chuckles.

"Hell, if we're talking about me, green will flatten me like a pancake."

"Yes, I know."

She stares at me. A dumb glimmer of recognition crosses her face.

"I know you, don't I? You were there when that gash came to visit me in the clink."

"That gash gave you that suit you're wearing, didn't she?"

Nia snorts. Before our abortive conversation can continue, Tina rounds a corner, her normally prim lilac scrubs ripped, bloodied, and in a general state of disarray.

"Oh, Tina," I breathe.

It's the first time since Zanib attacked me that I've felt any measure of actual relief. Seeing a familiar face in Nia is...well, it's not exactly good, and certainly not reassuring, although by the looks of it she seems to be on our side, whatever "our side" constitutes. It just sort of is. But seeing Tina is an actual relief.

She doesn't respond. In fact, her eyes fall to the deck. This is not the woman I remember. Never exactly warm, Tina had nevertheless been friendly, and I had even thought we had bonded after what happened to Becs.

"You know the drill, Nia."

The skin-wrapper nods and lowers the beam rifle to the ground, then kicks it towards Tina. Tina hops over it as it approaches and it passes under her feet. Then Tina places a jotter on the ground and slides it over to Nia. Nia snatches the jotter off the deck before it stops sliding, and plugs it into her suit via a socket similar to the one she had plugged the phone line into.

"Suit integrity report," Tina orders. "Vocal. Volume medium."

The jotter's tinny mechanical voice responds, "100% suit integrity has been maintained for the past seven hours."

Seven hours? I've been out for a while.

"Like I'd bloody well take it off," Nia sneers.

Tina lets slip a small sigh of relief. She recovers her jotter and hands Nia back the rifle.

"Against the bulkhead, please."

Nodding, Nia backs up against the bulkhead. Tina reaches into her kit and pulls out something I never expected to see in a nurse's black bag: a paint gun. From point-blank range she fires a green X-mark onto the shoulder of Nia's suit. For the first time, I notice she has a similar mark on her scrubs.

Not looking me in the eyes, Tina crouches down less than a meter away.

"Cover me," she says, pointing her face in Nia's direction but still not looking at me.

Nia crosses the corridor and puts the business end of the beam rifle directly to my ear.

"This seems..." I start to say.

"Quiet," Nia growls, shoving my head with the barrel of the weapon.

Tina unpacks her kit and pulls out a second object I never thought I'd see a nurse carry: a teaspoon. Finally, she's forced to look at me. She looks first at my blind eye and then at my good one, and seems to decide this is the one she's going to operate on. I'm suddenly leery about what I fear is coming next, but Nia, seemingly sensing my nerves, helps to calm them by tapping the side of my face with the beam rifle to remind me it's there.

Tina administers three shots, two below the eye and one above. I'm not sure what they're for until she grabs my lower eyelid and secures it to my cheek with what appears to be a safety pin. I'm only vaguely aware of this as I feel no pain.

The shots were, apparently, some kind of local anesthetic. She then pins my upper eyelid to my eyebrow.

I know I'm breathing harder than is strictly healthy, but I'm unreasonable worried about what's coming now, and as she sterilizes the spoon before my eyes, a funny inversion of a drug fiend holding a flame under a spoon, I'm beginning to seriously panic.

"Look down."

"Couldn't you do this to my bad eye?"

She seems to become herself again for an instant, at least the Tina I remember.

"Sorry, Paige." Then the coldness returns. "If you are Paige."

She glances up at Nia and they nod at each other. My breaths are coming like a steam engine. And then the spoon is in my eye socket. The pain is dulled by the narcotics, but the sensation is still horribly invasive and grotesque. I try to look up at the spoon digging me out of my own field of vision, but it's so painful that I understand now why Tina told me to look down and I comply, just in time for my ocular orb to pop out with a sickening squish. Luckily (if that's the right word) it only falls a few centimeters into Tina's waiting, latex-gloved hand. I'm now completely blind, my one eye scratched to bits and the other "safely" ensconced in a nurse's palm. My breaths are still flying, fast and shallow, and I guess from the warm sensation and the seemingly endless seconds passing that Tina is shining a light into my empty eye socket with the hand that is not clasping my evacuated eyeball.

She is very gentle in replacing it, far more gentle than she has been at any other point in this procedure. My eye rolls around, sore and painful, but luxuriating in being back in the healthy womb of its socket. The lack of freedom feels like a tincture.

Tina wraps her arms around me. I suppose I should be comforted, but this is more for her right now. I pat her gently on the back.

"Worm-free, I take it," Nia sneers.

I look up at the skin-wrapper and hope my eye isn't too swollen to give the evil glare. Tina releases me, and I'm surprised to see her wiping her nose. Had she really cared that much about me?

"We thought everyone else was gone. We thought there was no one else left. You're alive and uninfested. It's like a miracle."

Oh. It's not me, then. It's just the idea of me.

"I'm not going to be alive for much longer if I don't get some food and medicine."

She analyzes my wrecked body with a clinician's eye.

"Shit, but you're a mess. I'm sorry. And that trauma to your eye isn't helping matters. But it is necessary. You see, there are these eels..."

"Yes, I'm caught up on that part," I say through clenched teeth.

She pulls out a neurostim pack, a cardiac pack, and, to my surprise, what looks like a medical version of a crank armband. She even hooks in a saline pack after gauging how low my blood is. (I worry that in this brave new world of hematophage infestation, exsanguination is such a major concern that the nurse just carries around saline packs.)

I must be worse than I thought. Even when Helena was shot and left unconscious she hadn't rated this level of medical attention. Tina straps me in three ways from Sunday and finishes off by handing me a bland, oaten protein bar. It is an orgasm crossing my lips.

All is now well with the world. Well, not really, obviously, but my tit and my eye and my cheek are slowly mending, I'm full of dope and saline, and I'm finally filling my belly. I'm even off my knees and among friends... well, a friend and a temporary ally, if I'm being generous.

"What's been going on?" I ask, after taking the full requisite thirty seconds to luxuriate in my recovery.

Nia and Tina exchange a glance.

"What's the last thing you remember?"

"Asking you for advice."

I briefly bring them up to speed on what happened to me with Zanib, and the long period of lost time. They nod in sympathy at my every description of battling with the hematophages, and they both seem interested to note that when I slapped my armband on Zanib, it affected the hematophages as well.

"This is interesting news," Tina says. "I suspected as much, but we haven't really tested using drugs on the infested."

"It's been our experience up until now, that killing the host give the eels the means to escape to reinfest others. We lost a lot of good people before we got wise to that."

"Which is why they granted you parole, I take it?"

"Yes, actually," Nia replies, ignoring my sarcasm or perhaps simply unfazed by it. "At this point it's a war between the infested and the clean. Any other distinction is... trivial."

I guess it's heartening to know that in the human experience there are still some situations that can force you to trust a person who, less than a day ago, attempted to murder you and all of your friends.

"What happened while I was out? I gather things went a bit... sideways."

I gesture at the strange alignment of the ship.

"Cute," Nia says.

"Something happened over... there," Tina explains, gesturing in what I take to be the direction of the *Manifest Destiny*. "Something bad. Prosser didn't come back. But Helena and Tampa did. And they called for immediate demolition."

I stretch back. Between the food and the medicine, I feel halfway human again.

"And the explosion turned us on our side?"

Nia tugs on Tina's sleeve.

"We need to get back. Is she stable?"

Tina nods and crouches down to help me up. I could use another few hours sitting there, resting, but I don't exactly feel safe hanging out in the hallway. The *Borgwardt* looks like a warzone. The bulkheads are riddled with scars from beam rifles.

"Actually, we made it clear of the explosion," Tina says, punctuating the sentence with a grunt as she hauls me to my feet. "Everything was by the book, just like clockwork. But then the engines failed. We hadn't even broken the atmosphere."

"Sabotage," I say. It's not a question. Tina nods anyway. She helps me down the hallway toward the galley.

"And we landed like this. Sideways."

"At least now we know how the infestation got on board," Nia growls, "this one's girlfriend."

Tina nods and looks at me. I don't say anything. Sure, it was Zanib's fault. But it wasn't really her fault. She was doing her job. She had taken all the appropriate precautions. And, perhaps most important in my eyes, she had suffered more than anyone for her mistake. I would defend her to the end.

"Up until now there's been a lot of...tension. Most of the crew blames the colonists for bringing the infestation on board. I keep telling everyone they all came up clean, but there's still a lot of mistrust. I...know you probably don't want to drag Zanib's name through the mud, but this information will make things better."

"I understand."

We're standing outside the hatch to the galley. With the ship's new alignment, the hatch is a hole in the deck we have to clamber down into. Tina pulls out her paint gun a second time.

"Stand there against the bulkhead. Er... the deck. You know what I mean."

I nod and put my back to the bulkhead. Tina trains the paint gun at my shoulder and fires a pellet. It doesn't sting much, and I'm left with a small green X on my shoulder.

"Here's what you need to know," Tina says, and the canned speech she gives next is so emotionless and rote that I'm sure she's given it a hundred times before now. "The galley is a safe zone. I've cleared everyone who's inside. When I clear them, I give them a green mark. The paint guns have all been confiscated and they're all accounted for. All the green paint, too. Right now, the only person on board who has access to green paint is me. And by Diane's orders, only I can use it. When I use it, it will be in this hallway. We call this the green room.

"The green room serves the same purpose as a prophylactic airlock. I don't want to conduct the test inside the galley safe zone. If there are eels, I don't want anyone clean exposed to them, or their eggs. I don't know enough right now about how the infestation starts to risk that. If you go outside the green room, you will have to get checked again before re-entering the galley. I know it's unpleasant, but it's the only method we're sure of right now."

"If I have to leave again, I'm just going to wear a boom suit, like her."

Nia smiles grimly behind the plasteel.

"Sorry, this is the only one in the uninfested zone. The rest have been jettisoned."

"Let me guess," I say, "saboteurs."

"You got it. I was the only soul on board wearing a suit when they were jettisoned. So, my eyeballs get to stay safely in my head."

"Any questions?" Tina asks.

I'm about to shake my head, but one pops, unbidden, out of my lips.

"Is Becs in there?"

Nia and Tina exchange a look. I'm starting to get tired of them doing that.

"No," Nia states flatly.

It's clear they don't want to elaborate, so I clamber down into the galley. The place is, surprisingly, less of a disaster area than the rest of the ship. The tables are all dented and many of the chairs have twisted legs, presumably from when the office turned on its side and it all came crashing to the new deck. However, the survivors have mostly righted all the furniture, and cleared it to the sides. I spot Diane just as I think to myself that this is probably her doing. So, she survived. I feel weirdly relieved by that.

I scan the rest of the room. I don't recognize too many of the others, but I've only been on board for the better part of two days, and I haven't worked with a lot of my office mates. Grace and Jaime are here, and their people. Tampa is, too. And Helena is standing and walking towards me.

She promptly wraps her huge hands around my neck and begins crushing my windpipe.

# TWENTY-EIGHT

If I hadn't already had my eyeball popped out today, not to mention being attacked by hematophagic parasites, and nearly killed by my zombified roommate, this would be the worst experience of my life. As it is, being choked out by Helena only really rates the fourth or fifth worst experience of the day.

"Helena!" I hear Diane shout, as the blood rushes out of my brain.

I can feel someone else's fingers vainly prying at the security goon's. This is Tina, I'm vaguely aware of, though I feel more like I'm observing the situation from a corner in the ceiling where I'm safely floating above it all rather than experiencing it directly.

"Helena! I will not raise my voice again!"

The shaking and choking halts. For a moment, I think Helena is feeling ambivalent, but slowly she unwraps her fingers from around my neck. She shoves me away from her, but it's not an angry shove, it's dismissive. Tina starts to fuss over me, but I shake my head. I'm fine. Not really. But I want to seem fine. The medi-packs are still working me over. I'm sure they'll fix up my semi-collapsed trachea the same way as my cheek and eye.

Diane is standing in front of me now on her crutches, surveying me as though I am a budget report.

"I think you'd better go cool down," Diane says to Helena, without taking her eyes off of me.

"Yeah, yeah," Helena says, the most dismissive I've ever heard her treat Diane.

"Let me know when you've gotten hold of yourself."

Helena says nothing. She clambers up onto a table and starts pulling open a hatch on what is now the far bulkhead of the galley, which was formerly perpendicular to its current horizontal position.

"Where are you going?" the director asks Helena's receding back.

"The freezer," the goon replies, without looking over her shoulder, "you know, to cool off."

I can't tell if it was supposed to be a bon mot or if Helena just can't even stand to be in a room with me anymore. She goes through some acrobatics but manages to pull herself into the sideways walk-in freezer.

"I'm so sorry, Paige. Obviously, we can't tolerate this sort of inappropriate behavior, even in times of distress. Perhaps especially in times of distress. Would you like to file a report or speak to worker's compensation?"

I stare at her, aghast. Is she really still worried about all that?

"Uh... no."

She nods.

"Well, it's your right to do so for the next 90 days. Please do not feel pressure to forget this. I certainly won't."

"Okay," I say.

Diane stands there, silent for a moment, as if gauging how long is appropriate before launching right into business talk. The director sits down with Tina, Nia, and I (I still can't get over how quickly everyone's come to trust the skin-wrapper, but I guess needs must as the devil drives.) I don't feel much like talking, certainly not like reliving the pain of losing Zanib by recounting it a second time. Luckily, Tina and Nia are unusually eager to tell my story on my behalf. I don't feel obliged to correct them on a whole lot, though they've jumbled some of the details. Mostly they're interested in the information I've brought them about how I overdosed Zanib to stop the hematophages and how Zanib brought K.P. on board, who must have taken control of her and started bringing others on.

"It all seems quite obvious now in hindsight, doesn't it?" Diane says, shaking her head ruefully. "The worms were Patel's project. Meanwhile, uneven heads have been blaming the colonists. Ladies, could one of you please give me a hand?"

Nia and Tina assisted Diane in clambering up onto the tabletop. She clears her throat, and I never heard a room fall silent so fast.

"Ladies, can I have your attention please? Thank you. There's been a great deal of...shall we say...rumor-mongering of late. We've finally managed to confirm the origin of the outbreak. It seems that one of our own scientists brought the worms on board in the course of her normal duties."

"Who?" someone shouts, attempting to sound angry though the fear in her voice is palpable.

"I don't think it's appropriate to say at this time. Suffice it to say, she has paid with her life. I was aware of what she was doing and approved it. Ultimately the responsibility is mine. Therefore, if you must have a target for your animus, make it me."

Diane pauses, waiting for more outbursts from the cheap seats, but thankfully she has shamed them into silence.

"I would like to take this moment, therefore, to offer a public apology to Jaime and her crew. It's clear now to anyone who was still in doubt, that the infestation was not brought on board by your people, but rather by our own intemperate actions. I apologize for any discomfort or loss of esteem this may have caused you or your personnel. Hestle takes such slander very seriously, and we will work hard with you to see that it is made right as soon as we have returned to corporate space."

Jaime rises, seemingly unflustered.

"Thank you for your kind remarks, madam director. While we expected no trust from your people, we have, instead, been greeted with great kindness and compassion, excluding a very few bad apples. I accept your gracious apology in the spirit with which it was given, and we will seek no further remuneration for any intemperate words."

"Then that will be the end of it. Thank you, Jaime. And thank you everyone else for listening. You can return to your duties."

Everyone's "duties" seem to consist of muttering rumors in hushed tones and the occasional card game, but they return to them, nevertheless. With the help of the others, Diane retakes her seat. She seems to notice me again, as though for the first time.

"You're sure you're going to be all right, Paige? After what Helena did?"

It's all I can do not to roll my eyes.

"I'm not worried about it," I say, and I genuinely mean it, "But why is she so pissed at me?"

"I couldn't say for certain," Diane says, though I can tell she's equivocating.

It's pointless. Nia blurts out the truth in her own usual, tactless manner.

"She's still pissed about what happened to the cook."

I look up sharply.

"Becs? Why? What happened to her?"

The others fall silent, even Nia.

"Why won't you tell me? Fuck, what could be so much worse than parasites crawling out of people's eyes?"

"It's... worse," Diane states flatly.

"Tell me." I'm starting to feel like a broken record.

Diane takes a deep, thoughtful breath.

"I suppose you have a right to know. Have you got your jotter?"

I pull it out and place it on the table.

"We put all of the communications systems into emergency lockdown, for obvious reasons. No need to give the worms any advantage. However, I've had all the ship's computing rerouted to the galley terminal over there."

She points at the cash register Becs had previously manned. It had fallen along with the rest of the furniture, and been returned to an upright position. It seems funny, running an entire massive office's computers out of a cash register, but there's nothing normal about this situation anymore.

"If you plug in your jotter you can watch the security footage from Pod Nine during the security team's foray there."

To my surprise, Diane reaches out and takes hold of my wrist.

"Though I want to suggest again that you don't. I know not knowing is difficult and it is painful, but sometimes not knowing is better than knowing."

"I don't believe that's ever the case," I say with absolute conviction.

Diane nods.

"Then you can use this code to access the records."

She punches in an alphanumeric which populates the field as asterisks and leaves it to me to press the enter key. I rise, tentative despite my conviction to find out what happened to Becs.

"Don't do it," Tina warns as I walk towards the cash register.

"Fuck her," Nia says, "Let her see what she did."

# TWENTY—NINE

I'm so ruined by full-color interactive holography that I've almost forgotten how to watch a simple, 2-D recording. But, of course, it wouldn't be cost effective for the company to render countless hours of security footage into real-time holographs. In a way, watching the simple black and white images flash by on a screen is infinitely creepier than being immersed in the middle of a movie.

Helena leads the way into Pod Nine. This, I take it, is immediately after I left them. Prosser and Tampa join her, all three swiveling their heads like exotic birds. They're wearing boom suits this time, a precaution against a second gas attack, I guess. Helena fires her rifle at something off screen.

"Did I get her?" she asks aloud, her voice tinny through the boom suit microphone.

Prosser advances, puts her finger to the ground and holds it back up. She has chocolate sauce on her fingers...oh, no, wait, I see. It's blood. The lack of color in the feedback is playing tricks on my eyes. But, of course, it's really blood.

Then my wheels begin spinning. Beam rifles cauterize the wound as they go through. They'll still kill you, but you certainly won't bleed. I just saw it with Eden, the infested custodian. The far more experienced security goons have reached the same conclusion I'm already grasping for as they regroup and begin to move away from the blood spatter.

"They're baiting us," Prosser growls.

"Be careful," Helena warns, "First the gas, now this trap. They may look like savages but they're smart."

"And this is their home turf," Tampa adds.

The security guards play leapfrog, covering one another as they move into new positions to cover each other for the next movement. It has an elegant, almost balletic, hypnotic quality to it as I watch it in absolute silence.

Pod Nine itself is a nightmarescape. Substances that I suspect would have been difficult to identify even viewing them in living color drip from the bulkheads and ceiling. The deck appears to be coated with dung and offal. It must smell like a sewer. The goons are fortunate to be encased in self-contained boom suits, though none of them breaks their silence to state out loud what I am thinking as I watch them.

The dance ends suddenly and unexpectedly as Prosser makes an apparently wrong move and Helena's hand goes flying out, holding her back by the ribs, like a mother holding her child's chest as a vehicle crashes.

"Don't move," Helena warns.

Gingerly, Helena prods a pile of goo on the ground with the end of her beam rifle. She strikes something, and a crudely constructed bear trap snaps closed, its teeth jagged and composed of salvaged ship parts rather than sliding together perfectly. Helena angrily kicks the bear trap off of the end of her rifle, rather than prising it open and off.

"Thanks, boss," Prosser says.

"I just want to napalm this fucking ship and these fucking people," Helena mutters.

"But the cook, boss," Tampa chimes in.

"I know. That fucking Ambroziak. I can't believe the director listened to her. I knew this was a bad idea."

Heat flushes my cheeks. I have to look away for a moment. When I look back, Prosser puts a hand on Helena's shoulder.

"Forget it, boss. Head in the game."

"Head in the game," Helena agrees.

They return to leapfrogging. They kill another colonist. Uncover another trap. Once, Tampa nearly slips in the fecund matter coating the ground. One of the others (I can't identify which) steadies her before she does.

When they finally find Becs, I wish they hadn't. I wish I hadn't chosen to watch. I wish I hadn't lied to Diane about what I thought was best for the company. I wish I hadn't signed on with Hestle, or come on this expedition, or started working on my doctorate, or ever been born.

Becs – what's left of her, more accurately – is lying on a slab which I can't identify as either sectarian altar or dinner table, but appears to be engaged in the business of both. Crouching around her are the denizens of Pod Nine, mouths stained black with blood and some gnawing on strips of her flesh.

It is worse than I could have possibly imagined and I had imagined many awful fates for Becs. They have stripped the flesh from her legs down to the bone. Her chest is gaping open, her organs dug through and strewn about like a horn of plenty. They have been eating her, and she has been screaming and fighting back. It's unclear exactly when she died.

The security detail had spent only a few minutes assembling, and maybe twenty minutes exploring before finding her, yet it seems to me that Becs was doomed from the moment we breathed in the gas. Why did they choose her and not Helena or me? Perhaps a superstitious reason. Perhaps Becs was the lightest to carry. Her end was an undignified one, and a horror beyond imagining.

Helena takes the only action a reasonable human being could take when faced with that horror. She calmly, slowly, evenly begins gunning down each and every one of the colonists as they cry and plead for mercy. The ones that try to run she shoots first.

After a hesitant moment, Prosser and Tampa join in. I cannot see their faces, but I suspect they are not exulting in the same way as they had in destroying the skin-wrappers. In spite of their lost humanity, the dregs of Pod Nine seem more pathetic than anything else, like a pack of jackals unable to bring down their prey except through cowardice and trickery.

When every colonist in sight is dead, punctured through with a clean, cauterized beamhole, Helena stands with her weapon still leveled, as though desperately craving more targets.

"What do we tell the director?" Tampa asks.

"We report exactly what happened. We have no responsibility to hostile strangers," Helena says.

"They shouldn't have started this war if they didn't want us to finish it," Prosser agrees.

Of the three, Tampa seems the most reluctant to report on their massacre, but even that only really seems like hesitation. What is the "right" reaction to cannibalism?

A thump from a source I cannot spot, even as I go back to rewind and pause, startles all three of the goons and they turn in circles, hopelessly pointing their weapons in every direction. Helena is the first to identify it.

"Fuck me," she mutters, "would you look at this?"

The three goons approach a glass panel. It is identical to the hydroponic garden we saw on Pod Eight. There is something about this one, though, that has them upset. I can't identify what it is. What are they seeing?

"Is this their water system?" Prosser asks.

Helena nods. Prosser taps on the glass.

"It must be contaminated with that stuff outside."

I realize that the hydroponic garden has turned red, tainted by the blood ocean. It's something I never would have identified watching a black and white rendering. It took the women who were there long enough to notice it in person.

The bump sounds again, and the goons are startled again, but this time the source is obvious. One of the hematophages has latched onto the plasteel, suckling at it as if desperately trying to get at them.

"What the hell is that?" Tampa asks.

"Local fauna. A bloodsucker. Remember? Just like the xenobiologist predicted. What'd she call it?"

"A hematophage," I say aloud.

"A lamprey," Helena says.

The head of a colonist jumps. I jump with it. It starts to turn, turning towards the security goons. Slowly, lovingly, the hematophages within wheedle out first one eye, then the other, avoiding the telltale pop that usually accompanies such an action.

I see it before anyone who was actually there does. I know what's happening long before anyone else has figured it out. But they're trapped in there, in the tiny little rectangle in my jotter, trapped in the past, unable to avoid what's happening, unable to be aware of it like I am. It's like watching "The Manifest Destiny" holovid and knowing the damn ship is going to crash from the very first image and no one on screen can do a damn thing about it, despite all their attempts to stave off the inevitable.

The hematophages slither out of the cannibal's head as the goons continue talking to each other. I can't hear a word they're saying because I'm too fixated on the actions of the parasites. They crawl along the deck, seemingly pained by being out in the open air. Of course, they must be. They're used to swimming around an ocean of bodily fluid. They only leave to take up residence in an unsuspecting host's body. Being in the open air must be torture for them, like fish out of water or humans with their heads forcibly held under.

They seem to debate, and I watch as they undulate, their bodies bundling together and apparently exchanging some form of communication. These are no dumb animals. I don't know why I still thought of them as such, even after everything I've seen, but somehow, I thought it was us providing them with intellect, and not the other way around.

The breeding pair seems to have agreed to a plan, and working together, they each bite into the pantleg of Prosser's suit and pull in opposite directions. The hematophages must have jaws with preternatural strength to be able to rip open a boom suit. I know they're not impenetrable, but I didn't think the action of any human or animal alone could pierce one. Up until now. Only now do the goons notice what I've been watching, horrified, all along. Prosser's suit begins beeping, announcing, "Suit integrity compromised! Suit integrity compromised!"

Prosser and the others are turning around again, utterly unable to identify the threat. Tampa even looks up at the ceiling, the exact opposite direction of where she should be looking. It's too late. It was too late the moment they started pulling at her pantleg. Prosser is shrieking in horror. They've slithered into her suit. The secured, protected atmosphere has been turned against the security goon, ensuring that she is trapped with the parasites as they slither up her leg.

Prosser is shrieking louder and louder now. Helena and Tampa are utterly flustered, unsure what to do. Prosser pops off her helmet and casts it aside, not hard enough that it breaks (nothing, essentially, can break plasteel) but sending it bouncing around the room. She is trying to slough off the rest of her suit. She's still unable to articulate what is happening to her, and is howling in something approaching what I imagine to be the Platonic ideal of pain.

The other two finally rush to help, stripping Prosser of her suit as quickly as they can fumble the pieces apart. Once the pants of her suit are off we can all of us, both those present and those voyeurs who might be viewing later, see what's happening. One of the hematophages has already disappeared from view. Prosser is choking, hinting that it is crawling up through her esophagus and seeking the sweet climes of her brain. The other is squirming around, its tail poking out of Prosser's tight underpants.

With a mighty yank, Helena rips Prosser's panties right apart. The other woman is now naked from the waist down, with a ridiculously encumbering boom suit still over her upper half. The problem, though, is with her genitals, as the second half of the breeding pair of hematophages is burrowing deeply into her vagina. Tampa has her beam rifle leveled at Prosser's crotch, but she looks to Helena for instruction. This is utter madness.

Suddenly, around them, other bodies begin disgorging hematophages. Tampa begins firing, missing more often than not, but occasionally scoring a hit on the parasites and causing them to scream, a disturbingly human-sounding noise, as they sizzle and die. The whole room becomes a shooting gallery full of tiny, serpentining targets.

Not every colonist is disgorging parasites, but way too many to manage are. Who knows now if the denizens of Pod Nine had been reduced to their degraded state by years of isolation and space madness, or by the semi-rampant rampages of the hematophages among them. Perhaps a combination of the two. In any case, it's clear that this is what awaits us on the *Borgwardt* if we can't keep ourselves clean and defeat the threat.

"We have to get out of here," Helena is the first to realize.

The parasites are not tough, but they are small, wriggling, and difficult to shoot. Helena even tramples one underfoot. They are closing in on the two women who remain their potential prey.

"Please don't leave me!" Prosser shouts.

The second hematophage has completely disappeared. Prosser loses all ability to speak and begins coughing, the second half of the breeding pair now making its own way up into her brainpan. Blood begins to trickle from her ears. The first hematophage is enjoying a tasty feast of grey matter.

I am fixated, fascinated. This is like nothing I've ever seen before, or even been able to imagine, though I suppose I knew that Zanib, Eden, and the others must have become infested somehow. The reality of it, though, is an utter nightmare.

"Don't worry, kid," Helena announces bravely, putting her arm around Prosser, "We'd never leave you. We're all getting out of here. Tampa, grab the cook's body." She turns to Prosser, as though conspiratorially. "Nobody gets left behind on my watch, right?"

"No!" Prosser shrieks, and the blood is flowing thick and fast from both of her ears, and now her eyes, nose, and mouth, "No, please, no, fuck no! Please, Helena!"

Helena grabs her by the chin.

"I got you kid! I won't let you go!"

"Kill me! Please kill me! They're eating my brain!"

Helena is a far better person than I. Monsters worming across the ground, she still lifts her rifle and puts a beam between Prosser's eyes. Following her orders, Tampa throws Becs's body over her shoulder, though it sends her sweetmeats flying all over the room, and inadvertently some of the hematophages begin creeping in other directions, drawn by the smell of organ meat. Helena reaches down and grabs Prosser by the neck of her boom suit, firing a dozen more times into her head and turning it to absolute Swiss cheese as the parasites emerge from her eye sockets to seek a new host, most likely Helena herself.

The security goons are running now, running for the exit, bits and pieces of Becs's offal trailing behind them.

"Ops! Ops!" Helena is shouting, frantically.

"Hey, security team," Kelly Overland's voice intones, still attempting to be as friendly as possible, "we're monitoring your situation and reinforcements are..."

"Tell them to fuck the fuck off!" Helena shouts, "As soon as we're clear, you need to dump all the plasma we've got into this fucking ship. Send it back to Hell!"

# THIRTY

I stop the playback. The jotter indicates that it's logging me (by which it means Diane) out. In a shrewder moment I might have told it not to and hung on to Diane's password for a while to dig around in company records. I am not feeling shrewd right this moment. Nor am I feeling deflated. Nor guilty. Nor sad. I am an empty vessel, devoid of these things you humans call feelings. I am a robot of meat.

No one is looking at me. No one is thinking about me. They're all focusing on their own business. Diane and a few others are worried about operations and sending out forays. The others are trying not to get underfoot. There is little for a shipping supervisor or a budget tech to do under this new warlike footing.

Tina is busy tending to the wounded. She stops by and checks on me, tells me everything's healing up nicely. She gestures to one of the cooks, who seems genuinely excited to have something to do. The woman drops off a tray for me, apologizing that they can't do much beyond cold sandwiches and that sort of thing with the ovens and other equipment all standing perpendicular. I tell her it's fine, in such a subdued tone that a wave of disappointment washes over her face and she walks away, chastened. I suppose that was one of those occasions where you're supposed to ebulliently praise someone for whatever they've done. The truth is the tray she's laid before me is an outlandish repast, even if none of it is cooked. I should have thrown her a bone. I feel no compunction about it.

I feel no hunger, either. It's all bled out of me. But I know in some intellectual sense I need raw proteins and vitamins to make up for the ones my body has lost, so I begin shoveling it in. It's all fresh vegetables and meats and cheeses and salads, and my tongue should be luxuriating in it, but my mood has dampened it all down to tasting like ash.

Tina clambers up the emergency ladder into the green room. I gather from the buzzing that Quinn, the outcast security guard, has returned from a mission. The others gather together into a small crowd while Tina is away conducting the spoon-in-the-eye test. Though they have ostensibly been cleared of any wrongdoing, the colonists still gather on one side of the galley and the *Borgwardt* crew on the other, seemingly shunning each other. Diane knocks with her crutch on the freezer hatch, and Helena re-emerges. She gives me the stink-eye but Diane is watching closely and ultimately Helena simply folds her arms and joins the crowd.

Tina clambers back down the ladder first. She simply shakes her head sadly at the crowd and returns to her business. Everyone in the room deflates. As she passes by me, I catch Tina's hand.

"What's going on?"

She sighs.

"Quinn was supposed to get the engines turned back on. I don't think she ever even made it to ops."

Well, that explains the palpable sense of disappointment. Quinn is descending very slowly, a rifle slung over her back. She reaches the bottom of the ladder and claps her hands together nervously, as though shaking the dust from them. She looks around at the assembled women.

"Madam director," Quinn says, "may I speak to you? In private?"

Diane does not betray any emotion, but the rest of the crowd is upset, even disgusted.

"Yes, of course," Diane replies, looking around for some way to logistically make that happen. She can't exactly say, "Step into my office."

Helena practically pushes women out of the way as she emerges from the crowd and steps towards Quinn. Immediately Quinn has the look of a spooked rabbit.

"Where's the rest of your team?"

Quinn shakes her head mournfully.

"What the fuck does that mean?" Helena shouts, stepping up into Quinn's face. "Report, you piece of dogshit!"

"Helena!" Diane shouts.

"They... they didn't make it!" Quinn responds.

Helena looks for a moment as though she is going to slap Quinn, but then seems to think she's not worth it.

"I should've known. I should've known you couldn't handle it. You have no business being a security goon anyway. If this was fifty years ago, I would've already had you shot for dereliction. Those women's lives were in your hands!"

"The same way Prosser's was in yours?"

Helena starts an abortive charge. This time, I think she's going to kill Quinn, like she didn't kill me. But to everyone's surprise Quinn raises her beam rifle and points it directly at Helena. Helena halts on a dime.

"What do you think you're doing?"

"Ladies," Diane shouts, limping over into the scrum as fast as she can, "this is not the manner to..."

"You back off, Helena, you fucking bully! I do a good job. Maybe I can't do as many pull-ups as your favorites can... correction, as your favorites could... but I'm good at my job."

"Pointing a gun at your supervisor, you call that good at your job? Because I call it grounds for dismissal."

Diane doesn't step in between the rifle and Helena. That would be suicidal. But she does stand slightly to the left of the squabbling goons.

"You'll both be dismissed if this doesn't stop promptly. I can assure you of that."

"No need to worry, madam director," Helena says, without taking her eyes off Quinn, "this one's always been all talk, zero walk. She doesn't have the intestinal fortitude to swat a fly, let alone gun down a grown woman in cold blood."

"You know a lot about gunning down people in cold blood, don't you, boss?"

Tampa emerges from the crowd.

"Quinn. Come on now. You don't want to do this."

"What the fuck do you care? What are... what are you people doing? Don't you know what's going on out there? There's worms crawling into our heads and you all just keep acting like it's another day at the office. 'Nice to see you, Sam. Nice to see you, Jean. See you at the water cooler later!'"

Quinn is quivering, sweating. I don't like the look in her eyes.

"Quinn," Diane says quietly, "put the gun down now. We'll forget all of this. All of this business. It's forgotten."

"You might think it's forgotten, but I don't forget shit. I'm a fucking elephant," Helena says, stepping forward.

"Why are you always," she pauses, floundering for words, "picking on me? It's not the end of the world! So what if I didn't get the engines started? All we have to do is survive. Remember? AginCorp is sending a super-dreadnought out here. They're not going to ignore our distress call. They'll probably love having a hold full of Hestle employees to wave in corporate's face."

Diane purses her lips. Quinn looks wildly between her and Helena. The rest of the crowd is chattering now. Diane looks at the crowd. It's obvious she has something on her mind, but wouldn't normally say it in front of this many people. Helena feels no such hesitation.

"You've fucked us, Quinn. There's no rescue mission. There's no race any more. We heard from corporate two hours ago. Our saboteurs on Yloft have managed to scrap every rival mission. Nobody's coming for us for days. We're dead now and it's your fault."

Unable to vocalize any longer, a shriek like a steam engine comes from Quinn's mouth and she points her rifle directly at Helena's head.

"I didn't do anything! I didn't crash us in the ocean!"

"Go ahead. Do it. You don't have the..."

I guess the next word out of Helena's mouth was going to be "guts." Perhaps another more colorful synonym. I'll never find out. A perfect, thumb-sized, cauterized hole unfortunately appears in the speech center of her brain at just that instant, cutting short whatever she was about to say. Helena blinks after she's already been shot. She blinks as though confused. I don't know if it's a nerve impulse or if she's somehow clinging to life for a few instants after having her skull drilled clean through by a beam, but either way, she stands there and blinks before finally collapsing into a puddle.

Tampa tackles Quinn immediately, wrestling the weapon out of her hands, though there is precious little fight left in her. It seemed that having discharged her rifle all of the fight has gone out of her like air out of a balloon. Tampa looks up at Diane.

"What do I do with her, madam director?"

Diane slowly reaches up and takes off her glasses. She stands there, polishing them absently for a moment, then replaces them.

"Get her out of here," she whispers.

"Where?"

Diane stares at her. I wonder if we're all finally going to see the director lose her cool. No. Not this time, anyway.

"The freezer," she says flatly.

"The freezer? You can't put me in there. That's cruel. I want to talk my union rep. I want to talk to equal opportunity."

"Yes," Diane agrees, her voice a million light years away, "we'll of course provide you with all of that. But for now, throw her in the freezer."

A bang resounds through the galley. Then another, then another until we're all looking up at Nia, standing up on one of the tables, pointing at a plasteel screen which, due to the addled nature of the ship's alignment, is now running vertical instead of horizontal.

"Anyone know what this is? No need to all answer at once. This is the water that we need to survive. And you know what's all around us? An ocean of parasites who want to get in. They're going to get in, they're going to taint our water supply, and then that's all she wrote. There won't be a civilized planet or station in the galaxy that won't shoot us out of the ink after that. Even corsairs will fire on sight rather than board."

That last statement, coming from a skin-wrapper, is perhaps even more sobering than anything else. There's being an outcast, and then there's being an outcast even among outcasts.

"Now a lot of you don't trust me. I don't give a shit. I want to live. I don't trust a single one of you. Guess what? I don't give a shit. I want to live. The colonists don't trust the ink surfers? Guess what? I still fucking want to live. Crew doesn't trust the colonists? I'm not dying over that. Even your own security detail is gunning one another down? Guess what? I. Still. Fucking. Want. To. Live."

She surveys the room. Everyone is chattering. The energy is electric. For the first time since her downfall, I can see how Nia became a corsair captain.

"Now you people brought me on board here. Otherwise I'd be happily floating dead in space right now. So, guess what? You're responsible for getting me out of this mess. We need to get the engines fixed and get out of this fucking ocean. I'm going to go do that. And I don't care who comes with me. And I don't care about your regs. And I don't care about anything right now except for number one! Now who's coming with me?"

In a movie, this would be where a cheer goes up through the crowd. In real life, it's where I stand up. My medi-packs have finished their work. I'm not at 100% but I can stand and probably hold a gun if I have to.

"I'll go."

"All right, we've got the historian. Who else?"

Jaime also stands.

"I agree. Now is not the time for petty distinctions. For any distinctions, really. I'll go as well."

"Bully! Three's good. Four would be better."

Grace rises. She raises her hand. Says nothing.

"That's a fourth. Madam Gash of a Director... we're taking the guns that are left. That's not me really asking, it's more like telling."

Diane looks up at Nia, then over at me and finally at the colonists.

"If the four of you can get my office moving again I'll throw you a fucking parade."

# THIRTY-ONE

I feel like a character in a horror flick. It seems like there's always gibbering and running feet off in distant corridors. And it all seems so distant and indistinct until the moment a monster drops on me from out of nowhere.

"Don't get distracted," Nia says. "All that smoke and noise is for the rubes. We've got this on lockdown."

"You're pretty good at this," I say.

She smiles.

"Did you forget how I make my living? Piracy is pretty much nothing but creeping through scary wrecks where everyone wants to kill you."

"The only difference here is," Jaime intones, "your former enemies did not wish to eat your brains."

Nia snorts.

"I take you've never tried to board a Gore-Fa gunrunner. Those fucking punks play for keeps. Hey, historian. Which way to ops?"

Sadly, of the four of us, with my two or three days of experience I know the ship best. I'm finally doing what I was hired on to do: direct people around a ship. Only, in this case, it's not a derelict vessel no one knows anything about. We already firebombed that historical landmark. Now it's our own office, and we're trying to get it back under control.

I point the way to operations.

"I don't trust these damn things," Nia mutters.

I turn to her, confused. Is she talking to me? Grace is habitually silent and Jaime is bringing up the rear.

"What damn things?"

She slaps the stock of her beam rifle.

"Light particles are no good for shipboard combat. Give me a good old-fashioned plasma thrower any day."

"Weird," I reply, "somehow I prefer not to smell the burning flesh of my victims."

She might be smiling, but it's not clear behind her plasteel screen and lipless mouth.

"All these beams bouncing around. It's not safe. Right now, we don't know what it's doing. In space there'd be explosive decompression. In here, that gunk could be leaking in. Those things could be slipping in."

"Through a bullet hole?"

"What do you know about how small they start out? Or how flexible they are? I saw an octopus squeeze into a Mason jar once. More concerning though is the sewage and water system. I don't know how long we have until that's tampered with."

"They're probably tampering with it right now," Grace growls.

I glance back at her, and heft my rifle. I can't really bring it any closer to me than it is, but moving it around a little makes me feel better.

"How many people are unaccounted for?" I ask.

"Seven," Nia replies. "Well, that was counting you. And the custodian, she's dead now. And your friend Zanib Patel. That means we're down to four."

"Four's not so bad."

"It would only take one to spike the sewage system."

"That's what you were doing when you found me, then? Hunting down missing people?"

Nia nods. It's strange to see her head move behind the plasteel but not the helmet.

"We have to assume everyone who's missing is infested. And one of your operations people is still missing. That's... that's a big concern."

"Not Kelly Overland?"

"That's the one."

Shit. I had really liked her.

"Who else?"

"The office secretary. Another custodian. And... I forget who the last one is. It's on my jotter."

"But they might not be infested, right? We don't know."

"No, we don't," Nia agrees, "But we have to assume they are. Those are boss gash's orders."

"Diane said that?"

Nia nods again.

"You were supposed to shoot me?"

She turns and fixes me to the spot with one of her signature ghoulish grins.

"You're lucky you weren't too twitchy."

"Are they always twitchy?"

"Not always. There's only one way to be sure."

Grace makes a slurping, popping noise and motioned as though she was sticking a spoon into her own eye.

"Yup," Nia agrees. "We've reached ops, by the way."

"We have?"

I look around. I knew we were almost there, but never saw the hatch.

"You're standing on top of it."

Embarrassed, I step away from the hatch to operations. I guess it's good that I've gotten so used to the office being on its side. At times like this, though, it's embarrassing to forget.

"What's your name again?" Nia asks me.

"Paige," I reply.

"Right. Whatever. I want you to use your jotter and get this hatch open. If the parasites have jammed it or anything, get in contact with your boss and she'll give you a skeleton key code."

I nod and kneel down to start getting into the hatch's operating system. It's not exactly anything fancy, but I can understand why she hasn't asked Grace or Jaime to do it. Our computers would be way, way out of their league.

"All right, you two," Nia says, pointing at the colonists, "get up here with me and point your guns down. Keep your heads back away from the jamb. If you stick your head out, you make yourself a target."

"How are we supposed to shoot at anything if our heads are supposed to be out of the way?" Jaime asks.

"A mirror," Grace replies.

"Hey, I like you!" Nia says. "Best tactical tool in the arsenal."

She reaches into one of the pouches of her suit and pulls out what appears to be nothing more than a vanity mirror, with some sticky tactile substance on the rear. She tosses it gingerly so that it sticks to the erstwhile ceiling, which had previously been the bulkhead opposite the hatch to ops. We all look up into it and can see the hatch to ops reflected. When it opens, we should be able to see inside.

"It takes some adjustment to get used to. Remember right is left and left is right, but up and down are still the same. You'll have a couple of wild shots at first no matter what, but you'll adjust."

"Maybe we should try talking to Kelly before we kill her."

The other three look at me, at least two of them appalled.

"You want to risk your life on that? Go ahead."

"I will, thanks. Just don't anybody start shooting."

I punch a few buttons. The hematophages haven't locked the hatch down, so I have some hope that Kelly's just dead and not infested. That's actually a pretty depressing thought. I'm at the point where I'm wishing death on my friends because it's better than the alternative.

The hatch opens and the other three flinch, almost as one, moving their heads out of the field of view of anybody who might be within. I glance up at the mirror. It's too dark inside to see anything.

I reach up and grab Millie, my illumination globe, and push her into ops. She can't illuminate the whole room, but I can see a series of desks festooning the wall like trophy animal heads. Unlike the galley, where the table and chairs were light and (theoretically) not a falling hazard if the office went tumbling, the desks in ops are all heavy and bolted to the deck, which is now the bulkhead to the right as I'm looking in.

"Hello?" I cry out.

Nia pulls her beam rifle out of the hatchway and swivels around, scanning the hallways. I may be making enough noise to attract other hematophages.

"Who is it?" a raspy voice from within replies. I can't tell who it is. It sounds like she has strep throat.

"Paige Ambroziak."

"Good to hear from you, Paige!" the raspy voice replied.

"Is that you, Kelly?"

"It's me."

"I'm excited to finally meet you in person. You think you can come out? I'm afraid we're going to have to keep guns on you, but you understand, don't you?"

"I can't come out, Paige."

"She's infested," Nia growls.

"I'm the only one who cares if you live or die, Kelly." That came out wrong. "I'm sorry, that came out wrong. I mean you need to work with me."

"It's not that. I can't come out. I'm trapped, you see."

"Can you turn up the lights?"

The lights in ops rise and I have to turn away. They're not bright. Not particularly bright, anyway. But we've been walking around in dark hallways barely illuminated by emergency lighting and globes for so long that just normal illumination is enough to make our eyes water.

With the lights up I can now see that the desks on the far wall are lined in perfect rows like little toy soldiers, except for one. One fallen soldier.

Kelly is lying below us, pinned under the fallen desk. The bolts which should have kept it screwed to the deck dangle in their loops. Kelly looks up at me and smiles wanly. She's a pretty girl. Young. Too young. She is also as pale as a ghost. Only her torso is visible. Her legs and hips are pinned under the desk.

She waves at me as though we've spotted one another at the zoo or the park. I wave back.

"How are you, Kelly?"

She coughs.

"Not so good. I'm stuck."

I look at the other three members of the team.

"I'm getting her out of there. I don't care if you three help."

"That's not the mission," Jaime states flatly.

"The mission takes us right through ops and into engineering," I say.

"Nevertheless," Jaime says, "helping that woman will take an unacceptable amount of time."

"What's 'unacceptable' in your definition, Jaime?"

"Any amount of time is unacceptable," Jaime says. "We are in the unenviable position of racing the clock while having no idea how much time is left on it. As Nia pointed out, any moment the parasites could flood the water systems. Then all of this is in vain."

"I'm glad someone else around here makes sense," the skin-wrapper states flatly.

"So, if you get stuck, it's okay if we leave you behind?"

Nia stares at me.

"I'd be disappointed if you didn't."

"Well, you're a prisoner. You're lucky to be walking around. That's one of my crew-mates down there. She matters."

"Funny how you always seem to go from self-serving to self-righteous on a dime. Bearing in mind how little I matter, what if your imaginary friend down there is already infested and this is all a trap? If she's been alive all this time, how come she didn't reach out and tell us?"

"Because shipboard communications were shut down, remember? And she doesn't have one of those little phones in there."

"Maybe. Or maybe she's fucking infested. We could eliminate that little variable by drilling her right now."

I glare at her.

"Who would pretend to be trapped like that? She's not a skin-wrapper, you know."

Suddenly I'm shocked at Nia's strength as I'm lifted off my feet by the neck and slammed against the bulkhead.

"You don't like me," the skin-wrapper says, leering at me, forcing me to look into her lidless eyes and flayed face. "That's fine. I don't care. You can take shots at me, too. That's fine, too. I don't care. But do not ever suggest that I would fake illness as a ruse."

I've seen her before but this is the first time I've ever really been forced to look at her. It's easy to forget that in spite of everything else, in spite of being a walking, talking ghoul, in spite of being a reaving corsair who burns people to death with plasma, Nia is, at her most fundamental, a woman grappling with a terminal illness. She takes it seriously. All the snark is a defensive measure.

"I apologize," I say. "I mean it. I didn't think."

She looks me up and down. She seems to take me at my word and lets me drop to the deck.

"Listen," Kelly says, "I can hear you fighting over me. But it doesn't really matter. I'm not just pinned, you see. I'm dead. I'm dead already. My spine's been severed. Really, you won't even be able to move me."

The four of us return to the hatchway and peer down.

"We can get Tina down here," I say. "She'll be able to do something. At least put you into stasis or something until we can get you back to a proper hospital facility."

"Honestly, Paige, I'm at peace with it. You really want to do something for me, though, I'm dying for a glass of water."

I look at Nia. Her face is grim. Well, it's always grim. Grimmer than usual.

"We need to get to engineering," she states flatly.

Kelly nods. She presses a few buttons on her jotter and the hatch to the engine room opens.

"All right, you're all clear!"

I look at Nia and the other two.

"We have to go that way anyway. You can shoot her now, I guess. You know, to be sure."

Nia says nothing but simply begins climbing down the rows of desks which were bolted properly to the ground. Grace, Jaime, and myself follow, our beam rifles strapped to our backs. When I'm about halfway done navigating my way down the maze of desks, I realize that if Kelly is armed now is the perfect opportunity to gun us down. We're sitting ducks, our arms and legs occupied and our rifles out of reach. And if we do reach for them, we fall.

I'm struck by a sudden sense of overwhelming and impending doom. I've made the wrong choice, yet again. Allowed my emotions – this time, sympathy for Kelly and guilt over what happened to Becs, rather than raw, unchecked ambition as last time – get ahold of me. Whether she's infested or her story is true, Kelly is dead either way. It would probably be a mercy to drill a bolt through her forehead at this point. Certainly, it would guarantee our safety.

Nia reaches the deck first. She helps the rest of us down. The hardest part is navigating around the big missing hole where the desk that crushed Kelly should have been. It's like getting used to climbing a ladder only to find halfway up that it's suddenly missing a rung.

I approach Kelly's prostrate form.

"Hey, kid," I say.

"Hey," she replies weakly.

Her skin is flawless. That strikes me. She's not wearing a drop of makeup. She's just got the natural skin of a teenager. She probably is a teenager. Not even twenty yet. Probably joined Hestle as soon as possible at seventeen. Or maybe even before that as an intern and just got offered a job fresh after graduation. Her skin must have gone from betraying her at every turn in her oily early teens to that rare brief moment of perfection before the long march of time leads to crows' feet and pockmarks. She's perfect. Except for her spine, severed at the tailbone.

"You're that pirate," Kelly says.

"I'm that pirate," Nia agrees.

Kelly shrugs, then scowls at the pain it causes her to do so.

"Politics make for strange bedfellows I suppose. Did you... by chance bring any aqua?" I pull out my canteen but look at Nia first.

"I didn't bring a spoon," she says.

"It's all right," Kelly replies, misunderstanding and reaching out with her arms, "I don't need a spoon or a straw. I can drink it all right."

Nia shrugs.

"It's your neck to risk."

I crouch down and hand the canteen to Kelly, who eagerly swallows too much and begins choking. That long dreamt of perfect sip turns to pain.

"Are you guys finally going to fix the engine?"

"Yeah," I reply, before realizing what that means.

When the ship has power again and rights itself, Kelly will die. Her living situation is more than simply precarious, it's unsustainable. A jostle, a shake, and she'll be gone. We'll be turning the whole office ninety degrees.

"Kelly, I'm sorry."

"It's all right," she says, shaking her head. "I've already entered the commands for the ship to right itself and head for Yloft. It'll go on autopilot the whole way if it has to. I sure won't be able to pilot it at that point."

"You did that knowing it'll kill you?" Jaime asks.

"Well, I have my duties," she replies as though it's the simplest thing in the world.

"Yes," Jaime replies, "I suppose we all do."

"Well, don't let me keep you. There's nothing really you can do for me and getting the engine started is pretty much urgent. But, Paige, there is something you all should know."

Nia, Grace, and Jaime, perk up, surprised at the statement.

"Shipboard communications are shut down. It's supposed to stop the... whatever they are...from communicating with each other. At least... that was the director's orders. But, you know, I have access to override that from my station here."

"You do?" Nia asks. "Then why did you never try to contact us?"

"That's what I wanted to warn you four about. I did. Several times. But somebody shut me out. I don't think your safe zone is really safe. I think someone in there is infested."

# THIRTY-TWO

We spend the rest of the trek to the engine room in eerie silence. Kelly's revelation was shocking, but there's nothing we can do about it. At least, not until we reach a phone, and the nearest one of those is in... you guessed it... engineering.

We hear grunting and the banging of metal on metal as we round a corner. Without giving the order, all four of us douse our globes as one. We all become sober, silent killing machines as we approach, our footsteps muffled as though we have trained as trackers and stalkers all our lives.

Nia takes point. She turns back to me.

"It's the secretary," she whispers.

"Alone?"

She nods. I step around her and walk into engineering. It is the first time I have been in the room. In the dead center of the room, held in place by eight super magnets installed in the deck and ceiling, though now it is technically on its side, is a gravitational singularity about the size of a pea. I allow my footsteps to echo and announce my presence. Myrna, the red-headed secretary, is angrily bashing at a control monitor for the singularity.

I don't know much about engine rooms, but I do know that they are designed with about three hundred fail-safes and dead man switches designed to prevent the black hole that powers the office from being knocked loose and potentially expanding exponentially. Nothing – not lives, not money, not nothing – is more important to the company than preventing an apocalyptic event originating on one of their ships. If there's even a hint that the singularity could be knocked loose of its cage, the entire engine room will collapse on itself and destroy the singularity. Most modern ships are not lost due to the actions of corsairs, or corporate espionage. They're lost due to minor containment breaches in the engine room. It's like sealing up a sinkhole with cement, but better that than the sinkhole collapsing a whole city.

"Myrna," I say loudly.

She has obviously heard my footsteps, but she is still banging away impotently.

"Not so much anymore," Myrna replies, her voice low and guttural.

Each of her eyeballs pop out in turn. The hematophages emerge from her eye sockets, the male fat and plump and on the right, the female lither and skinnier and on the left, just like in Zanib. They bob and weave in the air, as Myrna, her eyeballs dangling from bundles of optic nerve around her chin level, raises the wrench like a baseball bat, about to take a swing at the control module.

"If you do that, you die. This whole office will implode. You know that, don't you?"

Nia, Grace, and Jaime enter, their weapons leveled as well.

"Arrgh!" Myrna growls. "Stupid, stupid, stupid! This human is one of the stupidest among you. She knows nothing about this system. She can barely even understand a damn manual."

Despite the tenseness of the situation, I have to suppress a smile. Myrna, the idiot, has turned out to be our greatest natural defense against the hematophages. She was too dumb to make a valuable saboteur.

"I'm not lying to you. That's a black hole. There are fail-safes in place to..."

"Gah! We know you're not lying."

The Myrna-thing drops the wrench, which clatters to the deck.

"Of course, you wouldn't let a singularity go unprotected. This entire solar system would be destroyed. Of course, there are fail-safes. But this..." Myrna gestures at her own head, "is so stupid! We are frustrated."

"You're about to be dead," Grace growls.

"Hold on," I say. "We've got the drop on her. No reason we can't talk. For once."

"You think you can negotiate with them?" Jaime asks.

"I'm not negotiating. I'm just talking."

Nia makes the hand-flapping "talk talk talk" gesture, but at least she holds her fire.

"Maybe we don't have to be at war. What is it that you want?"

Myrna makes a disdainful noise. She begins pacing like a caged animal. The hematophages continue to bob and weave in the air around her head.

"We need to get off this planet. We're dying off. It won't be long now before our entire species is extinct."

"Good riddance," Jaime states.

"This is your fault, alien. You killed our planet."

"Killed the planet? You mean the fleshworld? It's dying?"

"It's been dead for centuries. When your little seed ship landed here, it murdered our planet. The ecosystem collapsed. There's no longer nutriment in the ocean. We used to swim in an ocean of blood. Now we have to occupy your bodies to get fresh nourishment."

"That must mean there aren't many of you left."

"Very few. Our numbers are down to the dozens. Those of us who must stay in the ocean are dying by centimeters. It's like eating watered-down gruel. And soon it won't even be that."

"What if we can get you to another fleshworld?"

The Myrna-puppet barks in laughter.

"How dumb do you think we are? We know there are no other fleshworlds. You would make us promises so we would back down from our plans. And then you'd betray us. It is the human way."

"What are your plans then?"

Myrna laughs again.

"We feel like a villain in a third-rate entertainment fiction. Yes, of course, you can hear our plans. We've been planning to reactive the seed ship. We've been working at it restlessly for decades."

"That's impossible," Jaime breathes. "The engines were spiked when we first crashed."

Myrna points at Jaime.

"You see? You see how long we have toiled hopelessly? And then your craft landed. Now we can finally go free. When we get to civilization we can ride around in so many of your bodies."

"You have to know we wouldn't allow that," I say, "but we could work something out. We could develop a new food source for you. It might not be ideal but you wouldn't have to kill to survive. I'm sure you don't want that."

The male hematophage turns its maw to me. It is eyeless, but I can't escape the feeling it is staring at me.

"Why would we care about killing vermin to survive?"

Jaime steps forward. Like Diane, she is a stoic, but I wouldn't be surprised if, in some alternate universe, there were tears in her eyes.

"Vermin? You think my people are vermin?"

"We've battled you for centuries. You disgust us. With your pink, oily skin and your tiny, disgusting hairs. You have all these limbs and parts and you can barely do anything. You're the most disgusting creatures we can imagine, and what passes, futilely, for your intellect is a joke. Our world had poets and philosophers and theologians before you killed it. I know more and understand more than your species will ever be capable of even beginning to comprehend. You're like bugs to us. I feel no shame in stamping you out. I delight in it; I revel in it."

"The feeling, I suspect, is mutual," Jaime says.

She raises her weapon. I'm almost tempted to tell her not to do it, but I've tried reasoning with them. They are far, far beyond being reasoned with.

Jaime grins. It is the first time I have seen her do so. She opens her mouth and blood pours from it as she attempts to speak a word. I think it is "treason."

And treason it is, as Grace removes the blade from the back of her friend's neck.

# THIRTY-THREE

Grace's hand grabs the strap of Jaime's rifle and wraps it around her offhand even as Jaime slips out of the strap and tumbles to the deck. It is almost an elegant move, an unexpected martial pirouette. But now Grace has two guns, one pointed at Nia and the other at me. We both have our weapons pointed forward, more or less in Myrna's direction.

For once, Grace's eyeballs do not pop out of her head, although I almost wish they would after I witness what happens next. Instead, each of the hematophages messily devours her eyes from within before lurching out into the open air.

"No more need for deception, we suppose," the Grace-puppet says. "Weapons on the ground."

I unsling my rifle instantly. I know I'm beaten. This sort of business is out of my league. Nia seems to measure her options, but ultimately comes to the same conclusion I have and slowly lowers her own weapon to the ground.

"Now kick them over to our colleagues."

Nia is forceful with her kick, sending her rifle spinning into Myrna's waiting grasp. Her eyeballs are still dangling, and become entangled on the stock of the rifle as she retrieves it. I am less emphatic in getting rid of my rifle and it doesn't slide very far, but no one seems very concerned about it.

"How long have you been infested?" I ask Grace.

"Almost three years now," she replies.

Nia and I are visibly confused.

"But... you took the test. I thought..."

"Did either of you see me take the test?" She's smiling. "It's a shame, you know. Jaime was clean. If you'd sent her to the infirmary instead of me, you might all be safe now."

"And the security goons didn't see anything?"

Grace is still smiling.

"We stepped behind a curtain. For modesty's sake. And our babies infested your nurse. Jaime wasn't crazy. Several of us were infested. And still are. Your so-called safe zone is a joke. The person administering your little spoon test is one of ours. We could take you all out at any moment."

"Then why don't you?" Nia asks. "Aren't we just vermin?"

"Oh, you're vermin, all right," the Grace-thing replies. "Unfortunately, you know how your technology works better than this host body or that one. We could probably muddle through. Instead you're going to fix the engines for us."

"And just why the hell would we do that?"

Grace grins. Each of her parasites, such as they can, grin as well. It's an eerie sight, three smiles in tandem coming from a single, gestalt entity.

"Your lives are precious to you. You can have them for a few minutes longer."

Nia laughs. It is a horrifying, grisly display. She is caught up, as if in a fit, unable to stop laughing. She's gone practically hysterical. The two infested don't seem to know what to do. They even look to me for guidance, but I have none to offer. Finally, the short barking of the skin-wrapper's laughter comes to an end, more out of exhaustion than anything else.

"'Precious,'" she repeats. "You think my life is precious to me?"

"We could be persuaded to negotiate on such a minor matter," Myrna says. "We could let you two go unmolested. In an escape pod, perhaps."

"You don't get it," Nia says.

"I get it," I say, belatedly.

The hematophages are looking back and forth between us, their rifles leveled at each of us.

"Explain it to us, then," the thing that was Myrna spits out.

"She's a skin-wrapper. A terminally ill patient suffering from cancer so bad that flaying off her skin and living in zero gravity is better than the alternative. She's probably been prepared to die since the day she came to space. Is that about right, Nia?"

"You said it a little fancier than I probably would've, but that's about the gist of it. I'd die in a second before helping you."

"If you really mean that..." Grace starts to say, raising her weapon.

"Oh, I do," Nia replies, cutting her off.

She puts her hand on the knob in the center of her chest plate. The infested both jump, not sure if she's reaching for a weapon or what. But I know what she's reaching for. With a flourish, she cranks her boom suit's internal gravity up to the maximum.

Her ghoulish countenance is grinning, even as it begins quivering.

"This is going to be pretty gross," the skin-wrapper states. "I'm just sorry I won't get to see it."

Waves of visible energy ripple through her exposed muscle and sinew. She tips her head back, laughing manically as her body begins to quiver and quake. The hematophages and the infested are mesmerized, perhaps mortified, watching as the gravity inside Nia's suit begins to redline. They're distracted, and I wonder if that's why Nia did this rather than letting herself be shot. I suppose it is a unique way to go. A story I'll tell for ages. But she also seems to be giving me an opening. Her lidless eye twitches, and I wonder for the briefest of seconds if it's a wink, but it scarcely matters as both of her eyes begin to melt.

I drop to the deck and grab my rifle. I really hadn't kicked it very far away at all.

All the muscle sloughs away from Nia's face, exposing pure bone. Then her skull begins to compact in on itself. Skull and teeth splinter and fracture. Nia, at least, what's still left of her in the suit, staggers backwards, tips forwards and then her brain and chunks of skull spatter the inside of her plasteel visor. The chunks of grey matter drip away from the screen faster than usual in the artificially-heightened gravity, like water swirling away down a drain.

Nia's empty suit begins to collapse. It flutters to the ground, empty, until only the boots are still upright, full of what looks like maybe half a meter of leg in each. It occurs to me with a sickening feeling that of course her legs are not still there. Her pureed body has sunk into her boots. What was formerly the skin-wrapper captain is now reducing to two pantlegs filled with red pudding.

The infested turn on me. I have the beam rifle in my hand, but there are two of them. What are my options? I glance at the singularity, frozen in time and space, sitting on its side. I can attempt to breach it, which will cause the entire ship to implode. I'll die. We'll all die.

I can attempt to shoot it out with the infested. Two against one. And I'm not much good in a firefight.

I can do what they say. Take the deal. Which they almost certainly won't honor. And even if they do, civilization will still collapse. Mostly thanks to me.

Only one option seems reasonable. I put the beam rifle in my mouth and finger the trigger.

# THIRTY-FOUR

"Stop."

My eyes are pinched shut, but I know, deep in my heart, that I don't have the guts to do it. I take the rifle out of my mouth and lower it to the ground.

"Your friends," the Myrna parasite says, her eyeballs still dangling around her chin. "You haven't forgotten about them, have you?"

"They'd rather die than let you win, too."

"Maybe. Let's ask them." Myrna takes out a jotter and speaks into it. "Lift the communications ban."

Suddenly the room is filled with holograms. The galley as I left it behind is here in the engine room with me now. Diane, Quinn, and Tampa are still alive, sitting at a table, unmolested. Tina's parasites have emerged from her eye sockets. Several of the colonists from Pod Eight – obviously not as clean as we thought after being screened by one of their own – are also proudly displaying their parasitic colors. Tina drops the body of one of the clean crew members, exsanguinated by the eels poking out of her brain.

"Galley here," Tina says. "Things are pretty much over down here. We're keeping the remaining uninfested as snacks or hosts."

"Slight change in plans," Myrna replies. "We haven't got the engine working yet. The pirate killed herself. We've got the historian. She might be able to do it... properly motivated."

Tina hisses.

"Just infest her!"

"Now now," Myrna chastises, "we're civilized beings here. We can take into account the feelings even of vermin. What would it take for you to start the engine?"

I shake my head.

"There's nothing. Nothing you can offer me."

"Not even your life? The lives of your friends? You could be the hero here, Paige. No doubt the company would reward such behavior. Instead of a complete breakdown of an entire mission, just a really big fuck-up. What do you think, madam director?"

Diane's face is an icy, implacable mask. Myrna walks up and crouches down beside me.

"She won't talk," Myrna says. "That's fine. She never talks. You know, Myrna despised her. Resented her. Never let it show. Did you know that, madam director? Did you know your own secretary didn't have a shred of respect for you? She let her work drop. She wasn't half as dumb as you thought she was. She just didn't respect you enough to do things right."

Diane's mouth doesn't even flutter. The hematophages are barking up the wrong tree if they think they're going to get under her skin. But, no, that's not really what she's going after at all.

"What about you?" the Myrna-thing asks, the female hematophage snapping around in front of my lips until it's practically kissing me. It's Myrna's mouth that continues moving, but I know it's this particular eel that is speaking. "What do you think about your director? It doesn't really matter now, does it? You can be honest."

"I don't have anything to say to you. Kill me. Or don't."

"That's pretty gutsy coming from someone who obviously doesn't have the guts to kill herself. You want to know what we believe you think about the director? We think you couldn't care less about her. We think you couldn't care less about anyone in there. We think people don't mean a whole hell of a lot to you at all. You know you're supposed to have relationships, affection, dislike, but you don't. You look at people the same way we do, like vermin. Creatures you have to tolerate to survive in a cold universe."

"With one small difference: I'm not a lamprey hitching a ride in someone's brain."

"Aren't you?"

My witty rejoinder is cut off, never to be recalled again, because the room has succumbed to the sounds of hissing. Only, it's not hissing. Not in the sense we would use it. It's the hematophage equivalent of cheering. It's the lampreys who are making the noise, the need to manipulate their hosts forgotten in their momentary joy.

All the infested in the galley are staring at the plasteel of the sewage and water system. For a moment I wonder why, but then I see the red cloud. Then the cloud disappears as the red waters of the dead fleshworld rush in. All of our freshwater is lost, tainted by the first drop of hemoglobin. The *Borgwardt*'s water system is wriggling with hematophages.

"Ah," the Myrna-thing says, "the last of our passengers have come on board. Now, Paige. I can infest you. And my children can eat your brain away and hope that they're smart enough to rely on your muscle memory and the deep-seated knowledge hidden away in your brainstem. But I think having you fix the engine would be better than rolling the dice on all that working out. Don't you?"

I'm beyond responding. Beyond even caring. I am numbness. I am like a great draught of Novocain. I hold out my hand. Allow Myrna pull me to my feet. I put my hand out.

"Jotter."

Bemused, Myrna puts the jotter in my hand. I hook it into the engineering computer.

"Troubleshooting mode," I say.

"Troubleshooting mode locked by order of the director," the jotter's tinny voice responds.

I turn to Myrna and Grace.

"And if I do this you'll let me go? Uninfested?"

"Of course," Myrna coos.

"Not you. I want to hear it from you."

I point at Grace. She approaches and the roly-poly male hematophage lurches sickeningly towards me.

"What do you care what we have to say?"

"You haven't made a bunch of empty promises."

I have to wonder… I can't be sure, but I have to wonder. They claim to be more intelligent than us, to have greater minds. But at some point, when you're digging around in someone else's memories and occupying their body, how can you know where you begin and they end? There must be some kind of osmosis. The Tina-thing acts just like Tina. The Myrna-thing acts just like Myrna, albeit off the leash she usually keeps herself on. It stands to reason that the Grace-thing would act like Grace. Or at least enough for me to trust her if she gave me her word.

She nods, ever so slightly.

I turn back to the jotter. I tell it Diane's code, which she gave me earlier to view the assault on Pod Nine. I memorized it because of course I did. Diane rises.

"Paige!" she says sharply.

The Tina-thing kicks out sharply, knocking one of Diane's prosthetic legs out from under her. She crumples into her chair. I'm not sure where she would have walked or what difference it would have made, but the point has been adequately made.

"Don't do this, Paige. That is a direct verbal directive."

"Run it by EO and the union first," I reply. "I don't have to listen to you just because you're management."

Everyone in the holographic galley is on their feet (with the exception of Diane who can no longer get to her feet) shouting different things. I'm pretty sure the equal opportunity officers and the union stewards are urgently telling me to listen to management. That'd be funny if it still mattered. Hilarious, if it had ever mattered.

But it doesn't. I'm not listening to any of them. I'm listening to the jotter, and watching it, as it gives me moron-level instructions about what's wrong with the engine and how to fix it. It even comes with blinking diagrams and issues me codes as I need them. With Diane's password, fixing a singularity core is no harder than changing the toner in a photocopier. Without it, after having been spiked correctly by the crew, no engineering team in the galaxy could reverse the spike.

When I look up from my fussing, everyone in the room, real or projected, is staring at me.

"Is it fixed?" Myrna asks, looking like she's going to fall over if she leans in any closer.

I make circles with my hand over a handle switch.

"As soon as I pull this," I say.

"Pull it," Myrna says.

"Paige, don't you dare!" Diane shouts.

I look to Grace.

"You're going to kill me along with the others, aren't you?"

Grace shrugs and nods. Her hematophages have retreated back into her headspace. They are peeking out through her eye sockets, dagger-toothed mouths flexing inside the skull, but happily ensconced in the warm womb of Grace's head again.

I nod and pull the switch. The hematophages all begin hissing in glee again.

"I figured," I say.

"You can consider this your notice of dismissal," Diane states flatly.

"Have a little faith, madam director," I say, clipping a carabiner from my belt onto a control panel. "Kelly, have you been listening?"

"Yes, Paige," my "imaginary" friend responds.

"And you know what to do?"

"Yes, Paige."

"What... what's happening?" the Myrna-thing says, her eels writhing around in the air like mad.

Grace has already figured it out.

"She's outwitted us."

The *Borgwardt* suddenly rights itself, and everyone falls to the side. Kelly, I reflect, is dead now, her last act being to sacrifice herself by inputting the commands for us to right ourselves and blast off into the atmosphere.

Grace points her rifle at me. She's willing to take me out as a last act of vengeance against the human vermin. But it's already too late for her and Myrna before she can even aim at me. We've passed the atmosphere. Her shot goes off, but it goes wild as she's sucked into the hatchway out of the engine room. She strains against the jamb, attempting to force herself back in, perhaps to grab purchase on something more solid. But it's no use. Myrna slams into her, and both are sucked out into the hallways.

They'll be bounced around like pinballs out there. Their bodies, both those of the hosts and the parasites, will be pulverized by striking every flat surface in the Borgwardt half a hundred times until they're finally sucked out into their ultimate destination: open space. I'm sucked out as well, but the carabiner I've attached to the control panel is holding me fast. I'm just a dog on a very short leash, enjoying the zero G.

Millie, my ever-faithful glow globe, is not so fortunate and is ripped right off of my belt. The loss of the puppy-like tool would be cause for sadness on an ordinary day, but today has been so full of loss it barely even registers. Nia's suit is sucked past me as well, her pulverized remains sloshing around like river water in a fisherman's set of soggy boots.

"So long, skin-wrapper," I mutter, surprised to find myself waving goodbye to a woman who, only hours before, had been my mortal enemy.

The blood in the sewage system is draining away, too. I can hear the hematophages screaming in terror. It is the most horrifying noise I have ever heard, and in the last few hours I thought I had grown utterly desensitized to such things. Funny to think that creatures which were also my mortal enemies, even at that very instant, and an existential threat to my very race, not even a member of my race as the skin-wrapper had once been, could be capable of eliciting such a dread feeling in me.

Their screams are beyond the screams of the damned. They are shrieking in an agony beyond all knowing for me. Perhaps they really are more intelligent than us, more emotional, more poetic. Their shrieks as their lives are snuffed out resemble those of creatures who have thought long and thought hard about...well, not the human condition, I suppose. But the condition of any living, sentient being. I've exterminated a race of poet-philosophers with a single pull of a handle. I'm a perpetrator of genocide, one of a very few. Probably the only one currently living.

I'm blacking out. It's hard to ignore. All of my problems are swirling away, but all of my oxygen is, too. Kelly must have blown an airlock to allow explosive decompression, and one of the outer facing sewage pipes as well. I hope she timed it to stop at some point. I have no idea how long it would take to clear all of the hematophages out of the office, but if it's more than five or six minutes I'll be suffocated as well. Even if I'm not, I may not have enough air to make it back to Yloft, the nearest outpost.

A chair is flying at my nose. I flinch, then realize as it passes right through me that it was a hologram. There's a sinking feeling in my stomach. I hadn't even noticed it at the time, but Grace and Myrna weren't the only ones sucked out. The holographic projector is still projecting. It's just that Diane, Quinn, and all the survivors have been sucked out as well. The hematophages are gone, but the last of my compatriots have left with them.

I'm passing out now. No more oxygen. I hope Kelly entered a stop command on the explosive decompression. I can't really blame her, though, if she didn't.

# THIRTY-FIVE

"What do you think you could have done better to prevent this?"

I don't look up. My head is pointed downward, at the deck. Showing my eyes would show earnestness. A lot of people seem to genuinely believe you can intuit someone's feelings – some even say soul – from their eyes. The truth is that's all horseshit. Eyes don't smile. They don't laugh. They don't cry – well, they do, but you can tell when they're crying because salty liquid is pouring from them.

The truth is that eyes are just white and black and a little bit of color. Whatever you see in them is exactly as meaningful as looking at the stars and seeing ancient gods fucking one another, or looking at planetscapes and imagining a face or a skull. Eyes are empty, but they reflect the human desire to anthropomorphize every fucking thing.

The purpose of this question is to show contrition. They want you to list a mistake – ideally a whole litany of mistakes – and show your chagrin. Admit you were wrong.

"I could've not taken the job."

The goon is no Yloft station bunny, or I'd know her. Hestle imported her for the purpose of getting to the bottom of my ass, probably at great expense. She's probably a shadow-hunter, likely a former shadow herself, recruited for the purpose of rooting out her black-hatted kin. She'll have conducted thousands of interrogations like this, on subjects far cagier than me.

I'm surprised, then, when her response is simply, "Excuse me?"

I don't look up. I know my hair is hanging over my face and consequently my voice is muffled, but I just don't give a shit.

"I knew I had Hestle over a barrel. They would've paid any amount for me. I wasn't the best but I was the best available and in the ink sometimes that's all that matters."

The corporate shadow-hunter adjusts her spectrometry spectacles. She's trying to get a bead on my biochemistry. Her lenses are telling her all about my body temperature, heart rate, all the vital signs as we speak. I'm not controlling any of them myself, but I'm sure they're all steady or normal or negative or whatever the right medical/procedural term is. The only thing that can't be controlled is my blink rate. So, I have to keep my eyes hidden. Windows to the soul.

"You think this is some kind of joke?"

The urge to surge forward and throttle her is overwhelming. This comes from me, not them, I know. Stifling the urge is their doing. I remain downcast.

The purpose of this question is to get you back on track, prove that you still respect the questioner. Prove that you know not to push too far. A simple "no" will suffice.

"Gash, I have seen things in the last twenty-four hours that would make your stomach curdle. I've seen monstrosities coming in and out of orifices. Rivers of blood, choking people I know. Do I know what you want me to say? Yes. I always know what everyone wants me to say. All the time.

"Most people are so stupid that keeping them happy with a few lies is about as complicated as a game of fucking checkers. Do I respect you? No. Do I respect your process and your oh-so-vaunted procedures? No. I don't give a shit. I don't give a shit about you. I don't care if you dock all my pay. I don't care if you toss me in lock-up. And the answer you were looking for is," here I affect a perfect little schoolgirl voice, "No, officer, I don't think this is a joke."

I have no idea where that came from. Any of it. I scream. I yell. No noise comes. I snap my fingers. Nothing happens. My nerves are ignoring me.

The shadow-hunter turns and looks over her shoulder. The entire bulkhead behind her turns phosphorescent, then translucent. An entire control bay is behind us, row after row of panels, all manned, all blinking lights reflecting off the faces of the women manning them. A security goon, probably my spy-hunter's superior, judging by the fanciness of her epaulettes, half-rises from her seat and depresses a button.

"Fuck it," she says over the intercom.

The shadow-hunter sighs and pulls the glasses off her face, rubbing the sore spots behind her ears as she folds them up and tosses them onto the table.

"You're free to go."

"Go...?"

"Don't leave Yloft."

I rise. I couldn't have left Yloft anyway. They still have my transit chip. I step out of the interrogation chamber and into a prophylactic airlock. When I step out, the *Borgwardt*, still thrumming, gas-filled, and red lit, is through a bulkhead to my left. Yloft way-station, clean, bustling, and like something out of a campfire tale, is to my right. Ahead of me is a bulkhead leading out into open space, hinting by its markings that there are times a fourth ship or station needs to be brought into the orgiastic mix.

But I know the truth. I've studied these prophylaxes in my research. There are tales – lots of them, really – about lone survivors like myself. Something about sole survivors stirs the imagination of every ink surfer. They all have a weird desire to be one, to witness something so profound that nobody else could walk away from it. I guess I should say "we." I guess I'm an ink surfer now, a station bunny no longer. And yet, now, being a sole survivor as well, I desire almost anything else.

The stories are all identical, down to the last detail. A lost ship, tumbling through the ink. The older ones always seem to have the lone wolf in deep freeze. The newer ones don't feature that detail so much anymore. The hulk is recovered, dragged somewhere, preferably an independent entity like Yloft. A security goon, always in glasses, looking for the truth, not really caring what she finds.

Then the airlock opens into the prophy. Then as the survivor waits to find out whether she's been freed from quarantine or not, the fourth hatch, the empty hatch, opens, and she tumbles out into the ink, never to be seen or heard from again. Silenced by forces beyond her control, for reasons out of her imagining, and always portrayed as an accident. Maybe Sally Slap-Giggle, the station bunny who pressed the wrong airlock button gets a slap on the wrist. More likely, she gets a secret bonus, funneled through gray channels. Most likely she gets both.

I stop and stare. It's a classic story. One I've heard a thousand times before. We all tell it. Now I'm living it. I stare and stare and wait for the open airlock to open and suck me into oblivion. I've never wanted anything so much in my life.

Instead, the bulkhead on my right hisses and rises. Yloft.

Damn you. Damn you!

I scrabble to reach for the emergency override. My hands twitch, but beyond that, my nerve impulses don't even respond.

Please, please, space me! Please!

But it's no use. I step out, like a child born into the world through my mother's womb for the first time. I have no choice.

I don't even have to pass through customs. Deandre, a geek from the comptroller's office, replete in a severe bun, gray suit, and briefcase, hands me a badge.

"Hey, Paige," she whispers, blushing, "good to see you again."

"Hi, D," I mutter.

It'll be good for the transient quarters on Yloft. I never was a fan, but then I lived here and knew all the good places and bad. Without another word, Deandre nods and turns and disappears into the crush of people.

My feet take me where I'm supposed to go. I pass right into the Mercado, where the scents of sizzling meats from a hundred worlds mingle with the crisp aroma of dried spices and (semi-) fresh veggies. My stomach is doing more than growling, it's roaring, churning, but they won't let me stop off for a bite to eat.

Acquaintances all nod at me, but it's not the same anymore. I'm not one of them anymore. It's hard for a station bunny to trust an ink surfer, even if she used to be one of them. I'd be heartbroken if I wasn't so focused on other things. Then a loud clank of metal on metal, followed by a tinkle of follow-on clatters cuts through the din. I've practically walked into Peavey, who is holding a wooden bowl of clammer's stew, but her heavy metal spoon has just clattered to the deck. She's staring at me and I half think she's going to spill the rest of her clams and hydroponic beans onto the ground.

They want me to barrel past her, but she's literally blocking my way.

"A... A... Ambroziak," she stutters.

"Peavey," I growl, eyeing her soup.

"I didn't... I heard... I thought you were lost."

I smile at her darkly.

"And you thought that was going to put this thing between us to rest, did you?"

She turns white as a sheet. Funny to think that this girl who had the guts to try to off me has been terrified of me ever since. I think of her as a hyena striking once in the darkness. I'm a lion with a whole pride behind me. She can't get close to me. Even now, my friends are all around me. But are they, really? Do they even know me? Do they know what's inside of me? What I'm carrying? Am I too far gone for them? Am I just a spacer to them now, like any other fucking tourist who stops by the station?

A wave of nausea and pain sweeps over me, a clear message to deal with this undesirable distraction as quickly and efficiently as possible.

"You come to see me, Peavey. You come to see me straight away. I'm going to be in transient."

"What number?"

I nearly double over. I don't even know. It's on my key, but I can't be bothered to look.

"I don't know. Look me up."

I reach out, my hand trembling, wondering if I can take her soup from her. It's killing me. The walls of my stomach are dissolving in bile and acid. I could just reach out and triumphantly steal my enemy's meal, but they won't even let me do that. I push past her like she's a turnstile. It's straight to the six bulkheads that make up my cell in transient.

There's room for a bed. It's seated nearly as high as I am tall. Beneath the crusty, soiled mattress is what passes for my closet and drawer space. I don't bother checking it. I don't have anything. Everything I own is still aboard the *Borgwardt*, in quarantine. The company goons can deliver it to me or not, whenever they're satisfied.

In the corner is a commode, cattycorner to a sink and a greasy mirror. Jackpot. My hands are still tingling, trying to refuse the orders they're sending me. But it's like trying to hold your breath in space. I tear off my shirt, buttons flying. I jam it into the commode, blocking the piping, and flush and flush until I'm certain it's completely stopped up.

I rise, shaking, and turn to look in the mirror. They are no longer hiding. I feel the sickening press of slimy, slug-like flesh against both of my eye sockets. Out of my left eye slithers the thin, tubular hematophage female.

On the right is the thicker trunk of the male's body. I feel his tiny prick as it catches at my eyelid before sliding out with the rest of him.

I can see them and I can't. My real eyes are dangling from their nerves, useless. But the hematophages are sending me signals sufficient enough to do their bidding. I can see what they show me, as though through a glass and darkly. Their dim, serpentine forms undulate perversely in the air before me.

They do not speak directly to me, any more than I would speak directly to my razor or the toaster about my intentions for it. Still, I can't miss the fact that they seem to be laughing at me, as their bodies intertwine and they kiss right before me. The male's prick slides easily into the female's hole, a dance I have felt them perform within my skull a thousand times.

They can survive in open air, though they prefer the warm and hot environs inside my head. It is a peccadillo for them, a kink. They make me watch. That might be a kink, too, but I don't think so, any more than I would care if the toaster or the razor was on the nightstand as I touched myself.

I am frozen, rooted to the spot as they mate yet again. There is nothing I hate more than watching them engage in their slimy, grotesque alien congress, but I must. The end of their bodies are attached to a squishy, jagged hunk of meat. It is the minimal part of my brain that they did not devour, the bare minimum I need to walk, talk, and cogitate such as I am doing.

I know I am no longer whole, no longer there. They have devoured so much of my personality, my past, my feelings, my longings. I am not myself. I am no more than a meat puppet. I cannot even weep for my lowered station in life. I'm not capable of such emotions. I'm not even sure how much of what I'm thinking right now is even really me and not them.

They are intelligent. Deeply, darkly, perversely, malignly intelligent. And I don't know where I start and they begin. Mechanically, there is a separation between the base of the male's body and the nerves he has jammed down into my hunk of brainstem, but the thoughts and emotions flow freely between the two physical forms like a sieve. No doubt they are vaguely aware of my vestigial desires and fears, as one might recognize the real desires of a saddled horse even while spurring it to behave differently.

All these thoughts, all this that I think of as "me" may not even be mine. They may be his. And hers. She is the quiet partner, yet by far the dominant one. I feel her wants and needs pour into me so heavily, so constantly, it is like they are no longer even hers, they are mine, were always mine. I want – no, I need – to protect the babies.

I can see them there. Eggs, translucent and glistening like soap bubbles, accumulating in my brain pain, filling up my skull cavity. Soon my head will be so full that the hematophages and their kin will begin to press against my skull. I wonder what will happen then. Will the eggs ooze out of my ears? Will my head explode? What then? Will they continue to make me walk around, still a vehicle, just now missing a face?

My query is, strangely, answered, almost instantly. They have finished copulating. I feel a warm surge of pleasure pass through me. My own vagina is dripping. They would never give me a thought, never consider me enough to even let me touch myself as I bask in the vicarious pleasure of their sex.

All I want to do is lower my hand to my warm, quivering pussy and stroke. Instead I reach out and slash my own wrist against a ragged edge of the mirror. They've done with me, then?

No. As the blood begins to drip I drop to my knees. I let it fill the commode. I am weak, woozy. They, too, are affected by the loss of blood. Finally, I clutch my severed artery with my other hand, pinching it closed. I dip my head into the toilet, now filled with my own blood, and feel the eggs as they drift out of my skull cavity and into their new nest. When I finally pull my head out again, the pressure within what was once my nasal passages has considerably lessened. The babies have a new home.

My face is soaked in my own blood. I feel their circular, suckling mouth running up and down my face and my hair, licking away the red like a post-coital sandwich. But then it's no longer post-coital. They're fucking again.

They forget about my wrist and I take my other hand away from clutching it. I feel a brief surge of hope. Perhaps they are so ignorant of human anatomy I can die. If I can only die, they will be stranded. Stranded without a vehicle. The babies will perish without someone to refill their nest with blood and, ultimately, chunkier effluvia. The others will find me and realize how close they came to a full-scale hematophage infestation which would've overrun Yloft, and shortly afterwards, as a bustling port of call, would've spread to every corner of human civilization.

But I'm a fool. Even my own emotions betray me. They feel my surge of joy and realize something is wrong. They slow their humping long enough to force me to wrap some spare bedding around my wrist. They are angry with me for interrupting their recreation and punish me with pain. But it doesn't matter. There is no physical pain they can cause me greater than knowing that I have become the vector for monstrous space lampreys to wipe out my species.

I used to want many things. Money, love, respect, a place in history, awards, the praise of my fellow academics. Now I want only one: the feel of a sharp piece of metal destroying the barely animal remaining chunk of my brain. But I know I'll never get it. I'm far too instrumental to them, especially right now.

A ding signals someone outside my hatch.

"Who the fuck is it?" I roar. This is me. The real me. What's left of me. That tiny little chunk of brain, raging. They let me rage.

Peavey responds with her name, her voice tiny and distant, even though it's just on the other side of the hatch.

I grin. That's me grinning and them grinning, too. At least we can agree on one thing. "Come on in," I reply sweetly.

# THE END

Thank you for reading THE HEMATOPHAGES. Whether you liked it or not I hope you'll take a moment to leave a review on Amazon or your favorite book review site. Reviews are vitally important to me as an author both to help me market my book and to improve my writing in the future. Thank you!

- Stephen Kozeniewski

# ABOUT THE AUTHOR

Stephen Kozeniewski (pronounced "causin' ooze key") lives in Pennsylvania, the birthplace of the modern zombie. During his time as a Field Artillery officer, he served for three years in Oklahoma and one in Iraq, where due to what he assumes was a clerical error, he was awarded the Bronze Star. He is also a classically trained linguist, which sounds more impressive than saying his bachelor's degree is in German.

## COMING SOON

*Stone Wall* by Dominic Stabile

*Episodes of Violence* by David Bernstein

*Brain Dead Blues* by Matt Hayward

Find these and other books at www.sinistergrinpress.com

72125803R00180

Made in the USA
Lexington, KY
28 November 2017